On earth as it is

By the same author

Fiction

Flight Paths of the Emperor (1992)

Poetry

Stalin's Carnival (1989)
Foreign Ghosts (1989)
The Ecstasy of Skeptics (1994)

Steven Heighton

ON EARTH AS IT IS

The Porcupine's Quill

CANADIAN CATALOGUING IN PUBLICATION DATA

Heighton, Steven, 1961-
   On earth as it is

ISBN 0-88984-155-9

I. Title

PS8573.E45IO5   1995   C813'.54   C95-930880-6
PR9199.3.H4505   1995

Published by The Porcupine's Quill, Inc., 68 Main Street, Erin, Ontario NOB 1TO with financial assistance from The Canada Council and the Ontario Arts Council. The support of the Government of Ontario through the Ministry of Culture, Tourism and Recreation is also gratefully acknowledged, as is the support of the Department of Canadian Heritage through the Book and Periodical Industry Development programme and the Periodical Distribution Assistance Programme.

Represented in Canada by the Literary Press Group. Trade orders are available from General Distribution Services.

Readied for the press by John Metcalf.
Copy edited by Doris Cowan.

Cover image is after a collage by Mary Huggard.

Contents

Heartfelt thanks to Mary Huggard, my parents, the editors of the magazines and anthologies that published the stories (and especially the editors of *The New Quarterly*), Caroline Adderson, Allan Brown, Mary Cameron, Judith Cowan, Melanie Dugan, Michael Holmes, Christine Klein-Lataud, Janet Madsen, Tom Marshall, Kent Nussey, Jennifer Oulton, Michael Redhill, Jay Ruzesky, Mark Sinnett, and Geoffrey Ursell. Vanny Doutch helped me with the Khmer in 'The Patrons'. Susan Huggard helped generously with research and a hundred other things. I'm grateful also to the indefatigable Inksters at The Porcupine's Quill, along with their office manager Michael Carbert, and Jason Van Zyl, and Doris Cowan.

The assistance of the Ontario Arts Council and the Canada Council was important to me and I'm grateful to both of them.

I especially want to thank John Metcalf for his tireless support, criticism & encouragement.

'Townsmen of a Stiller Town' is for Kent Nussey & Lydia Joss.

'The Patrons' is for Vanny Doutch.

For Mary

Everything may change in this demoralized world except the heart, human love, & our striving to know the divine.

— MARC CHAGALL

To Everything a Season

A time to embrace, and a time to refrain from embracing

– ECCLESIASTES

I *Winter Earth*

How does it happen for the last time? The lovemaking. Two bodies joining once, twice, a thousand times, then never again. How?

* * *

OVER THE CITY a vault of winter clouds as grey and cold as limestone. Like the walls of the old house, the walls of the garden, where the raised beds of frozen earth pushed through snow like islands in an ice-bound lake.

Through a circle he had cleared in the frost of his study window Alden looked out across the garden and over ranks of snowy roofs to the lake, where the ferry was crossing to Wolfe Island. At this distance it seemed to glide above the ice and only the mist rising around it from a slim, tenuous lead of open water proved otherwise. The newspaper open on his desk advised commuters that tonight the channel would freeze hard in the few hours the ferry docked; from tomorrow until the lake warmed in early March, the much longer, winter route would be used.

Perfect. Yes! And those scales – the ones in D minor! You won't forget! So – next week at the same time!

Holly dismissing her last student downstairs, playing her own voice with virtuoso skill – touching all the lively, pert, high trilling notes.

Alden! Alden! Her own voice again, weary and dissonant, tuned back to the cracked muffled chords of old age by the departure of outsiders, the front door's slam.

Alden got up from his hard chair and stood facing his

great-great-grandfather Caleb MacLeod, the 'rebel and exile', who glowered out of his framed old charcoal sketch as if from a prison casement. Chastened, Alden pocketed his glasses, crossed the small dim study and pulled open the door. The glassed-in parchment map on the back rattled softly as the door swung to. Alden's study was papered in maps, framed and unframed, contour, weather and relief maps, ancient, old, or recent, the former tools and current mementoes of thirty-six years in the Geography Department at the college. Alden had been – and in retirement remained – an authority on historical cartography, especially as it applied to the mapping of south-eastern Ontario and the Thousand Islands. *The Garden of the Spirits*, the Iroquois had called it, *Garden of the Gods*, before they and their names were written over or erased.

After Holly's Sunday afternoon lessons a blessed silence settled over the house. After eighteen years with his own children at home and with students at school, then fifteen more among the swelling undergraduate hordes, Alden had been ready for retirement, for the cozy undemanding silence and setness of the old limestone house, for a study untrespassed by students who sprang lately from a world for which he had no maps, and which continued to spawn junior colleagues of an increasingly remote and radical stripe. *Postcolonial revisionings of the mapping process. Marxist demography. The cartographer as rapist.* Before his departure Alden had made a few listless bids at befriending and understanding his new colleagues, but they had not really wanted that any more than he had. He did have a few friends – one left in the department, the others retired – and they still met sometimes for a drink or two, at the faculty club, Friday afternoons.

He had always been more comfortable with maps than people anyway.

Alden!

He started downstairs. Holly had taken on the piano students soon after Caleb and Annie left home, within a year, one after another, the house suddenly silent after all that time. She had said the students were to give her something to do besides the garden and her winter reading – and he had seen her point. It was good for her to get out of the house and to meet new people. But in the last few years her back problems had worsened, and her students had begun to come to her. And, inescapably, to him.

He could hardly object, out loud, to such a necessity.

She was waiting for him at the dining room table, a dull grey cardigan over the ochre paisley dress she had worn for her lessons. He sat down across from her. Her three students, who came one after another for an hour each, had made distressing inroads on the plate of biscuits she had set out earlier in the day – but a few of his favourites remained. He heard the kettle steaming in the kitchen. Snow fell behind her, beyond the picture window giving onto the garden, and it seemed to fall around and onto her head, whitening her hair, which had been white now for a decade and grew whiter each year so her shrinking face seemed each year redder against the white, her blue eyes refined to an eerie brilliance.

'Really, Alden, there's no need for you to hide away in your study whenever they come.'

He selected a small piece of her shortbread.

'Or to look at me like that.'

'I was watching the snow. Behind you.'

She half turned in her chair and winced, her rouged mouth pinched and puckering. Alden started to his feet, and then, seeing she was all right, settled back down.

She said, 'I would have thought it was too cold to snow.'

'Well, the paper predicts the ferry channel will freeze tonight and they'll have to change to the winter route tomorrow. So tonight would be better for the island.'

'Yes ... '

'Is your back too painful? We don't have to go.'

'Alden, *please* ... ' That faint, exasperated quaver betraying deep weariness. A yellowing key, accidentally touched, on a worn old piano.

'I only meant – '

'No, I want to, we go every New Year and we'll go tonight. I want to.'

'I realize the food isn't as good as it used to be.'

She smiled. 'That's us. We don't taste things the same way.'

She started to get up for the kettle but he waved her off with a brisk teacherly sweep of the hand. He rose and strode smartly past her as if entering a crowded classroom.

'To hear you talk,' he chided from the kitchen, quickly finishing his shortbread, 'you'd think we were in our eighties.'

He poured a stream of boiling water into the white stoneware pot she had already sprinkled with leaves. He checked his watch. Beyond the kitchen window snow sifted into the garden, filling the furrows between the raised beds; tucked invisibly under the sill, the stiff frozen stalks and clenched, faded flowers of the snapdragons would be sinking under the snow.

Alden brought in the teapot and cups and saucers on an heirloom tray. As he served her, Holly frowned and fidgeted with the brooch pinned over her thin breast, the grey cardigan that grew looser by the week. How much longer, he wondered, would she be able to go on teaching? He did wish she could still go out to do it.

They drank tea in silence. The room went darker, the clean corners growing dusty with shadow and the dust seeming to creep outward and suffuse the whole room. Above the piano there was a small Krieghoff that had been in Alden's family for years and by the time he had finished his third cup of tea the voyageurs heaving their sledge through snowdrifts, pipes pluckily chomped in their mouths, were almost imperceptible.

He squinted again at his watch.

'Shall we get ready?'

She swallowed the last of her tea, as if bracing for an ordeal.

'You really don't want to go,' he told her, sensing her fatigue and how it mirrored his own and accusing her of both. But her back, he thought, her spine – the bones there dissolving. A woman who had loved more than anything else *to go out*, for dinner, for walks, for drinks and dancing when a sitter was found and it was Friday night or even on weeknights when the children were older and Alden willing to go along. To the theatre, then, or a pub by the harbour – or, more recently, on her own, to the warm houses of students where she would be offered such delicacies, Alden, such delicacies, you can't imagine! Things we never had when we were young. *Sushi, samosas*, blue corn chips with homemade *salsa*, pickled ginger! How our old city has changed!

Each New Year as they got ready for the drive to the ferry and the island for their annual celebration she would grow spry, sprightly as Caleb and Annie years before at Christmas: the drive down Princess Street crowded with students under the green and spruce-blue lights and then aboard the ferry, pulling out, the half-hour passage with the boat grinding through the ice-clogged channel or taking the longer route past Fort Henry and the lights of Marysville to the winter dock, then a short drive to the old limestone inn, the Sir John A., and the table they reserved each year by the window with the city lights mirrored in long tapering rays over the ice....

He helped her upstairs and in their bedroom turned on the dim lamp on the oak table between the beds. Her idea, these matching single beds; not long after his retirement she had pointed them out in a catalogue and said that with her pain and her waking at night for pills it might be better for him, he might rest a bit better. 'Well,' he'd said after a time – a short time during which his mind flashed over a broad, sombre spectrum of feelings – 'I suppose it's a good idea. It would be better for you, I suppose, your back.'

And he'd added, 'Besides, we never really make love anymore.'

'We never much did,' she'd snapped. And after all there had been a time when only he was indifferent – once the children were born, and his academic standing and responsibilities increased, when sex had seemed, as often as not, just too much fuss. He wondered sometimes if he had left his most passionate efforts in the lecture hall – or perhaps at his desk? He could not be sure. He couldn't say. He could only wonder how a man put in thirty-five years at 'an esteemed institution of higher learning', reading and thinking and teaching, and forty-one years in the institution of marriage, perfectly faithful (in marked contrast to his colleagues, or most of them); how it happened he raised two good children and cared for his wife in health and now in sickness and did everything one is supposed to do only to end up so baffled, bled dry, alone in a study scanning the legends of priceless old parchment maps for a clue to where he was and what had happened. *One of the country's foremost authorities on. The author of respected volumes concerning.* Lies, on one level. *A stranger to his most basic desires.*

He eased shut the bathroom door and shaved for the second time that day. The light above the mirror granted, as usual, no quarter at all: his dull eyes trapped in a cobweb of wrinkles: deep shadow in the wattled folds of his neck. But a full head of silver hair, swept off the forehead and back from the sides, still handsome.

When he stepped back into the bedroom the lamp was off, the room almost dark. Holly sat on the side of her quilt, knees in the furrow between the beds – her knees bare. She was naked. They always undressed separately these days, not exactly hiding from each other but with a kind of coy, Victorian stealth, discreet contortions and turnings-away, Holly stiffer, more clumsy all the time, Alden more precise and methodical.

It had been a while since he'd seen her naked. Thinner now. Sitting on her bedside in the near-dark.

'Alden ...?'

Faint stirrings, a quickening in the belly, not the rushing spring-melt of early youth but an echo of that, muted as so many things now seemed, as if age were gradually cooling, burying him in drifts of softly falling – what? Not only snow. Cheques and bills? A storm, maybe, of calendar leaves blown from the old black-and-white films of his youth. Blurring his eyes, frosting his brows and hair. His ears filling up. His senses shrouded, deadened – but alive.

He undressed. Snow slipped past the darkening window and for a moment a gust rattled the pane and snow whirled and flocked against it.

'Of course I want to go,' she said softly as he eased down beside her. 'I still look forward to it. Every year. Here, kiss me.'

Her face looked different, smoothed out by the near-dark; in bright light her papery skin seemed almost translucent, as if she were melting from outside as well as from within, but this dimness filled-out and deepened her face so she seemed now more solid, substantial, less likely to fold up and crumple if he held her.

And as they lay back together on her bed and began again, with great patience, for the first time in a year and the second in three years and for the last time, a thought drifted through Alden's mind and he wondered if it mattered and thought it must but then he lost it, he let it go and only recalled later, when they arrived an hour late at the Sir John A., that he'd been worried about missing the next ferry. Their pale bodies stirring like snow outside the window, blending, settling through grey air then churned to life by occasional gusts and floating down again to sift white over the frozen earth like seed. But cold. And as Alden made slow and difficult, blissful love to Holly he wondered why they had never much done it and why they did not do it more often now in spite of everything, to let it heal and bind them, and he vowed he would not let the intensity and purity of this moment melt away, he would keep it alive inside him, he would make this happen more often, again. But afterward as they lay on her bed he felt the warmth and rapture beginning to fade and bleed away: stored heat drawn from the body of the earth as summer ends, and autumn, and ice embalms the dead stalks of flowers and glazes over the lake – an old woman's eyes dulled, glassed-over with time.

So they came home later that night from the island to their separate beds, and went on as before, and Alden failed to keep his vow. And kept on asking himself how, and why. How was it that the love and gravity stored in the lodestones of the body – the organs and the brain – were strong enough one day to draw two people together and the next day not quite strong enough? Or the next, or the next. A threshold crossed. The body's brief half-life ending.

He holds her arm tightly as they come downstairs, he in a wool suit, dark grey, she in a pleated maroon skirt and jacket. Telling her he wants to clear snow from the steps he carefully bundles up and hurries out around the house for a shovel. The air is clear and cold. Orion's belt hangs over the chimney like three sparks and, in the back garden, light from the picture window maps a gold square on the beds of soil. Huddled by the limestone in deep shadow under the kitchen are the stalks and wizened heads of the snapdragons; each year he records the date they last until and this year has been the latest ever. A few hardy survivors, closest to the wall, were still waving gamely from the snows a month before.

A faint high trilling of music. Through the dining room window Alden sees Holly at the piano, hunched painfully over the keyboard, her face flushed and her lips, half-open, budding into a smile. He can't quite make out the piece she is playing but he stands a long time, leaning on his shovel in that parcel of light, and watches.

2 *To the Sea in Spring*

That spring I was twenty years old and I was going out to the coast – the ocean. West.

Jess and I had been working since March in a small hotel in Banff where we'd wound up after leaving Toronto. I first met her there in a Queen Street place called the Cutting Edge where I knew the bass guitarist in a local band – the Cargo Cult. Back then I was serious about guitar and this friend kept promising me a place in the band but nothing ever seemed to come up. 'Caleb,' he kept at me, 'it won't be long,' but in those days I didn't know how to wait. Night and day I was busking Yonge Street to keep afloat and sharing a small attic off College with another guitarist – Kathy. We weren't getting along too well. I couldn't really cover my share of the rent and I was thinking I'd maybe go home and finish school – which in hindsight didn't look too bad – but I kept thinking of Kerouac and Ginsberg and of Neil Young heading west in his beat-up old hearse, and wondering what they would have done.

My dog-eared second-hand Scriptures (*On the Road, Dharma Bums, Desolation Angels*) made it pretty clear: the safe smooth expressway back to school and a white-collar noose was mortal sin and I would lose my soul. Go West, young man. 'Man, you gotta Go.'

Jess herself had left art college a few years before. She was twenty-three. She was waiting tables at the Edge but wanted to leave since she'd just broken up with the sax player for the Cult and he was giving her a hard time. He was also a friend of a friend, bitter about Jess and by all accounts a mean drunk so there was nothing left when we hit it off but to skip town. We caught the eighty-nine-buck cross-country Greyhound and rolled out across what Kerouac (that exile Canadien) might have called *the big gone breathtaking vastness of Canada* sharing smokes and necking in the cramped seats and trying without much luck to go farther as the lights of prairie farms and wheat-towns washed past behind our reflections like phosphorescence on the sea around a ferry. When the sun came up on the snowy outskirts of Swift Current and sloped in the windows it made her long ringlets of ginger hair glint and it ripened her face and hands to a freckled grain-gold. Jeans and snug sweater dazzling blue, wide eyes as green as – what? I settled for the Strait of Juan de Fuca – another name from my father's maps. I'd never been there. But I'd be there soon. Jess doing quick sketches of me or 'gesture drawings' of the other passengers while I cheerfully played requests, rock, folk, or country, my pliant voice always the voice of the song's famous singer.

I was happy. I was who I wanted to be. Not the feeble *myself* I'd been tied to at home and still cousined to two and a half hours west in Toronto but something better, infinitely, a character I'd come to love, to chase, somebody with a myth and a story. And the myth and the story gave me a future. I still hadn't read *Big Sur*.

We got off in Banff, for Jess, for the mountains. She'd seen them with her folks when she was a child and the minute we cleared Calgary and they soared up out of the snowed-in plains and foothills she said we had to stop there, and we did.

So I got a job in the great north woods/Working as a cook for a spell.... Well, really a 'cook's helper.' Who helped by washing the dishes, pots – a dirty job, but I could take it for a while. Jess got another waitress position and we shacked up in a small lopsided room in the old staff barracks behind the hotel. The place smelled of sawdust and mildew, stale beer. Browsing elk and blasé 'garbage-bears' peeped in the windows of the staff lounge like boorish, unshaven tourists, drawn I guess by the sounds of our jamming. One night the bellman with the off-key twelve-string brought in a Yukon mickey and the jamming kept going till way past dawn and when I wrote home I made sure my folks knew all about it. I told my father how much his maps and atlases had made me want to light out and see the world.

Jess and I walked hand in hand in the snow with our necks sore as Michelangelo in the Sistine Chapel from looking up at the Rockies. That was how she liked to put it. She kept a little sketchbook in her jacket pocket with a small box of charcoal and in the barracks after work she could sit for hours by the window, drawing. I could never sit that still – not even for Kerouac's *Lonesome Traveller*, my latest Book. Hearing sounds of guitar or voices or bottles clinking up the hall or in the lounge I'd be pulled out of the room irresistibly, a passenger sucked from a damaged jet. Between my impatience and the way she'd always put her pencil down soon after starting to draw me, smile, say, *Caleb, let's get undressed*, she never did quite finish a portrait, though more and more that's what she wanted to do – sit in the room drawing or reading or cleaning up and saying we should look around town for new jobs, a nicer place. And still I kept telling myself she really loved our nights off, singing and drinking, dancing, then at midnight under a sea of stars stumbling out for coffee and rushing back to the lounge and jamming again till dawn. But now I see. Like when you read some complex, eerie book and wake up a few nights later in a sweat because out of the blue some small, subtle detail makes terrible sense? That's how it is with me now. I'll remember something she said in passing, some subtle gesture, and I get to know better what she was, what she wanted. I haven't seen her in a dozen years but each year that goes by I get to know her more. Too late. Guess I've finally fallen in love.

I can see it now – what she liked best was what we did only on the nights we were tired, or I was – a possibility *On the Road* hadn't really prepared me for. We'd lie in bed after making love and read together, taking turns reading aloud, the wings of an open book balanced on our chests. In March we'd read parts of *The Horse's Mouth* (I'd chosen it for her and she'd liked it, though the artist Gulley sometimes riled her) and now in April it was *On the Road*. In hindsight I see she never liked the book too much and only put up with it for my sake. As she had to – as she put up with me. For a while.

Then one night in bed she turned to me, propping her head on one hand – long ginger curls spooling over her cheeks, breasts flopping together – to ask if I didn't think those guys were sometimes a bit, you know, a bit *immature*. They were in their thirties, after all.

I sat up in bed, cradling in my right hand The Book.

'Now Caleb, don't get angry, all I mean is ... I mean do you really want to be driving around the country wrecking cars when you're middle-aged? Drinking till you pass out? Like a schoolkid. Looking for Mom.'

I told her The Beats were just more alive than most people. Burning with life, with a hunger for life. Wanting to swallow it whole. *Living*.

'Sure. And treating women as if they're just a bunch of – just – '

'What?'

She brushed a curl off her breast and looked down, smiling slightly, shaking her head.

'Bullshit,' I told her. 'Jack was compassionate. He always was. Look, I'm not *making* you read anything, I can get by just fine reading this on my own.'

She sighed. 'I know it.'

'What's that supposed to mean?'

She just smiled again, said she'd had enough of books for now, and asked me to turn out the light. She took my *On the Road* and set it on the floor and pulled me down to her.

In late April I was promoted to the position of third cook, which meant I got to ladle soup and slap eggs onto plates as well as help with the dishes. Jess and I saw each other on the job all the time, me passing her breakfasts over the steam table while the Swiss-German chefs made bad jokes in broken English about me slipping the pretty painter the bacon. I just shook my head and smiled. Jess never seemed to hear, so I didn't think it mattered. I ignored them when they ribbed me about Chantal, too, since she was from a small town in the Gaspé and barely knew a word of English. It was strange – we'd barely exchanged a word since meeting and it wasn't till the chefs started smirking and teasing me about her that I realized they'd long seen what I was just starting to feel.

In early May Jess told me she'd tracked down a nice apartment in town that was free from the first of June, and I said I guessed that sounded all right, but when were we going on to the coast? She suggested a week's holiday after we moved in to the new place – the overnight bus to Vancouver and maybe a couple days on the island, Long Beach. I told her that sounded fine to me too, but I warned her once we got out to the sea we might never want to come back.

'I think I will,' she said, setting aside *Mad Shadows* and turning in bed to face me. I put down my own book; it was one of our quiet nights but we weren't reading together much anymore. 'In fact I'm sure I'll want to come back. I've never been any place like this before. It's the light, I think – so much clearer than back east.'

'Really,' I said. 'You think so?'

'Caleb you *know* I do. You told me it was growing on you, too.'

I was hungover and tired. I was now struggling through the terminal stages of Kerouac's canon and the later books painted a pretty bleak picture of life for a Lonesome Traveller, getting old. All I really wanted then was to make love – to forget – and go to sleep. So I told her she was right, the light here *was* really special, it was growing on me too, it must be perfect for her drawing and painting and all.

She kissed me and I reached for the bare bulb above our heads.

The light really was something through May and Jess spent all her free time outside painting the landscape as it thawed, and, especially when I was least in the mood, talking about June and our new place. It had been a rough month in some ways and I wanted to avoid more arguing, so I just nodded and told myself – and her – how tired I was of the barracks crowd anyway. Meantime my body, without my knowledge, went on mapping out its own plans.

It was a few days before the end of May when Jess tried again to draw me. She sat me at the foot of the bed so her drawing would take in most of our little room and even the window where evening sunlight flooded in with the year's first mellow wind. Her hair riffled over her forehead as she studied me, her face still, eyes now and then dipping to the page.

Like all the other times I'd posed for her I found myself torn between vanity and impatience. The scratch of her charcoal mixed rhythmically into the undertow of sounds from the lounge up the hall: jamming guitars, singing, voices always swelling into laughter and then subsiding in a slow tidal rhythm, waves breaking on a shore. A shore where new friends sit by a bonfire and sing, smoke strong hash and pass around bottles of wine? Or was it the Big Sur coast where Kerouac's dream of a highway endlessly running finally slowed and skidded over the cliffs ...? I was almost finished *Big Sur* and strangely enough that elegy to the Beat years, along with my own growing fatigue, just made me more restless and anxious to prove it didn't all have to end in nausea: Kerouac kneeling like Narcissus in the shallows and puking, weeping into his own wavery image; me going back east hat in hand to my father and maybe ending up an accountant or a prof and stodgy recluse like him....

Whatever feelings had surfaced in my eyes, Jessie seemed to find them riveting. Frightening. I'd never seen her stare so intensely, her own eyes so transfixing and transfixed that she hardly ever seemed to look down at the page. As usual I was anxious to see the drawing in process, to see what was there so far. Then another wave of laughter from the lounge. I found my fingers tapping on my knee, as if in time to a music I couldn't hear. *I don't know, Caleb ... those guys are in their thirties after all.... Do you want to be driving around the country wrecking cars when you're an old man ...?*

'Caleb?' She was frowning at me, setting down her charcoal. 'Caleb, what is it? What's wrong? You look ... '

'What?'

'I can't finish with your look changing that way.'

'I'm tired,' I lied, 'that's all. I need a walk. Think I'll go on up the hall, see what's happening, maybe have a drink.'

She turned over her pad and came to me.

'You don't *need* another drink, Caleb – that's why you're so tired to begin with.' Her mouth tightened. 'Unless maybe you've just been working a bit too hard on your French.'

I glared at her. She looked away.

'You don't need another drink, Caleb, it's the last thing – '

'A change of scene, that's what I really need. A real change. They're going to fire me soon anyhow.'

A sharp rapping at some door a few rooms down, then footsteps rushing up the hall.

She was shaking her head, eyes downcast, smiling tightly.

'Caleb ...?'

I watched her blackened fingers form fists. I looked up at

her. She seemed to force the words out, an actress delivering a line she didn't believe in:

'Caleb, I swear, you touch her and I'll get my palette knife and ... '

'And *what*?' I grabbed her wrist, as if she held the knife already. 'I know you wouldn't.'

She shook her wrist free and gripped my hand and held it till it hurt. 'No,' she said softly. 'Of course not. Of *course* not. But isn't that what I'm supposed to say? Something like that? Anyway you half-deserve it, you know, you and your stupid – stupid Dharma Bums and their – goddamn empty – '

She was pushing me back onto the bed and kissing me sharply, clawing at my shirt. I found myself kissing and biting her lips and roughly undressing her as we fell back into the blankets. She made a quick swiping motion with her arm. There was a muffled thump as my books slid off the bed to the floor. All the angry blood seemed to be draining down out of my face into my body and suddenly I was hard and wanting her as badly as I ever had, or maybe ever could – as if I really did love her and we were back in Toronto on our first night together.

Looking back now I try to remember just how it was that last time, but who can ever remember how it felt, how it feels to make love? Especially the last time, and you never knew. Details, that's all. As if Nature's worked things out so we have to fuck again and again to remember and that need to remember keeps us doing it, keeps us feeling unhappy – restless. Feeling my jeans slide round my ankles, the breeze on my thighs. Warm melon-musk of her breasts in my face, my mouth. Her tongue seeming to paint its way down and down my belly to my cock then rushing up again to my nipples and throat then a force like my own anger seeming to fuel her hips so she rammed herself down onto me with a cry and bit her own lower lip, hard, her body so brine-wet we slid smack together and I bit her neck and shoulders scratching as we fucked and the welts and bruises she left me were still there two nights later when I got to Vancouver and the sea.

Lights of the north shore and the mountains above, lights strung up like Orion over the freighters in English Bay and the sweep and spread of it all tugs your eye and heart way out after the close stony walls of the Rockies. The sea. For the first time ever. And every time after is a first time.

Because afterwards I left Jess calmly sleeping and found a party up the hall, but I couldn't leave her words behind. The anger ebbed back, blood rising back out of my heart and body into my face – ashamed. Drinking made it worse. *Cale,* my friends said, *you're so quiet tonight,* and Chantal slipped her arm around me and asked if I was okay.

No. I thought of rushing back to the room and waking Jess and telling her she was wrong and bound for a life of clock-punching dullness and domestic mediocrity – but I just kept drinking and some time before dawn I tumbled into bed with Chantal.

Late next morning I collected my things off the floor of a room I now thought of as Jessie's. She was at work. My *On the Road* lay atop a neat pile of my stuff she'd stacked in the corner by the door. The cover was partly torn, as if she'd started to shred it with the palette knife that lay on the floor nearby – then stopped. For a moment I thought of taking the knife and thrusting it through last night's portrait – very dark and blurred, the borders of the head rough and broken as a shoreline – then I grabbed a pencil instead and scrawled in the margin a brief, bitter goodbye.

I stood and stared down at it for a minute or two, then hurried out.

My pack with guitar strapped on the top felt so fine, so light on my shoulders as I hiked to the station. Chantal was already there. Such black, black hair, her eyes pale blue; *like the waters off Vancouver Island.* I scrawled a postcard to my folks and we boarded the Vancouver bus and pulled away twelve hours over the mountains and through the interior to the sea – Golden, Revelstoke, Salmon Arm, Kamloops, Boston Bar and Hope, the marvellous names from my father's maps scrolling through my mind with the warm foreign word Chantal kissed into my ear when we first sensed, on the soft wind gusting up the valley of the Fraser an hour from the coast, *la mer.* Our lips and tongues sweetly sore from hours of necking but no need now for speech and so few words we knew in common anyway and it seemed perfect like that and I was sure that was the secret, Chantal and I had dropped anchor off an island of calm: shared language led to strife and pain and ice-cold familiarity (my folks!) and paradise was a lover who could never perjure herself or you with a spoken word. The secret. We'd be together a long time.

Bullshit.

In the cramped, rumbling washroom just before we got in, I stared at my face in the mirror – dimly lit and warped, uneven, as in a mountain pool. Had Jess really seen through me? I leaned closer to the smeared glass and a reek of piss and disinfectant washed up from below. Peering into my eyes I wondered – I wonder – what Chantal saw there. The bus swerved and braked for something on the road and I pitched off-balance, felt my face crack into the glass and for a moment I was stunned. Numb, breathless. Awash in a dim reflection. Drowned.

How does it happen for the last time? The lovemaking. Two
bodies joining once, twice, a thousand times, then never again.
How?

* * *

In the early summer of 1839 Alden's great-great-grandfather
Caleb MacLeod found his way back to Brockville, his wife
Charlotte and their three small children. He arrived long after
midnight. He was filthy and sunburnt, his stern, bulging blue
eyes had sunk back in his skull, and the fierce determined jut
of the chin so striking in his portrait was hidden under a matted bush of beard. His prematurely thin red hair had thinned
still further and his fiery brows had thickened in the seven
months since his capture and five weeks since his escape.
Alden pictured him standing in the doorway before his wife, a
storybook giant grown thin as the cut-out silhouette figurines
his children would have eyed in vain through shop windows
last Christmas, soon after his capture. So changed now, face
flickering in the weak glow of the candle Charlotte has
brought to the door....

The story of Caleb's famous insurgency, flight and exile had
been heirloomed along through the generations as far as
Alden, then his children, Annie and Caleb, the known facts
hammered down during its passage to the gritty essentials, as
a fugitive will gradually jettison all but the most basic posses-
sions yet build around him a portable mansion of memories as
shelter for the long, fetal nights cringing under scrub-pines
and in caves and deserted cabins. Likewise Caleb's story had
grown in spirit as it shrivelled in fact, so by the time it was
entrusted to Alden his ancestor loomed as a mythic, romantic
giant who both inspired and intimidated his heirs. Alden
could trace his fascination with the rugged and fickle geography of the region to the story of Caleb's escape from Fort
Henry in mid-May 1839 – a few days before he was to be
shipped out for Quebec, Portsmouth, and Van Diemen's land –
and his five-week wilderness journey north to the edge of the

‹ 26 ›

Shield country, then furtively east and south again to Brockville. Alden felt certain, too, that the unruly wanderlust of his son Caleb's youth (Banff, Vancouver, Australia) had sprung also from Caleb senior – from his example as much as his genes. Alden, after all, had never much liked to travel or even leave his solid house, let alone his study. But who could tell? Perhaps his ancestor had been the same. After all, young Caleb's footloose enthusiasms had cooled and he now lived a steady productive life as a prison literacy and music teacher, married, in Winnipeg.

So perhaps Caleb senior, a blacksmith by trade, had loved the warm confines of his shop? Alden pictured him on a winter's day flushed with the crackling heat of the forge, his great red eyebrows singed and curling, the firelight mirrored above his temples on the bald scalp. He whistles quietly, mumbles to himself and grins. He savours the warm private manual work – the mundane spectacle of golden sparks cascading from the hammered anvil, its rhythmic clanging as intimate as his own pulse, his muscles rippling smoothly under the warm wool shirt and leather apron.... Alden did not believe, as some of his old academic friends believed about the radical new scholars in the department, that inside every rebel there skulks a sullen child anxious to seize the attention of the world, or, failing that, to destroy it. He believed he'd seen through a few bandwagon radicals but he had also met some young people – and older ones – who seemed driven by solid and reasoned convictions to challenge the status quo. Sometimes Alden saw their point, and for a while he'd done some teaching in the prisons, but he loved too much the stillness and setness of his maps and study ever to throw himself wholly into the fray. But his great-great-grandfather had done that – thrown himself in. Surely, though, the injustices of his age had been harsher, more sharply defined? Sometimes Alden was not so sure. But Caleb, a mild giant of a man who loved the confines of his workshop and the hearthlike heat of the forge – who loved his hearth, his wife Charlotte and three small children – Caleb had made up his mind and beat his dead father's ploughshare into a sword.

The story first joins him in the fall of 1837 when he is

thirty-six years old and established as one of four blacksmiths in the town of Brockville. He is a hardworking pious man who reads to his wife and children from the Bible each night before supper. His blood, steeped in the sober egalitarianism of his Scots forebears, has warmed at the despotic pranks and machinations of the ruling Family Compact, steamed at their summer decrees, and comes to a rolling boil in the fall of '37 after a run of incendiary sermons by local politicoes and the visiting radical William Lyon Mackenzie.

In November Caleb closes shop and canters toward York, or Toronto, with twelve other Brockville men. A few of them are armed with muskets; Caleb carries a kind of lance he has improvised by lashing a long, home-beaten blade onto a staff. In York, family tradition casts our hero willy-nilly in a starring role on a decidedly ill-starred stage: during the rebels' pell-mell flight from Montgomery's Tavern the gallant blacksmith holds off a body of militiamen with his shining lance and thus helps scores of comrades evade capture, even death.

Here the family storysmiths beat a hurried retreat and Caleb is seen back in his workshop, with markedly less work to lay on the anvil because customers have switched to other shops during his three-week absence, and the Tories among them, hearing rumours of his treason, have sworn never to come back.

Nothing is told here of Charlotte, but surely her feelings can be guessed. For three weeks no income, and now an income greatly reduced; three weeks alone with the children at night wondering if her husband has been shot, imprisoned, hanged; three weeks of rising alone, chilled, stirring the embers and feeling their faint lukewarm breath waft up to her face, blinking down at their dim, infernal glow. *Van Diemen's Land.*

Unrest smoulders again through the hot summer of '38 and the autumn winds, like a bellows by the forge at dawn, fan it to high flame. More fighting in Lower Canada. A hundred soldiers and *patriotes* dead in the snow near Beauharnois. So the rumour runs. And in November a force of Canadian patriots and sympathetic Yankees is ferried across the St Lawrence below Brockville, hoping to seize Fort Wellington. Caleb and his comrades, undaunted by last autumn's debacle, are there to join them. The whole force falls back on an old windmill above the river and is soon besieged by British soldiers and local militia. Four days inside the yard-thick limestone walls while fire rages and fades in the buildings around the mill – then bursts through the oak floor of the mill inside. The crackle of musket fire echoing madly, the bark of British cannon, the thudding as balls pound the limestone and soundwaves smash through to pummel the ribs like the butt of a rifle.

Flame-red jackets moving over the brown grasses of the field. Like a brush-fire. Closing in.

Caleb is captured, trussed and carted with over a hundred others to Fort Henry in Kingston where a young lawyer named Sir John A. Macdonald defends their leader, but to no avail. The leader is to be hanged, along with ten others. And along with fifty-nine others Caleb is sentenced to transportation – to Van Diemen's land, in May.

In March when the worst of the winter is past, Charlotte and the children accomplish the rough two-day journey from Brockville to Kingston to say farewell. The children weep and shiver in the damp grey corridors of Fort Henry, Dickensian waifs clinging to the full skirts of their pallid, frightened mother. A rushed visit. Kisses for the children who hardly recognize their father, his face, his clothing, his smell. A few moments in private for Caleb and Charlotte – Charlotte torn by fear and regret and anger and desire and who knows what else? Her desire, such as it is, damped by dreary circumstance. Her fear by now familiar, hidden, like her feelings of regret.

And anger? But there is so little time. And so much anger.

Your smithy is lost and your children halfway orphaned and I –

But the guards have come. An iron door clangs shut.

In mid-May, a few days before he is to be shipped out for Quebec, Portsmouth, and Australia, Caleb escapes a work detail outside the fort walls. With the hammer that he wields to crush rock, his expert hands (so the story goes) neatly smash the shackles, and he is spotted (too late) in full stride over the newly green fields, his prison-trousers flapping round bloodied ankles as he lopes downhill for the river. A single erratic musket blast. A blast of Cockney cursing as the second guard's gun misfires. Already the balding red-bearded giant is at the river's edge, and gone.

It has been a warm spring and had it been otherwise Caleb could hardly have survived his first night: shivering, wet, in the soft needled shelter of a small pine, after running north along the Cataraqui and braving its unusually mild waters at a ford. In the morning he cuts inland and thrashes north through the wilderness above Kingston. Near Westport, it is said, he finds in a deserted shack some old moth-ravaged woollens and a bit of dried food. He stays for several days to recoup his strength, then moves on. North. Through the forest a stone's throw east of the Perth Road so that he hears and sometimes catches a glimpse of traffic on the road, a troop of red-coated cavalry cantering south – on the lookout for someone? – or farmers and settlers bound north from Kingston on one-horse carts laden with topsoil and seed-potatoes and sacks of grain. Caleb, a beanstalk of a giant not born for stealth, sidling through the undergrowth and darting barefoot for silence onto the King's road behind a clattering cart. Grabbing whatever he can. A few seed potatoes. A turnip. Sometimes only seed.

For a few days he camps on Foley Mountain, above the hamlet of Westport, where the farmlands end and the granite Shield rears up. At night he slinks down the pine-covered mountainside to the sleeping hamlet and scavenges what he can. There is little enough – a meat-pie on a sill, a small bag of flour in a shed behind the baker's. Two more days on the mountain resting, eating cold flour mush till his stomach rebels, regretting his forge and hearth but not daring to light a fire....

He sets out for home. Stronger now and more acquainted with stealth, he escapes even the mythmakers who lose him in dense forest east of Westport and only catch him in passing glances through the woods or darting at nightfall with his giant strides over the new-seeded fields north of Brockville. He surprises them, and Charlotte, sometime after midnight on mid-summer's eve 1839 when he appears, a bearded, sunburned ghost, in the doorway of his home.

The mythmakers usher him to the table where his devoted Charlotte serves him his first substantial meal in weeks, and they grant him a brief last look at his sleeping children before he and his wife retire for the night and he sleeps in a good bed for the first time in months – and the last time in his life. With a modesty and discretion suited to the authors of stories that may be told to children, the mythmakers do not shadow the reunited pair over the threshold of their room, or even grant us a keyhole peep, but in his later years, especially after he and Holly had moved to separate rooms, Alden often wondered what his forebear's last night had been like. Had *they* made love again? Caleb must have been mortally tired, Charlotte desperately afraid. And angry. But by all accounts Caleb was a fiery impetuous giant of a man and Alden felt sure, in his study under that smouldering charcoal gaze, that he would have squeezed his wife in a last mighty bearhug.

It is a sultry windless night so that even with the window above the bed propped open the flame of the candle on the bed-side table does not stir. Caleb peels off his matted clothing and washes quickly at the basin, sighing richly but with a now-instinctive softness as the water streams over his body and face. Charlotte sits on the side of the bed in her summer night-gown, bare feet on the floor. She stares into the flame of the candle then looks down at her lap, the patient hands folded together – a little too tightly. Caleb in his old nightshirt on the bed beside her. Mumbled words. Where will he go in the morning? Away. Again? He must go away again.

No. *No.* But she admits that, yes, men have come to the house many times, men with firearms and pointed questions. Her hands clench tighter, the knuckles blanched and angry – then she turns on Caleb with a sudden embrace. He responds with his usual clumsy ardour and the candle flame wavers in the breeze of their coupling. So thin he is under his shirt; yet still heavy. She kisses his balding scalp, the massive brow and eyes and beard. Their hands and fingers clawing and flickering like flames, impatient, as if fearing interruption – as if after long absence every half-forgotten half-embellished part must be re-explored and so relearned, reclaimed. *Stay*, she says, *for the sake of your children, hide here until they forget*, and he clenches her tighter till she can hardly breathe, or move, or say another word. This man she has cursed every day of his absence and craved, Alden thinks, every night.

As usual it is over too soon. Sadness, deeper than usual, and the old, embering coals of shame.

Van Diemen's Land.

They are sweating with the heat, as if the single candle is a hearth, a forge. They have never before made love in the light. Charlotte blows out the candle and Caleb, within seconds, is snoring heavily so she must lean across his long enfeebled frame and yank down the sash. She lies back, turning from him, the ache inside her unfilled. Anger flaring up to fill it. For with morning he will leave and start fading from his family's eyes to something as dim as the light this glowing wick still casts: a character in a story read once as a child, his name forgotten with the story's name, nothing left but an aura, a tone of voice, a few flickering details.

The story has it that he did not leave, he was taken. At first light a platoon of redcoated soldiers hammered on the door and Caleb was seized by four strong men as he leapt in his nightshirt from the bedroom window. And here the forgers of the story follow him for the last time as he is marched in irons down the cobbled streets of Brockville to the river and up the gangplank of a sloop bound for Quebec, then Portsmouth, then Australia. They lose him as the ship leans out and ferries him away with the current and a clean summer wind.

Who can add further chapters? His own son, thought Alden, the son he named Caleb, who has seen Botany Bay and Tasmania.

The story ends that Charlotte conceived her third daughter that night – Alden's great grandmother Sarah. Sarah in her cradle by the hearth in late March, cooing, her cries a dim high echo of her father's deep bass. Reading from Scripture, at table, in a much brighter season: *After the fire a still small voice.*

4 *The Fall Wind*

A Chinook wind blew in over the passes and the clean powder snow falling since Remembrance Day turned soft and wet and began to vanish. The streets of Banff, full of skiers and sightseers up for the day from Calgary, ran with meltwater smelling of spring, the sun in the clear sky was summer-hot. Jessie and Stratis stood at the plate-glass window of their busy café gazing up over the bright crowded streets and dripping roofs of the facing shops to the peak of Mount Rundle, where snow was being churned and spun by the westerlies like spume off the tip of a wave. And Rundle did look like a wave, a huge tidal wave of blue-grey water frozen solid in the second before breaking. So Jessie thought. She was a painter, part-time – a too-small part of the time – and she'd told Stratis how the mountain looked to her but he always said he just couldn't see it, a mountain was a mountain, wasn't it?

She turned to him. The sunlight through the plate-glass window did him good, brushed his greyed face with colour. For two weeks he'd been in a state of unexpected remission and ten days ago he'd come home from the hospital in Calgary. The doctors, Stratis warned her, were not optimistic. She knew that. She knew not to expect miracles. But on a day like today anything seemed possible, even likely, with Rundle holding its precarious poise against the blue sky, the sunlight, the Chinook breathing sweetly through the open door of the shop, winter deferred for a few more days, the shop full of cheerful customers and the new help, Glen, working out just fine – much better than the last student she'd hired in June when Stratis first went into hospital.

'Jess?'

Glen needed help at the till. Jessie spun round and in a few strides crossed the tiny Olympos Café. She and Stratis had long fought over the decor – he wanted posters and framed, doctored tourist photos of Greece, she planned to cover the walls with the sketches and paintings of Bow Valley artists – but from the start of his illness she had acquiesced, so in his absence the café had come to look exactly as he had always hoped. A few of her paintings he could live with, he said, gladly he could, but all that other stuff? There were enough mountains out the window, who wanted airbrushed Alps when you had the real thing a few steps out the door? So while a few of her watercolour landscapes still hung behind the till, it had been months since she'd hung any new work by friends. A yellowing map of Greece instead, the Acropolis from at least five angles and through lenses aimed with wildly differing degrees of skill, Mt Olympos viewed from the sea, sunny beaches with fresh-painted fishing boats drawn up, the Aegean in implausible postcard blue and the matching forgery of Grecian skies.

A tightness now in her throat and belly as she passed them, these aquamarine clichés, these touched-up dreams that would soon remind her of a fresh and unretouched sorrow. But no. Stratis looked so well these days; he was cheered by the café's increasing success, and the weather, and most of all by being back in Banff with his children. And Jessie. He had smiled weakly then laughed out loud and hugged her on seeing how she'd put up all those extra images of Greece.

'But soon my dear you will take them down.'

He said it softly, without malice.

Jessie had met him eight years before in Calgary, where, at twenty-six, she was trying to finish a Fine Arts degree part-time while waitressing wherever she could. Stratis managed the dining room where she worked weekends. He was the owner's son and he'd surprised her, over time, by erasing her stereotyped image of the Classical Greek Boss. 'My father, mind you, is the real thing,' he would laugh, his long black feminine lashes meeting. 'Me, I hate it here.'

Stratis had no particular interest in art and that suited Jessie just fine, she'd had enough of dating art students. Stratis's consuming interest, she learned, was family – not the one he had, mind you, but the one he hoped to have. He wanted a small business of his own somewhere a long way from his father's city and he wanted his own big family as well. So his lean olive features lit up and furrowed in a broad smile whenever a family with small children came into his father's place – partly, Jessie teased, because he didn't have to serve them.

'Strange,' he opened up to her one night after work, over his beer and cigarettes, 'we were never happy as children. I think sometimes I want to do right what my father didn't.'

Stratis was ready to settle down, it was clear, and Jessie had long been ready. So after getting her degree she moved with him to Banff, which she loved and he didn't think was really far enough from Calgary but did offer good prospects for the future. They both got work in another restaurant through one of Stratis's seemingly countless uncles. They lived frugally and began to save. They were made floor-managers, Jessie days and Stratis nights, and the money was better. After a year they got married and a year later they had their first child – a girl, Calla. Then twins, Larissa and Paul. They made an offer on a closing crafts-shop and did it over as a café.

With each passing year Jessie smuggled a few more of her friends' paintings into the café and deported a few more of her husband's Grecian atrocities. Stratis fought a stubborn rear-guard action and sometimes resorted to guerrilla tactics, one night replacing three watery Alpscapes with chromatically-similar Greek scenes, then pleading, 'Jessie, *pethi*, we're a Greek-style café, think of the customers!' And she had to nod. But this was no more than a minor check. Eventually, she was sure, the Olympos Café would be a kind of local art gallery.

The impending realization of her dream could do little now but depress her. As if the dream itself were partly to blame for what had happened? Stratis looked so thin here, silhouetted in the window with the mountain above him; snow churning steadily off the crest.

She showed Glen how to unjam the drawer of the till and, when she looked up, saw Stratis weaving his way back through the tables. He riffled the hair of a small blond girl who grinned up at him, her chin, lips and teeth flecked with nuts and sticky bits of *filo*. For a moment he seemed to flush, to glow with that contact, but as he neared the till his face faded again from rich colour to shades of chalk and charcoal, black-and-white. The furrows in his cheeks and around his eyes sank deeper. Deeper still as he tried to smile.

'It's such a nice day, Jessie. Too busy to leave Glen here alone. Let's close at four and go for supper with the kids.'

At home, after the children were in bed, Jessie asked Glen to come down from his upstairs apartment so she and Stratis could go out for a while. The Chinook was still blowing and the streets still ran with meltwater and the Bow River, sluggish and half frozen just a day before, was flowing swiftly in the dark. But the air did seem colder and Jessie wondered if it was more than just the absence of the sun. A change in the weather? They walked arm in arm along the river, slowly. The path was deserted. Then, straight ahead, a black, massive shape bulked out of the river onto the banks: a huge elk, his hide and antlers dripping, glistening in the faint lamplight, his body like a great barrel rocking back and forth as he shook off the cold water of his crossing.

Jessie and Stratis stood very still. The elk ignored them, his heavy snout upraised and snuffling the wind. After a few moments he ambled, with solemn dignity, into the pines.

They lagged back up Wolf Street toward the café. Stratis said he wanted to check the place seeing as they'd closed early – and since Stratis was the kind of man who would stop the car halfway to Calgary and turn round and drive back to Banff just to check if he'd turned off the coffee machine, Jessie was not surprised. She was not even exasperated, as she had been in the past by his worrying, his occasional laziness in the shop, his stubborn matter-of-factness (*a mountain is a mountain!*) – and his refusal to quit smoking till it was too late. How strange, how very wasteful such exasperation now seemed! Even about the smoking, perhaps....

Rundle brooded above them again, a tidal wave in silhouette. Jessie would never tire of its power, its tension, the sense of massive implacable movement, stopped. Yet always in motion; never complete. It was a masterpiece of tension and whoever could reflect it perfectly in paint – and not just its essence but its *shape*, which could never be improved on – would have a masterpiece on her hands. She had sketched and painted it many times, in charcoal, *conté*, watercolour and oils, in as many versions as there were tourist views of the

Acropolis. By the path near the bridge over the Bow River where she and Caleb had come walking years before, she would set up her easel in the sun. Mondays, for a few stolen hours. So that when she came home, Stratis – making the *baklava* that had added, with the children, twenty pounds to her frame – smiled at her freckles and said it looked like someone had sprinkled her face with nutmeg.

And she would laugh. But the mountain escaped her.

They came back to the modest clapboard two-storey on Marten Street and thanked Glen. Jessie noticed how uneasy the boy looked on seeing Stratis's face. And when she and Stratis were alone and she got a good look at him under the hall-light, she realized he did look worse. And she sensed he knew it.

He told her he felt fine.

In bed, the mountain and its halo of blue air were still above them – a kind of abstract Greek Orthodox icon, framed above their heads, in encaustic. Jessie's. She frowned up at it as she got under the down quilt beside her husband, who was almost asleep now but seemed to stir himself, to rub his long-lashed eyes like a child resisting sleep. And with those white pyjamas he had started wearing in the hospital after years of sleeping nude, he looked even more like a child. So small and shrunken, even now, after a week of eating well.

His body giving off the faint sour odour they had both noticed in June. For the last week it had been gone and his body had seemed, to Jessie, fresh and pure as a wind off the snowfields.

'I smell again, Jess. I stink.'

A kiss of denial. 'Hush.'

He puts his arms around her and pulls her naked body onto him. His clasp is so gentle, she thinks; and then she thinks, weak.

She helps him undress. Gently she holds him and rubs her body over his. He is so weak, not like two nights ago when he seemed almost as before, laughing, reminding her of when sex was something lively, raunchy, a terrific joke with endless variations and the same gut-wrenching punchline that seemed new every time. A warm fragrant gust of Chinook rattles the blinds and passes over them and perhaps it stirs him, wakes him a little, breathes strength back into his lungs because his cock hardens in her hand and quickly she guides him inside her and moves over him, and over him. They go on for a long time in near-silence, Stratis with his eyes closed and a look on his face so peaceful, the long lashes twinned, parted lips like a sleeping child's. She with her mouth open near to his. Exhaling deep as if to revive him. Now his eyes open, widen and he clutches her buttocks with hands so gentle she could weep, she arches harder and rubs against him and pulls back and feels a kind of fear as if the smooth motion of her cunt soon to clasp and suck the crisis from deep inside him with his seed will weaken him too much, bleed life from his core. He is coming, groaning weakly and she lets herself go, she pushes and as the storm breaks under her womb and pumps long sweet warming gusts to the tips of her arching toes and clinched fingers a breeze blows through the room and just to feel it caress her bare skin as she comes is too much, the sweetness is too much, the pain, god damn it, the sorrow. A second climax wells from her belly but this time it is all pain, an orgasm of pain that racks her whole body dredging up all the things she has kept down as she sobs and collapses on top of this man, this good man, this fucking heartless bastard who is going to leave her.

So soon. So soon his cock softens, wilts and slips out of her. She can't stop crying, her head pressed into the bony crook between his neck and shoulder. The sour reek of his poor body.

'It's all right, Jessie. Please. It's all right.'

It's not god damn it and you know it's not. It's not. You're going to leave me. What the hell am I going to do?

At four she wakes and his side of the bed is empty. For a moment she lies propped on an elbow staring at the imprint his body has etched into the sheet. That sour smell again, stronger.

She stumbles into the hall. A white form glides toward her out of the dark. 'Stratis?'

'The children,' he whispers, short of breath. 'Just checking. You know how I am. To close their windows.'

She guides him back into the bedroom, so cold now, icy, the

weather has turned and by dawn the unmelted snow in the yard will have a crust a child can walk on without sinking. Ice knitting up in the melt-pools and forming along the banks of the Bow. Cold air bleeding in through the walls and settling into the drawer by the window where she keeps all her portraits.

She tucks Stratis in and closes the window for winter.

'In the morning,' she says lightly – trying to sound casual, in control – 'darling? In the morning we should probably go see the doctors. In Calgary.'

His mouth is open as if to form a response, but he says nothing. Asleep, so soon. She lies beside him and studies the familiar yet subtly changed contours of his face, thinking of the weeks to come, and Rundle: the blue sky above it and the Chinook blowing snow like foam off the grey rock crest of a shape she will always be painting. Down the sloping backside of the frozen wave to a small graveyard of crooked limestone slabs. She has painted there, too, but she won't be able to do that again.

She leans over and sets her palm, like a mirror, an inch above the open mouth and feels the warm soft breath of her husband moistening her skin.

Coda

Alden and Holly stand in the blunt bow of the ferry crossing to the island and peer into a slim channel clogged with broken ice – ice that buckles and cracks and gets sucked under by the ferry as it grinds along. A cold wind burns their cheeks and stings their squinted eyes and they huddle together for warmth. Everyone else is in the heated cabin or in cars with engines running but Holly has insisted they leave their car and stand in the bow, as they used to do years back, to feel the wind. And it is bracing, it does slap them awake: Alden feels his chest fill up with a kind of boyish joy and expectation so that even squinting down stiffly at his watch he seems a young explorer – a mapmaker – poring over a compass as his ship nears new land. Wind and black water in the channel and the snowy hill where the old prison looms and the lights of the town like flickering amber spots in a damped, cooling fire.

'What were you playing on the piano,' he says, then has to shout over the roaring, '*what were you playing when I went out to clear the ice!*'

The trickling of the notes, so faint, but two or three in sequence clear enough to rouse the ghost of some forgotten passage.

'*Holly!*'

She kisses him, smiles, excited by the wind, her back forgotten, the fire-warmed inn and the dinner to come. The way she smiled at the keyboard, caught in the window while the snapdragons disappeared below.... Laughing, she says she's forgotten. Think of that! She recalls sitting down and playing the piano, but forgets now what she played.

On earth as it is

Father

STAVROS LEARNED THAT time does not so much dull a pain as seal it off, the way a membrane formed around the poisons in his father's gut after his appendix cracked open like an egg and for a year nobody knew, not even his father, till the surgeons cut him open for something else and there it was. A lunar, bluish ball, wobbling and amniotic, it still seethed with poisons, though they were securely shelled in and had done no obvious harm. But the doctors soon learned that the tumour they'd cut him open to remove was anything but harmless, and their white-gloved hands, palms up in attitudes of defeat, flittered helpless above the opened body like doves or small spirits escaping from the flesh.

Supposing all doctors knew exactly where to pry; supposing their eyes and their instruments were more acute than they are, more attuned. Surely on cutting into the body of a man or a woman they would find other organs like that, and the older the patient the more they would find. Could be that death comes in part because the sealed-up grief gradually squeezes out and destroys every essential life-organ. Could be the membranes make an imperfect seal and they leak, they drip – like I.V. bags, but toxic – so a tincture of past sorrow is always circling in the blood.

Still, with age Stavros shut away the night of his father's death – he was only six at the time – and another night a few summers later when he was staying at a Greek Orthodox boys' camp up in the hill country north of Toronto. That night had always involved his father too, though his father had not been there. He was safe in the earth and he was up in the stars – so his mother and brothers had reassured him, often – but now their words were no consolation because at night, north of the city, the stars were shining fingertips and tantalizing, close enough to touch, yet they were so cold, and far, and they did not touch back.

Our Father who aren't in heaven, that was how the first line of the prayer always sounded when they recited it at school each morning or in the camp chapel before breakfast. Anyway it was best to think of him safe in the earth – that was easier to think of, easier to believe. Easier to think of him rising out of the earth back into the world where people loved him than to picture him floundering down from the sky like some slingshot-shattered bird – or, in Stavros' nightmare, a bag of debris, discarded from a passing jet, split and spilling its rank, rotted contents as it tumbled back to earth.

Son

The boys, sweating, stumbled up a dark path cobbled with fist-sized stones and the boughs and unripe apples that had fallen in Sunday's gale. There was no moon. Up ahead clear of the trees a dozen flashlights flickered over the bare hill and the boys pressed on, shoving each other, swearing, loosing the odd clap of high-pitched laughter. It was hard to keep up with the counsellors. Father Yiannis would be up ahead too, scything through the tall grass with his massive strides, his long robes swirling round his ankles.

It's a perfect night for it, one boy whispered. The counsellors say it's perfect.

What do snipes look like anyway?

Nobody knows.

Your counsellor doesn't even know? What about Father Yiannis?

Won't say, the boy whispered, louder. Be quiet now.

I don't see how we can catch them if we don't even –

Quiet. They're afraid of people – we've got to be quiet.

Sounds of laboured breathing as the boys climbed. The pulsing hum of late-summer cicadas in trees that could not be seen: a buzzing that seemed to flag and fizzle out as the boys pushed on, like the sound of a childhood toy – abandoned, the batteries almost dead – dug from a cellar and played with one last time.

I don't even believe in them, snipes.

Yeah? So what are those bags for?

A flashlight-beam up ahead had caught a green garbage bag and the fisted hand of the counsellor who held it. The boys were falling farther back.

Santa Claus, jeered the skeptical one, carries a big bag too. And the tooth fairy.

This is different.

QUIET, a counsellor called back, his flashlight wheeling round at them like a single, blinding eye.

Stavros was not sure what to think. His father had taught him a bit about birds and he thought he'd heard of these snipes, but he seemed to remember they lived in marshes and along the sea. Still, he could not believe that Father Yiannis and the counsellors would lead the whole camp into the hills for nothing on such a hot night. And dark – Stavros seemed to be wading through the dark like an astronaut outside his ship, line severed, limbs flapping, half hoping to find solid earth under his foot as he reaches out. But only stars. Ahead of him a sudden bulking of shadow and he collided with something big; he was sworn at in Greek, he was shoved and crumpled back into the grass. He sat very still. The grass around him hissed like some living thing as the other boys rushed on. A good smell rose out of the earth – an odour of soil and wet weeds, sweet wildflowers, split apples – and he let himself glance up at the sky and pick out the clear constellations his father had taught him. No more than a few seconds passed but by the time he scrambled to his feet the flashlights far ahead of him were swithering like fireflies, growing fainter and fainter.

As he ran he felt the ground grow level and soon he caught up with the other boys, the counsellors, and Father Yiannis. He could not actually see Father Yiannis but he could hear his voice – firm, resonant and reassuring – booming above him out of the dark.

Father Yiannis was repeating what he had told them in the assembly hall a short while before: snipes were very fast and clever and the only way to catch them was on a moonless night because their eyesight was bad and they could not see you. But they had good ears and they could hear you even if you whispered so you had to be quiet – silent, absolutely – and you had to stick close by your counsellor. If you bent down and felt along the earth with your hands you might come across some snipes and you must squeeze them tight and hold them or they would run away. Snipes could not fly but they were fast on their feet.

The boys did their best in the dark to form up around their counsellors. Flashlight-rays strobed over the hilltop and were swallowed by the trees and the tall grass, then a whistle shrilled and the boys, panting, giggling in staccato bursts and urging each other *shhhh*, scattered into the night. Something slithered across Stavros' path. He froze in mid-step. Something else rattled toward him and clunked into his ankle: a small rock snared and tossed away by one of the others.

Stavros knelt and stretched out his hands, palms open, feeling for the earth and timidly touching it like the rough black hide of some massive animal. Fallen dead, or just sleeping? He'd had dreams. The same irrestrainable urge to reach out, same tantalizing dread: cold pebbles, dank slimy stems, a thistle prickling under his hand then his fingers squelching into something soft and pulpy and he gasped and pulled back as if the sick fox that two boys had cornered behind the chapel and beaten with planks three days before was up here on the hill, had crawled here to die, its mashy wounds splayed under his hands. He sniffed: the tart cidery rankness of crushed apple.

He stood and tugged at the damp, rolled sleeve of his counsellor Petros to ask him about the snipes – was it true, were they really so fast? Petros craned the flashlight up at his own face and set a finger to his clamped lips. A ghoulish, glowing skull, eye-sockets caved and bottomless, leered down at Stavros and he jerked back and looked away, first into the dark around him, then up at the stars: the Bear, the Serpent, the Dragon. He thought again of his father, teaching him the names. His throat tightened.

Caught one! somebody cried, and immediately the cry was echoed. An older boy in Stavros' group hooted in triumph and a darting flashlight beam caught him in silhouette, lowering his cupped hands into the counsellor's sack.

Chris, Stavros' only friend at the camp, lurched into him.

Caught anything?

Oh, Stavros breathed, it's only you.

What did you expect? The snipes can't hurt you.

I haven't caught any, Stavros said.

Me too. *Tipota....* Are they real, do you think?

They must be, Stavros said gravely, why else would we be here?

SHHHH! Petros loomed above them. Again his face was deformed by the rising light, made old, like the racked features of saints in the icons of the camp chapel, candlelit from below. *Here*, the face ordered, *feel the sack*. At once they ran their hands over the bottom of the raised bag, Stavros sure he felt on his palm the tickle and prickling of tiny, clawed feet.

I felt them too! Chris said.

They begged Petros to shine his light into the bag so they could see the snipes, but Petros refused – bright light would stun the birds and wreck the boys' fun, later.

Anyways it's almost time to go, Petros leered. The sacks are filling up.

Barks of triumph from somewhere nearby. Stavros' eyes were getting used to the dark and now he made out Father Yiannis – at least the pale skin of his face above his beard and below his cap – gliding toward them out of the fields. His long black robes were hissing, rustling invisibly in the grass.

Time to go back, he rumbled, teeth flashing in his beard. Have you caught many snipes?

I didn't catch any, Stavros heard himself blurt into the dark.

The skeptical boy snickered. Chris gave Stavros a poke in the ribs.

Now shut up, Petros said.

The assembly hall was even darker than the hills, and hotter. Stavros could no longer see the priest's face though under the high ceiling his voice was clearer than ever, firmer, more fatherly. But no longer reassuring. Stavros held himself stiffly on the damp bench, the other boys invisible on his right and, to his left, Petros: a mass of moving shadow exuding heat and a dense, sweaty smell. He wanted to reach out and tug at the young man's wrist, shown only by the ghost-glow of his diving watch. He wanted to ask what Papa Yiannis could possibly mean.

The instructions were simple enough. Apparently some of the other counsellors were up at the front before the lines of benches jittering with boys and when Papa Yiannis said the word they would upend the garbage bags and free the snipes. *But snipes run very fast,* the priest's voice cut through the darkness, *so the minute we empty the bags you must all start stamping up and down in place so that none may get away.*

The dark hall was still and solemn as a church before Easter mass. Stavros thought he caught from behind him a faint crackle of laughter, whispering, then silence. Petros breathing, calm and slow.

Jim the cook has promised to make us something nice of the birds for tomorrow.

More laughter, a few cries of alarm, disgust.

Snipe pie!

You are ready!

He glanced round frantically to find what the other boys were doing. The faces beside him and behind were pale circles, formless in the dark, like the framed saints at home above his bed whose gaunt features dimmed to anonymity when his mother flicked off the light. *Petro*, he whispered, but the young man did not respond. He was rising to his feet, Stavros sensed it. The other boys were rising too. A few of them chuckled and muttered softly. *Chris!* Stavros said, but his friend was not beside him.

ALL RIGHT, Father Yiannis' voice rang out, LET THEM GO!

In seconds the tumult of shouting and laughter and the thunder of feet thumping the pine boards reached such a pitch that Stavros gave up calling his friend and just hunkered on the bench, curled into himself, feet clear of the floor. The bench quaked and swayed. For a second he felt sure it would tip and hurl him under the feet of the howling, cackling boys, but he held on, a small thing trapped on the bough of a tree shaken from below. He peered into the darkness but saw no snipes. Now the awful pounding seemed to be inside him, gathering pace and strength, hammering out at his ribs and small chest.

The bench shuddered once more, swayed, and toppled.

Arms stretched and beating the air for balance Stavros fell straight backward, tensing his body, but the floor was not there and he was falling for what seemed hours as if a deep hole had opened up in the earth and swallowed him whole. All sounds were muffled and the impact, when it finally came, was muffled too, was painless. Dark and still, like in the grass stargazing with Patera on a summer night but under the ground the stars are hidden. With him. In the night-sky of the earth. Countless specks of ash aglow in a buried urn.

The lights burst on and he shut his eyes against the glare and his hearing rushed back: the thumping was over but the roar of voices was louder now, discordant, a crossfire of disbelieving cries and smug, knowing laughter and disappointment and the skeptical boy could be heard sniggering and when Petros and the boys discovered Stavros and helped him up there were a few noises of concern.

Dazzling faces ringed him. You fell right under my feet, Petros said, eyes wide with fear, his blanched face shoving in huge and close. You're all right?

THE SNIPES ARE ALL GONE, the priest boomed from the front of the hall, THEY ALL GOT AWAY. I AM AFRAID JIM LEFT THE SIDE DOOR OPEN AND THE BIRDS ...

Jim, the old cook, stood sheepishly at the priest's side, his felt cap in his hands.

Boys, I'm sorry....

Everyone watched Jim and the priest, and Stavros was forgotten. His ribs and right forearm throbbed, his eyes stung with sweat and the kettle-drum beating that had ceased for others when the lights came on was still pounding in his ribcage. But his heart slowed and lifted as he scanned the floor by the toppled bench and saw nothing but gum wrappers and a crumpled leaflet from the morning service.

I can't believe it, the skeptic said, nodding to show that he could, he could. Look it, check it out. He's still crying.

Chris was beside him. We hurt you when you fell?

He's all right, Petros said and his arm coiled out along Stavros' shoulder and weighed it down. Just a bit shaken. Aren't you, Stavro?

It wasn't just that I fell.

HE'S ALL RIGHT, Petros announced, as if echoing words Stavros had said too softly for others to hear. HE'S FINE!

The priest reared above them, lips bitten in his beard.

It wasn't just *falling*, Stavros said, glaring round at a pack of strangers. It wasn't! The skeptic pursed his lips at him, shook his head. The sweating faces of the priest and counsellor hulked above the others and frowned down in confusion, concern. Suddenly Stavros saw it had all been a prank, he was the last to understand. His eyes filled, brimmed over, and the ring of faces dissolved.

Don't worry, Papa Yiannis, he'll be fine. Fine.

How can you be so sure?

Check it out, the skeptic said, he's still crying.

Did you know? Stavros, half blind behind tears, turned on his friend: You were stomping with the others! Did you know all along?

The friend leaned toward him and whispered, *Not for sure, but I wasn't taking any chances.*

Each year, the priest sighed, there is a child like this.

Ghost

With time Stavros sealed away that night, but it ruptured open years later when, after high school, he went to Greece to visit cousins he had never met and to place in the family plot a small cask of his father's ashes. He had also brought with him a number of old volumes his father had willed the cousins on his death a dozen years before. By this time Stavros had forgotten almost all of his Greek but he could tell from pictures in two of the frail calf-bound books that one of them was about stars and the other about birds. Of course. His father had been a keen watcher of the skies and as a small boy Stavros had watched with him, always eager to follow his upstretched arm and pointing finger, to hear him pick things out, to name them – day-dove, starling, Orion the hunter – but then his father had died and with time, as his memory faded, the boy's interests had realigned themselves and he had forgotten most of what he'd heard. The constellations in the clean air above the Attic coast were as bright as any astronomer could ask, yet Stavros could recognize little now but Hercules, the Big Dipper, the Pleiades, Orion. As for birds, the coast teemed with them and the olive groves on the hillsides above the church and graveyard bristled with busy nests, but Stavros felt only a vestigial interest – though for the sake of his father's memory, he tried to feel more.

Still, the night before he left his cousins for Athens and the flight home he was made to recall his boyhood fascination with birds, and to remember the snipes, and that night at the summer camp. He was walking alone by the sea, near the graveyard. The moon was almost full and a small island an hour offshore mirrored its light so richly it seemed a second moon had plunged into the Aegean, only a sliver of it showing above the tide. Ahead, just up from the waterline, Stavros saw two small boys hunkered down, crawling or wrestling – or were they playing with something in the sand between them, the gibbering violence of their voices now translating into laughter? As Stavros approached they fell silent – froze – then sprang apart hissing, whispering, their repeated word clear: *Xenos.* A foreigner. Outsider.

The boys slouched, eyeing Stavros in the stumped, resigned manner of children who realize they've done something punishable but have no idea why others think it so wrong. They seemed to be awaiting his sentence, or absolution. Then at their feet Stavros made out something small, and dark – something thrashing in the sand. At first he thought it was a crab they'd buried deep in its own element, meaning no harm, then realized the waving leg was actually a wing. A head appeared, then the jerking neck of a small bird flapping itself free of the muck.

Stavros' feelings must have shown in his face. Before he could even snap the word *fige* – a simple command he still knew – the boys had spun around and scrambled away up the beach.

Stavros knelt in the dampness and pawed gently at the sand behind the bird's head. It cheeped sharply, twisting its tiny beak round to cast him what seemed a stern, affronted look. He smiled and made a soothing noise in his throat, eyes smarting from the sand and grit churned up by the wing. For a moment his scooping fingers pressed into the bird's back and he felt the heat of the small damp body quivering through the down.

Then, although the bird still seemed half-buried, its other wing snapped loose and it shot up out of the hole, its wet, softly thudding wings flashing in the moonlight as it surged out over the beach, the shallows, the eggshell-sliver of island out to sea.

Townsmen of a Stiller Town

Smart lad, to slip betimes away
From fields where glory does not stay
And early though the laurel grows
It withers quicker than the rose.

– HOUSMAN, 'To an Athlete Dying Young'

A WASHED-OUT SLUSHY week night near the end of winter, the Maple Leafs losing badly to the Canadiens, business dead slow, till a man's voice called in an order from an address none of them had heard before. A *preposterous* voice, Aunt Helen said, a real live one. She figured the place must be somewhere down near the hospital, maybe just back of it, she couldn't rightly tell – but one thing she did know, a new address meant new customers so would Tris kindly oblige her and put aside his vanity just this one time, for her, and get into his official uniform? Now?

A few months after fleeing high school with a skin-of-the-teeth diploma and going full time as driver at his Aunt Helen's Pickin' Chickin' franchise (TASTIEST SOUTHERN FRIED CHICKEN IN THE GREAT WHITE NORTH, ran the slot-lettered sign beside a giant neon silhouette of a grinning chicken chummily lifting a boater off his comb with one wing and with the other wing picking a banjo), Tris Leduc had staged a secret mutiny and begun removing his uniform anywhere he could between the shop and the places he was bound with his deliveries of deep-fried Pickin' Chickin', deep-fried Possum Chips, pan-fried Alabama-Style Biscuits, dip-fried Toothsome Tennessee Apple Tarts, and Carolina Corny Pone, fresh and steaming from the microwave.

Wearing the uniform had become hateful to Tris. Wearing it on late-night deliveries up to the base had always been a drag because it was so dangerous, though not nearly so bad as it was for the cadets themselves to wear their own uniforms in certain of the city's bars. And as certain locals would tell you, and without being asked, the city of Champlain Locks (pop. 22,501) had more bars per person than any city of comparable size in North America.

One problem Tris had faced since starting part time when the shop opened a year back was that the massive feathered headpiece reduced his peripheral vision to practically zero, forcing him, even in the dead of winter, to leave the driver's-side window down so he could poke out his beaked, wattled head when turning or pulling out to pass. Not that the cold was any real problem. Even with his comb and his left wing icing over, Tris found the suit unbearably hot, not to mention too tight, though the Pickin' Chickin' International head office in Athens, Ohio, had issued along with the suit a colourfully illustrated, jokey brochure that bubbled over about how 'marvelous improved new elastic advances' in the waist and chest material ensured 'our one standard suit fits every possible sized Cock, or Hen.' Tris was skeletally thin but tall and had what his Aunt Helen liked to call 'a heroic frame' – wide shoulders on a tapered waist, big bones, big hands – and every time he'd locked himself in the staff washroom to squeeze into the suit it was a battle. He felt like a crazy man or a scapegoat cramped into a strait-jacket, then tarred and feathered. But hardly a man. Glaring into the mirror before pulling on the last part of the outfit – the headpiece with its goggling eyes the size of softballs – he saw an overgrown kid dressing up for a Hallowe'en party, pale lashless eyes, a face so neutral and unlined it might have been sketched in thin pencil with a few listless, grade-school strokes.

Standing six-foot-three in his red-striped leggings, with the bulky headpiece in place, Tris bore a degrading resemblance to Big Bird.

The first stage in Tris Leduc's separation from the ludicrous suit came during a heat wave in late July. Between deliveries he'd gunned the ageing little Samurai down to Juno Beach on the Ottawa and leapt from the car, stripped out of suit and cut-off jeans and T-shirt and dived into the river in his briefs.

While he plunged and butterflied outward into colder and colder currents, groaning with pleasure, the laid-off millworkers drinking beer up the way, on Omaha Beach, had sauntered down and resurrected the crumpled yellow outfit lying by the car; and as Tris waded back up into air so humid it felt half again as dense and slow as the water, he saw a troop of hooting guys marching away up the beaches, a huge chicken hoisted on their shoulders like a team mascot or troop hero. The bird was facing backwards toward Tris, gaping beak tilted way back as it held a beer overhead with one fingered wing and poured a stream of golden liquid down its gizzard, the other wing thumbing the beak in farewell.

Tris did not give chase. He was completely delighted. He lit a cigarette and drove back laughing, cool and happily windblown – the Crash Test Dummies on the radio groaning away about Superman – and while picking up his next delivery reported to Marsh McDermott, back of the pick-up counter frying drumsticks, that the suit had been stolen.

Marsh was the only high school friend Tris still saw and that was only because Marsh was Aunt Helen's other full-time employee. From four till midnight six days a week he worked back of the counter with fryer and microwave, essentially warming over the pre-packaged items the head office shipped them in bulk every month. Marsh's red hair had once been long but now it was brushcut like a cadet's, which beat the shit out of wearing a hairnet on the job, he said. Besides, with the mills shutting up for good he thought he might as well join the army. HATE U., read the college-style crest on his backwards ball cap. His lean, red-bristled face was always slick with grease and sweat, a toothpick champed between long yellow teeth, bad gums. He'd taught himself to roll the toothpicks from one side of his mouth to the other with no visible movement of lips, but his big jaw muscles were always working, always pulsing with a tense, directionless energy.

When Tris told him about the suit Marsh looked up from the fryer and leered around his toothpick, then came over to the pick-up counter and turned down the old portable black-and-white TV.

'She's not going to like this, boy.' Marsh said everything through gritted, grinning teeth. 'That get-up cost her. Shit, did you see that?'

Tris turned toward the Plexiglas door and windows and peered outside. An eighteen-wheeler had just shuddered past and now as it cleared the city limits, where Main Street broadened into Highway 17, you could hear it gearing up, gaining momentum as it headed west for Mattawa and Sudbury and Lake Superior, the prairies, the Rocky Mountains and the coast.

'No, shithead, here, the *screen*, on the *screen*.' Marsh grinned violently and bore down on his toothpick. 'Our champ Mr Henke just walked another one. Man, shit on *me*.'

'Yeah,' Tris said distantly, 'but she doesn't need to know right now, I'll talk to her later. Anyway there's nothing I could of done.'

'Hey, you could of fought.' Marsh struck a staunch, heroic posture, jutting out his stiff lower lip, cocking up his toothpick at a plucky angle. 'For the honour of the franchise, son. It's like they've ripped off our flag or something. Team colours. Hey, don't you buy that stuff Athens sends us all the time about team spirit and loyalty and pulling together and all that shit?'

Tris grinned. 'What do you think?'

Marsh's toothpick drooped, he shook his head wryly and glanced smirking at the side of the TV as if primed to tell it a dirty joke.

'Hear that, sports fans? He's not a believer anymore.'

'Marsh,' Tris said, chuckling.

'He's in a slump. That's all. Eh, Patrice? Slumps pass.'

Marsh kept staring at the side of the TV but now with fierce concentration, then toothpick-crushing distress, his taut jaw working as the Jays pitcher hit a batter and scored another run for the enemy. Tris stared at the screen too, but blankly. Through high school he'd been as big a Leafs and Jays fan as Marsh – in fact they'd been fans together – but in the past few months his interest had staled, flickered, and at last flattened out like the electrocardiogram of a lost patient.

'Marshall? Marshall, something is burning!' Aunt Helen

was trundling into the narrow kitchen behind Marsh. *Mawshall*, she called him again, *Mawshall*, her accent suggesting that what was burning might very well be Atlanta. She'd only ever been South one time, on her honeymoon with Uncle Hector, but as she liked to put it the experience had been, for both of them, formative. (And for Hector, fatal. He'd joined the Champlain Locks Civil War Club and over the years had risen to General and then, at their annual Gettysburg re-enactment, leading Pickett's Charge in full regalia despite the heat, a heart attack had felled him in his tracks.)

Aunt Helen's blue-rinsed hair was as always piled up over her red heavy face. She was wedged into a peach dress suit with padded shoulders, her bulky form supported by ballerina calves and ankles that tapered to dainty points in cream-coloured icepick pumps.

She'd overheard them talking about the chicken suit. Now, as Tris lit a Players and repeated his story, she eyed him shrewdly and he could tell she didn't buy a word, that she believed he'd ditched the thing as she knew he'd wanted to for a good long while. Finally though she did report the theft to the police, insisting Tris come to the phone and give Desk Sergeant Treacy a conscientious description of the missing bird, and a few days later it was exhumed from a dumpster behind the Wholly Donut a half-mile up the strip.

He'd felt different at first. The first time he'd donned the suit a kind of schoolkid giddiness had overcome him and like a local boy on the first day of the Spring Circus he'd been irrepressible, giggling uncontrollably inside the headpiece, Marsh and Aunt Helen laughing along with him until sweat sprang prickling into his scalp and above his lip and his own ceaseless laughter, muffled inside the headpiece as if in a rubber room, began to alarm him. Still, for a few days it had been a party, a summer holiday, an *escape*, to see familiar faces along the main drag nudge each other and buckle over with laughter as he peeled out of a stop light in the heat of a June noon, window down, music humping, a cigarette burning like a fuse in his beak and one wing cocked coolly over the door. Then, summer fading into fall, the laughter had weakened and died out and people seemed instead to look away – to look away with a kind of embarrassment – like folks who'd really prefer not to hear, yet again, a good joke that has done the rounds.

Hear a joke too many times and you come to see its edges – some of them too sharp to touch. Tris was coming to see how, at the heart of every gag, there's a dark, hollow space, a kind of death, a loss.

October and the Blue Jays, bathed in radiance under the banked lights of the SkyDome, brought home another World Series; the Maple Leafs were shooting from the blocks. None of it seemed to matter. When Tris's high school girlfriend Amelia quit finding his uniform amusing there was little left for them to laugh about. He could hardly blame her for blaming him – his moods, his restlessness. Hell, he had a job! Not perfect maybe but he was still a lucky fucker and besides, she said, he wore that suit pretty well.... Then one night toward the end of fall, driving up a dark sidestreet as he now liked to do to avoid the downtown, Tris hit a detour and had to bear back toward Main. As he waited for a light at the corner Amelia suddenly appeared in the windshield's frame and crossed a few feet in front of the car with a big moustached Air Cad. They were walking with a kind of stiff, hypnotized urgency, hand in hand, as if they'd been ordered in a trance to go somewhere fast and were now obeying. Blindly. When the light went green Tris popped the clutch and screeched round directly behind them onto Main, sensing their startled faces turning as he peeled and fishtailed away.

By the time of the first snow Tris had found a good place to change out of his humiliating suit. A couple of minutes up the strip there was an old derelict drive-in, the Bill Barilko Burger Barn, and after dark he would skid in behind it and pump to a stop at the back of the parking lot by a gutted phone booth. For a moment before he cut the headlights he would stare at the huge graffiti spattered in crimson spraypaint across the diner's back wall. Like the wall of the St Valentine's Day Massacre. The words always made him shudder; glance behind him. Finally he would kill the lights and get out and after a few minutes the loathsome skin would lie gutted and buckled in slush by the shattered phone booth.

It won't be so long, Patrice, Aunt Helen would sigh

whenever she caught him out of uniform, *until this enterprise will be your own. Think of your own future if you're not inclined to think of mine.* And she would swab sweat and blue mascara from her tired eyes, like the tears he'd never seen her weep. And now – a slushy week night near the end of winter, the Leafs losing badly to the Canadiens, business dead slow – she eyed him as the phone rang for the first time in hours. Crowed, actually: it was a buff plastic rooster, head craned back, the receiver resting in its opened beak. She swiped it up before the second ring.

★ ★ ★

Bethune Street turned out to be a dark narrow fire-alley that ran off Lock. Tris had passed this way often but never seen it. A new address, 99 Bethune St (rear), and that meant new customers and since it was a dead night and his aunt seemed so tired Tris decided to give in to her wishes. Put on the suit. The headpiece at least. It wasn't so much to ask, surely? Helen Evans was not his mother – that had been his uncle's French cousin Lucie, killed when the pulp mill burned down in '78 – but she was as close as he would come.

Tris crunched to a stop in the slushy gravel before a wall of black-washed brick indented by a grey steel door, knobless and riveted like the door of a plane. The door was lit from above by a single bare bulb, the number 99 stencilled in black paint on the steel. Killing the lights Tris got out of the car, threw open the trunk and took out the headpiece. For a moment he smoked and stared at the grey door and its cone of light where a few flakes of wet snow swithered briefly and dissolved.

The buzzer by the door seemed to make no sound. The bag of chicken cradled under his arm steamed in the bitter air, a few snowflakes lighting on the paper, melting. Through the gauze surface of his eyeholes Tris's gaze was tunnelled to a small circle showing the stencilled 99, then his finger, still on the buzzer.

A quick spatting of footfalls behind the door and it swung inward with a groan: a short bald man in a labcoat stood there with an open-mouthed smile, marvelling as if sizing up a long-lost friend. When he pursed his lips his look turned knowing, almost scornful. His small dark eyes were shrewdly appraising, his skin swarthy, beard fussily trimmed, a fine dash of black along the jawline linking sideburns and goatee.

'Ah. Very good. You do deliver the food in disguise. What a piece of work, that mask! Well, no need to stand on ceremony, or out in the freezing – by all means come in.'

The man had a vague, unplaceable accent and spoke with theatrical precision, like a man on stage playing a dandy or a connoisseur. He seemed to list slightly to one side; that side of his body was smaller, sunken, as if there were only bones under the labcoat.

'You see there has been a heated debate downstairs as to whether you really do dress up. *My* faith never wavered. One has to believe, though, doesn't one? Even when all the instruments agree it is a dark cold day. Although I had hoped you would go the whole hen. Ah well. Through here, just tag along into the dumbwaiter. You're?'

'Pardon me?'

'But allow me first. Basil Mantha.' He held out a shrivelled hand and when Tris took it Mantha squeezed with surprising force, something sharp like a ring jabbing the boy's palm. The man pulled him on toward another steel door which hatched open to swallow them: the elevator was deep and filled with a green, anemic institutional light and against the chrome of the back wall stood a sheeted gurney. There was an odd, medicinal smell.

'I'm Tris,' Tris said, wondering if his weak voice had escaped the long plastic beak. 'Is this a hospital?'

'Well an abattoir it is not, let me put you at your.... Oh *Christ.*' Basil Mantha's polished head bobbed with fierce flamboyant impatience as he stabbed a finger into the control panel. It was whisky Tris smelled – rye. Cologne too. They were dropping fast. The elevator braked with knee-buckling abruptness and the doors clanked open. 'Excellent. End of the line. The lowest circle.'

Tris heard his own breathing inside the headpiece.

'*Come* on!'

Like a retired colonel with his dignifying wound, Basil Mantha limped briskly ahead up a broad dim-lit corridor and burst on through a set of swinging doors. Polio, Tris thought.

He had to run to get through the doors before they swung shut. Then, headpiece wobbling and chafing, he had to jog to keep up. Mantha was glancing back at him with his beady, satirical eyes: 'No, young Tristan. No. You must not. You just leave that chicken head on. By order of the City. If you can call it that. I called *you*, you see, for the novelty – we could use a bit of a. What. A *lift*. We've had such a night. And on Byrna's fiftieth too. Here, through here and we shall fix you a drink, young Dristan, something to unclog those fouled-up sinuses!'

'It's Patrice,' Tris said, but Mantha had already bustled through another set of doors.

Tris entered a small grubby room lit by a bare bulb hung on a string above a table strewn with papers, books, playing cards, mugs, a coffee pot, an old black manual typewriter and a half-empty quart of Golden Wedding. The damp cold air stank of coffee and tobacco. The bulb's light was weak and sallow, the air smoky, but Tris, scanning the room with his funnelled eye-sight, saw everything with heightened precision: the school-room clock facing him from the far wall, the brace of framed certificates beneath it, rows of filing cabinets and dented chrome sinks, and, beside them, afloat in a specimen jar, some kind of brain. The right wall seemed to consist of a door and a long window that gave onto another, darkened room, as in a recording studio.

'Tristan?'

Basil Mantha was reclining in a rollered office chair, the orthopedic heels of his polished shoes on the table by a pile of books. The titles on some of the spines were French, German. HOUSMAN, read the paperback on top, A SHROPSHIRE LAD. There was a second man and a woman, their lab-coated backs to Tris; the man's big, white-haired head was turning slowly side to side, brown smoke seeming to fume up from him. 'Jesus, Baz, you shouldn't have brought the delivery boy down here.'

'If you can *call* him a boy,' Mantha said.

With a drawn-out sigh the man worked himself free of his chair and turned around. By the time he reached Tris his glum, sour, jowly face had rounded into a grin that seemed to mix sheepish apology with tickled disbelief. He stuck his pipe back in his mouth, held out a shaky hand, grey eyes leaky and twinkling above the reading glasses slouched on his nose. 'Well, Baz – I'll be damned, you were right after all.' His slack throat shook as he chuckled. 'How do you do, son? Norm Joliffe. I'm afraid you'll have to, uh.... I'm afraid we're not being too professional tonight, been a bit of a bad one. Here, sit down a minute, take a load.'

Tris fell into the only free chair, across from Dr Joliffe and with Mantha on his left. Behind Joliffe was the wide dark window where Tris could not help seeing the obscure, goofy reflection of his goggle-eyed headpiece. Though against the dark background it seemed the denizen of a drugged nightmare, not a cartoon. He looked away. On his right a woman sat stiffly upright as if in a church pew. She was drunk. Under her drooping labcoat her chest and shoulders seemed fallen, her averted face shrivelled and puckered as a deflated balloon.

'And this is Byrna Starnes, our unit manager.' Dr Joliffe spoke gently, sitting back and drawing on his pipe, the bowl trembling where his hand braced it. 'The birthday girl.'

'Tris Leduc. Congratulations, ma'am.'

'It would seem I am due an apology,' Basil Mantha said. 'And you can hardly deny me now; not with the cock crowing here before you.'

'Like I said, Baz – you were right. Hot in there, son?'

Leaning forward to set the bag of food on the table Tris could feel Byrna Starnes's hooded eyes raking him as if she'd bet her life savings on his not wearing the suit.

'Just half,' she said.

'Oh Byrna,' Mantha said, 'you become so solemn when you tipple.'

Setting his pipe down Joliffe picked up the bottle and gave Tris a confiding wink. 'We'll pour him a drink then, see what he's more of – eh son? Man or bird.'

'I could just take it off,' Tris said.

'What am I owed then?' Mantha demanded. 'Brandy or single-malt next time – was that not the bet? No more of this rye. Malt *does* do more than Milton can to justify God's ways to man. Now had you bet cash – '

'He's not wearing the whole of it,' Byrna Starnes said with

stilted precision. 'My sister's children once saw him wearing the rest.'

'Yeah, well, jeez.' The doctor's eyes were abruptly wistful, watery above his glasses as he sat up straight, raised his mug in a toast and nodded back toward the window behind him: 'May they never get the rest of you son.'

'Hear hear,' cheered Basil Mantha, and abruptly Norm Joliffe shook his head and snorted out a hearty, companionable laugh as if he'd just been caught mumbling to himself and wanted to be the first to make fun of it. 'Well, what do you say, all – should we tuck in? But first – right, go ahead, Baz.'

Mantha was posing a styrofoam cup in front of Tris. 'Out of mugs,' he regretted fastidiously, 'do forgive us.' The doctor, muttering something about highway safety, dispensed a tiny dose and Byrna Starnes tugged open a can of Jolt Cola and topped it up.

'Can you really feed yourself a drink through that thing, son?'

'What if I take it off,' Tris said.

'Please do,' Byrna Starnes said – then let a smile graze the pinched corners of her mouth. 'Please. You look ridiculous.'

A paper plate appeared in front of Tris. Norm Joliffe, hands trembling less but still trembling, pawed clumsily in the food bag and brought out the cans of Mountain Dew, three Collard-Green Cole Slaws, a grease-sodden Banjo Box of Possum Chips, the Alabama Jumbo Bucket of chicken.

'Go on, son, help yourself.'

'Thanks,' Tris said, 'but, well. I can't stand the stuff anymore.'

He gestured with his beak.

'What's through that window there?'

'May I help you off with the neck, dear?'

'Right – *off* with his head.' Over the rim of his mug Mantha's small black eyes glittered with irony and something else, something far more brittle, bitter. 'No, young Tristan. No. You must not let us make a cannibal of you.' He seized a chicken breast and bit into it.

Tris pried off the headpiece and set it on the floor. As Byrna Starnes saw his face there was a pensive, rueful softening in her hard hooded eyes; Tris had to look away. But the doctor watched him too. Mantha too. And his own face in the window. Tris reddened, sipped stiffly at his drink. He liked rye and coke, he and Marsh had drunk a lot of it for a while, but now the lukewarm sweetness sickened him as if the bubbles surged up from something rotten at the bottom of the cup.

Somehow the eyes that watched him seemed both plaintive and predatory.

Finally Joliffe, voice shaky, spoke.

'How old are you, son? You in school?'

'Eighteen,' Tris said.

'So you're done. For now.'

'Yes.'

'You like the job?'

'A mind reader,' Mantha said, dabbing lips with handkerchief, 'is hardly called for in such – '

'Jobs do have their ups and downs, son, no question there. No question at all. Sometimes, though.... Sometimes a man really does get the feeling he's had enough.'

'Just so,' Byrna Starnes smiled grimly. 'One does.' Then, diluting Tris's coke and rye further with stale-smelling coffee, spilling most on the table: 'Bad driving tonight is it, dear?'

'Not so bad.' A dark stain was spreading and blotting into a pad of blank forms: *Name, Age, Race, Place and Approximate Time of Death.*

'He wasn't driving,' Byrna said.

'Who?' – but Tris instinctively looked up past Joliffe's face and tried to peer into the dark room behind him. His own squinting face stared back.

'Jeez now, Byrna, you know better than – '

'Ah, what does it matter,' Mantha cut in, '*sub specie aeternitatis!* Whatever *that* is, eh Tris? Someone else was at the wheel.'

'There's always somebody else at the wheel,' Byrna said.

'There was an accident?'

'Hit and run, dear. Of a kind.'

'To the Great Lay Public, yes, Byrna, hit and run, as you so colloquially put it. But to the initiated – since tonight you are one of us, Tristan – the term is, well. Roadkill.'

Byrna Starnes shot Mantha a glance that might have bored through steel. Joliffe frowned down at the carnage on the plates before him.

'You're kidding,' Tris said.

There was a silence during which Tris listened to the clock ticking and the soda's effervescence expiring in his cup.

Dr Norm Joliffe relit his pipe, drank off his rye and cleared his throat, as if preparing to deliver a complex prognosis. 'Know what I'd do if I were your age, son? The whole of life at your feet?'

'I know what *I* would do,' Basil Mantha said, 'but I suspect young Trismégiste here wants only to know what all the – all the scabby particulars – '

'Here, Baz, have another.'

'I would go to a city that cherished conversation. Bookstores. Fine wine. No wine here in Winesburg.'

'Maybe seal you up for a bit.'

'No wine but winos aplenty. How do they manage? Resourceful of them don't you think?'

'Basil – '

'*I* would look for a place where the alley behind Welfare is not littered with Aqua Velva bottles. Where no child cyclist is ever found throttled with her own kryptonite lock. Where – where people do not glare when they see one pull out a book in a restaurant as if one were holding a rotten smelt. Hah! Did I say *restaurant?* There are no restaurants any more. Only this – *Pickin' Chickin*. Only *chains*.' He shoved his unfinished food away, let his head sag forward. His ringed, withered hand moved quiveringly over the damp scalp, as if feeling for an old scar.

Joliffe sighed wearily as he set the bottle – close to empty now – back on the table. The shake in his hands was gone. He looked up over his bifocals and into Tris's eyes with a kind of avuncular sobriety; Tris kept trying to see behind him, through the window, where a pale oblong shape glowed faintly through the darkness and the marbled pipe smoke. At first it had seemed to be the white reflection of the doctor's hair, yet it did not move when he did.

'It was a fight at Henderson's Goal, Tris. The kid's an Air Cad, fresh off the base. French, from just over the river in fact. I uhh – I know his people in fact, they're relations of my wife. I knew the kid when he was, what. Just a kid. Haven't seen him in years, mind you, but still.

'Anyway the game was on in the bar, Leafs and Montreal I guess, and he and a couple other French Cads got into a mixup with some of the local boys. You know how they are about the Leafs. And I guess they were losing.'

'It was pretty bad,' Tris said.

'So they took it outside into the parking lot and went at it, I guess a few of the others wound up a *bit* hurt, Cads and local boys too, but not this one. A couple boys knocked him down, thought they'd really hurt him so they tried to scram but he dusted himself off and went after their truck like a damned fool and they didn't see him, that's what they told old Treacy anyway, said he got pulled in under the tires. Drove right over him and crushed his pelvis. Half his guts in the snow. Got him to hospital but it was too late.'

Tris felt his cup start to buckle, crack in his hand. 'I never even heard the siren,' he said.

'The boys in the pick-up – they came back. Brought him in to emerg themselves.'

'What are friends for,' Mantha said bitterly.

'Baz, shut the hell up, okay?'

Byrna Starnes seemed suddenly much drunker than before. She was mumbling something, eyes closed, thin arms crossed over her sunken chest as she rocked herself back and forth. Tris couldn't be sure of her words. *I do*, he thought he heard, *I really do*.

'We don't often see it this bad,' Joliffe said, brusquely setting down his pipe and stabbing his plastic fork into a drumstick. 'Hardly ever in fact. And he was so damned young. And *family*.'

'And dead ere his prime, Tris,' Mantha said loudly. 'But men may come to worse than dust. Even golden lads like you, Tris. Tall and pretty and six-foot plus. Ah who would not sing for –'

'Jesus, Baz, quit *quoting* that stuff. Leave the kid alone!'

Hate it here, Byrna Starnes was saying, eyes closed, body rocking. *All my heart.* Tris turned toward her gratefully, afraid now of facing Mantha, afraid of the clock above the man's bald, perspiring head. He knew he was late. Yet he could not turn to check. He could not tear his eyes from the pale supine form in the darkness behind Joliffe, who was now huddled with Mantha, Joliffe flushed, frowning as he scolded and shook his pipe in the small man's haughty face.

Tris felt something come to rest on his hand. It was so light and dry it could not possibly be another hand, it must be a fallen leaf – something that shrunken, weightless. It was Byrna's hand. Her hooded eyes were aimed straight at him though they seemed to overshoot his face and fix on something on the other side.

'It was better the year I was sixteen,' she said in a grave, conspiratorial whisper. 'You. You make me think of him, that one on the French shore. A fisherman. I never knew what he told me, it wasn't English. We were having a bonfire on Juno Beach, you see, Wilf dared us, who'd swim across the river and back? It was a joke, he didn't mean for anyone to. I was so excited that night though. Strong. I was sixteen. A good swimmer.'

'You swam across the river and back?'

'It's a long way.'

'It's a hell of a long way!'

'When I came up on the French shore a man was there on the bank, fishing – fishing, you see, and it was midnight! He was very tall, like you. Handsome. He put his fishing rod down, came over and he had a jacket and I was cold. I let him wrap it around me and then he, he held me and told me something and I got afraid and broke away and dove in. It was farther coming back. When I came in my friends were lined on the beach shouting with lamps and flashlights, a few out in canoes, they thought I'd drowned you see, they had to help me up the beach. I was too weak to walk. Dizzy. They were saying I was a hero but all I cared was to ask my friend Claire – she was French you see – she's dead now, cancer, we had her in last March, what was left – I asked her about the words but I must have addled them all, swimming, she couldn't make sense of it. What he'd said. At all. I so wanted to know.'

She closed her eyes and sank back in her chair.

'No one would be waiting for me now, you see. On the beach, with lights.'

'Well!' Basil Mantha clapped his hands, 'on that sprightly note! Byrna swimming the Hellespont again. What has become of our bona-fide Ottawa Valley wake? I believe we meant to show our poor grounded chutist back there the time of his. Well. And you too, Tristan, I fear we have made you even *trister*.' Mantha's voice now bristled with a vindictive, menacing edge: 'But then I suppose it never is too early in the morn for a – for a head-on collision with the realities of life. Here on earth, Tristan. The real one. *Bienvenue*.'

'You're drunk,' Tris snapped.

'And you, my boy, are a hollow man, stuffed man, head-piece filled with straw!' A large black beetle scuttled out from under the stained papers and raced over the table. Lip curling with cruelty, or in pain, Mantha flailed his dwindled arm and cracked the flat of his hand down.

'What was the cadet's name,' Tris blurted, turning to Joliffe.

'Not just Juno Beach either. On both shores. I've thought of it too, don't think I haven't. Swim out again like that. Stars would be the lights to guide you home.'

'Now Byrna,' Joliffe soothed, 'don't talk nonsense.'

'The cadet's name, Tris? *Mouton Cadet!*' Mantha's voice was raucous, his accent thick. He toasted Tris with the bottle: 'One more lamb to the slaughter!'

'I tried once too. Walked out on the ice to where it flows.'

'Everyman, Tris, that was his sobriquet. Now you may think Tris that is something that goes in the barbecue – *sobriquet* – right under the writhing, roasting – '

'SHUT THE HELL UP BASIL,' Joliffe said and spat something into his napkin.

There was a prolonged, awkward silence. For the first time in months Tris found himself wishing he had the headpiece on; he didn't know where to look. He stared down at a table strewn with bones, the scorched rinds of Possum Chips, Joliffe's pipe on its side, leaking ash over papers. *Length. Weight. Nature and Extent of Internal Injuries.*

'I should go now,' he said.

'You want to know where I'd go, son? With all of life at my feet?' The pathologist's leaky eyes were glazed and wishful; then they went hard and dead as stones. 'Where I'd go is somewhere folks didn't murder each other over a goddamned, stupid, piddlyass....'

His voice trailed off and he shook his drooping head.

'*I could have swum the Channel then ... I ran that group of friends ...*'

'I have to get going,' Tris said. 'I should get back.'

Tris picked up the chicken head and set it on his lap, then stood. A bone crunched under his shoe. He turned the head uncertainly in his hands, like an enormous hat.

'I'll see you to the door, son,' Dr Joliffe wheezed, starting to rise from his chair, but then he sagged back and did not try to stop himself. He, Basil Mantha, and Byrna Starnes all slumped gravely around the table staring at the boxes, bucket, bones and cups, the little Rorschach smear Mantha had made of the beetle, the green evil splat of a collard slaw slathered over some forms. Above the clock's ticking, the slow drip of a tap and a faint steady electric hum that seemed to come from somewhere past the darkened room's door and window. And Byrna Starnes, weeping.

'Don't go,' Basil Mantha said.

After what seemed a long time Tris heard himself mumbling, 'I'm sorry, it's late,' and Mantha wobbled abruptly upright and grabbed the bottle but instead of heading for Tris he cut a teetering half-pirouette and stumped toward the second room. 'Smart boy,' he muttered, pulling open the door, the empty bottle slipping, smashing. 'Smart boy to slip betimes away, from fields where honour. Does not. Ever.' He hobbled into darkness. Tris squinted through the wide window but could not see him. The lights blazed on, a blinding radiance, and when Tris could look again Mantha stood dramatically spotlit in a bare room under a ceiling striped with fluorescent tubes, the tiled walls and guttered floor glaring white, a black-board on the far wall scribbled with figures, a microphone dangling mid-air.

Beside him on a table of shocking chrome, under a sheet, the body. Two yellow feet splayed out at one end. Through the window Mantha transfixing Tris with a glare of triumphant allegation, an attorney facing the accused with clear evidence of his crime. He seems set to speak into the microphone – then with one theatrical sweep of the hand he uncovers the body, the face blanched, unblemished, a grisly pink zipper of puckered flesh running from armpit to groin and the groin itself a squashed, sunken mess.

Tris jerked away, groaning, dropping the headpiece and bolting up the corridor through sets of swinging doors with the sounds of violent contention dying out behind him. He stood jamming his finger on the elevator button. He kicked and shoved at the doors. A spate of flustered shuffling and he wheeled round: Basil Mantha, wall-eyed yet stately like a demented lord, was almost upon him. Mantha stopped, stood tottering. The steel doors at Tris's back lurched open and the small man rose onto his toes, put his dead hand on Tris's shoulder and pulled himself close while his good hand slipped bills into the boy's shirt. Lips puckering in his beard he huffed out a breath as foul and harsh as formaldehyde.

'Beauchemin, Marc,' he hissed, and pushed Tris firmly through the doors.

* * *

Spinning out of the slippery lot Tris heard behind him the buckshot rattling of gravel against the door of the morgue. He swerved onto Lock Street and then veered again onto Main and raced through the near-deserted, dying business section, past closed or boarded shop fronts and huge, useless signs saying FOR SALE or TO LET, past punctured hoardings littered with obscene graffiti and the sad, battered whores being hassled by cops outside Henderson's Goal and the small triangular park where the green copper bayonet of the Great War soldier was always sheathed in a hot dog wrapper or a chip bag or a condom, his upturned eyes gouged out.... Nirvana came on the radio and he jerked the volume to full. Over the opening chords of 'Come As You Are' the DJ was bellowing that Kurt Cobain had heroically recovered from his accidental O.D. and would be leading us all in song for a long time to come.

The strip melting behind him he was back in the town's strung-out neon peripheries where signs seemed more than ever to stutter vain promises, THE WHOLLY DONUT, THE AVALON BINGO PALACE, SIN-D'S ADULT GIFTS selling *Revolutionary New Sexual Aides*, Champlain Locks Pentecostal (HE SPENT EASTER ON THE CROSS!), MCDONALD'S, PACO'S TACOS, THE HOLLYWOOD DRIVE-IN (long since closed) – the gaps between them growing longer and lonelier the way spaces between towns would look to the Air Cads on their first night-sorties north over the river into Quebec and on for another hour to the Arctic Circle and the dark, unpeopled treeline and the sea.

The neon, banjo-strumming chicken loomed into view, lofty as Goliath, jauntily presiding over the scene. Tris slowed as he passed the shop. His aunt was in the front booth seated upright, with iron propriety, sipping her Jack Daniels and glaring at her watch; Marsh, behind the counter, elbows splayed on an open paper and bristly red head in his hands, would be rolling a toothpick in his gritted teeth while he reread the NHL player stats for the tenth time that day. Neither looked up or out to see Tris edging past.

He pulled in behind the Bill Barilko Burger Barn. He parked by the phone booth and let his forehead sag to rest on his knuckles, blanched and cold where they still clenched the wheel. Then he killed the engine though he left the lights on against the dark and sat listening as sounds rose to fill up the silence: the sly, steady tick of freezing rain on the windshield, clicks and weak metallic whimperings from the motor as it cooled, the dying whistle of a CF-18 on the base a mile east, and in the woods behind him a rifling crack: a branch, sap frozen, snapping off.

His headlights blazed against the diner's rear wall. Again Tris felt his pulse bolt and his cheeks redden, as if from a vicious slap, as he peered up and out at the words spattered there. Fifty times now he'd faced them. Maybe a hundred. Maybe the last time. There would have to be a last time.

YOUR MAMA HAVE ANY KIDS WHO LIVED ASSHOLE

Tris clawed at his shirt pocket then dug inside and pulled out the money Mantha had stuffed in: there were two tens and three other bills he couldn't place at first. He hit the light. Fifties. They were fifties. He flicked one over and the snowy owl on the back seemed to regard him with an air of composed, commanding dignity; fanning out behind the bird under a broad, dawning sky was an estuary, or an arm of the sea, and beyond the water a line of low mountains wreathed with snow.

Tris took out his wallet and slipped in the cash. Slapped the overhead light back off. From out in the darkness, like a call, came the gear-grunting of a tractor-trailer on the long highway west.

Translations of April

During the ice-ages that have repeatedly gripped the earth, brief ten- to twenty-thousand year thaws have alternated with hundred-thousand year epochs of glaciation. Human civilization has sprung up during one such fleeting thaw; a thaw which must be nearing its end, for we are still in the midst of the most recent ice age, an especially severe one, which set in some three million years ago.

> — MATHIEU DE SEPOURIN
>   *L'exploration et l'arctique*

... the lies and sadism will settle in the marrow of the language. It will no longer perform, quite as well as it used to, its two principal functions: the conveyance of the humane order which we call law, and the communication of the quick of the human spirit which we call grace.

> — GEORGE STEINER

1 *April*

Seven times you were a different garden. *A fleur de peau.*

You'll never get this, but I had to write anyway. Useless gesture – like the winter a few years back when my friend Leith finally put his insomnia out of business by swallowing two dozen Equanil and the next night I called his room, not so much because I didn't believe he was gone – though for a while it was hard to believe – as because I guessed his family would unplug his answering machine as soon as they got there and I wanted to hear his voice one more time. Lousy recording, but it was him all right. Especially at the end, that mock-grouching, gravelly fade-out, as if he really didn't give a damn whether you left him a gracious dinner invitation or went straight to hell. *Just leave me a message and I'll uh … do my best to … call you back later sometime …*

I did leave something on his machine. A goodbye. I know, I know what you're thinking, and it's not just you either – at the service his father gave me some pretty strange looks.

You don't have to tell me we do these things for ourselves.

This, too – this wanting to remind you about Montreal, that time in '81 we drove up there for the weekend and stayed in Leith's seedy, wonderful bachelor flat off L'Esplanade when he was away skiing near Bethlehem, in the White Mountains. You remember – it was the worst winter any of us had slogged through and even Montreal, that city of so much tenacious *esprit*, had wilted by mid-February into a dormant, defeated state, like a sunflower mashed flat under the snow. Drifts ten feet deep in the fire-alleys and ploughed into grimy, miniature mountain-chains along Sherbrooke, Duluth, St-Laurent. Leith's place was at street level and half the bay-window was buried. At two or three a.m. the room was half-lit by those halogen streetlights reflecting off the fallen snow and the snow still winnowing down and the light was a cool bluish fog that filled the room, hovering just over the bed. Nights like that everything is lulled, muffled, so by three or four, even in a city of three million, you can almost believe you're the only ones awake. Or alive – survivors in the snow after some Arctic disaster.

It's about something you said earlier that night. One of those odd, unspectacular things that quietly seeds itself in your mind and then keeps coming back, perennial, long after other things that seemed so unkillably real and rooted and vital have wilted, disappeared. That weekend in Leith Allen's ice-water flat with candles burning on the bedside table for warmth as much as ambience, Cohen dirgeing away on Leith's heirloom eight-track and us huddled under down quilts and Hudson's Bay blankets sharing Christmas mandarins and stained coffee mugs full of the only drink he had in the place – vodka. You had a cold and kept sneezing. Leith's toilet ran all the time so when its muffled gargling finally stopped we joked that the pipes must have frozen. And those old high ceilings, plaster embossed with ornate, smoke-stained Victorian mouldings I would lock onto with my eyes whenever we lay talking, as if our time together were a French film projected on the ceiling, subtitled, me watching for my own lines. I try to play it back now. The print is faded, a little. 'Look at me, Tobias, my eyes, look *here*,' you say, 'at *me*' – and I do. Unsettling the first time you realize you can't look into somebody's eyes, just her eye, as if you're only seeing half of her and all the rest is assumption, make-believe, your translation of whatever's there. *Look. Here.* Your head on my shoulder or chest you stare pointblank whenever you speak, or I do. I can't imagine what you see of me in the half-light without your glasses. Wishing it were dark. With my own strong eyes I keep brailling those mouldings and translating them into the shrewdest evasions.

I make the best part of my living now translating things yet often it strikes me that my own life consists of a growing sequence of mistranslated scenes, that I've never stopped mistranslating what I see and sense and hear. And feel. Like *à fleur de peau* – remember how you got that wrong? How I told you you'd got it wrong? This is to let you know you were right.

You're up at the window when you say the words, on your toes, squinting out at the snowdrifts. Knowing me, I probably never told you but those glasses of yours – I loved them, always an extra layer to peel off, so delicately, always the last thing to go. Except for them you're naked. The round muscles in your calves glow in the chilly light, two moons faintly cratered with gooseflesh. Fresh from lovemaking under the quilts and blankets you let the cold air tease and brace you. You stand that way a long time. I can see your breath. I'm trying not to remember what the rest of you, from the calves up, looks like. That weekend was the first time for both of us, our translation into another, long-rumoured place – the adult world – which for me is distilled and always will be in the icy bite of vodka, the incense-smell of sandalwood candles, the slick, shocking heat of lips open to kiss.

You ask if I know how you feel. It's still snowing, you say. Black hair showers straight down over your shoulders, breasts.

I focus on the white mouldings, like a relief map of Antarctica.

No, I say, trembling. The cold. *Tell me.*

A fleur de peau.

I tell you I don't understand. But I do. In first-year Translation a week before I came across a nineteenth-century French piece about Arctic explorers, how all they'd really discovered up there was that the absence of heat is the natural state of things, that life itself is a brief aberration, that the brash, barging optimism of their age was wishful and misplaced. Struggling to turn the stiff labyrinthine French into English I felt my own fascination with the north catch fire. But *à fleur de peau*: the phrase came up in a passage about Arctic summer and the permafrost that always lingers a few inches under the flowering hills. Shivering up in the airless stacks of the U of T library I'd reached responsibly for my Larousse, as I always did.

You look down then, at your breasts I think. Your glasses slip down your nose. You ignore them. Hands tentative, you cup your breasts, lift them.

It means my skin is flowering. For you.

It doesn't mean that, I whisper.

Then for who else?

No. I mean the phrase, *à fleur de peau*. Not flowering skin.

You turn back to me. You pad over and I look away, back up

at the cold plaster map. Afraid, maybe, of what I might say if I really watch you now. Some words once spoken can never be taken back and some, if not said at the right moment, never can be said. The same words, sometimes.

You look down at me with the most serious look, almost comically earnest – your glasses sliding down again – that look the muscles of the face start to forget soon after childhood, then stiffen too much to shape at all. Not without pain. You know the one I mean: feel something hard enough and your whole face fists around the hurt of it, hands shooting up too, helpless, Leith's father bending over the coffin, palms to his face, petals closing over the frost-broken bud.

Listen, April; Leith too. I hate the way things harden with time. Into ice, or rock, or plaster. The gardens in your flesh all petrified: every face in the subway a blank headstone.

Don't tell me I'm wrong, Tobias. Please. I've been thinking it all weekend, I saw the words on a billboard, we were on the metro, God it was just yesterday and as soon as I saw them – it was an ad for something, perfume I think, she was supposed to look like she was just, you know, falling hard – soon as I saw them I knew it was how, it was the right phrase. The only one. There's nothing like it in English. There must be in another language. Don't tell me I'm wrong.

You grin down then, a kind of fond smirk. You pedantic bastard, I can see it, you're going to tell me I'm wrong.

It means skin-deep, I say. Sorry.

Remember the mouldings were a wreathlike intertwined O set around a sealed-up fixture where a chandelier must have hung? O, I think now, or Ah: the only words we have for the skin's flowering. In the French poems on my course I'd seen them too, those – what? Not words exactly. Now a dozen years and how many books and translations later I've learned it's the same in every language – there's always a word like O and one like Ah and used the same way, always. But not really words. Definition of a word: a sound that can be defined. Look in your Oxford or Larousse for the meaning of O and Ah – or if you find one of your own let me know.

You're laughing now with that full-bodied, unabashed laughter, breasts shaking, a flush starting at the base of your neck and blooming up into your face. *Good old Doctor Toby,* you say, chuckling, *I knew you would, too.*

You set your glasses by the phone. I grip your wrists and pull you down to me. You're short yet somehow in bed you always match my length, the O of your mouth locked onto mine, your cold toes arching, curled into my instep. *Bastard* you say – you smile – *you're hiding in your books. Again. Look at me.*

I tell you it means skin deep, again.

You pull the quilt over my head. *Not in a book. You belong here, inside me. You too, I can see it. Flowering.* And once I've fought my way clear of the quilt I smother you with my open mouth so you won't say anything more. So I won't have to say what I do feel then so strongly, something inside feels ready to crack, hatch open, an egg in the high Arctic and I'm afraid the feeling won't still be there at dawn – a small skinned bird still pulsing on the ice. So I pull you onto me to have the ceiling, the ice-white zero above me, I need to anchor my eyes on some sign while we make love and say the subversive untranslatable things people say then so come morning you wonder if you're possessed each night by some passionate ventriloquist, the survivor of another time when the heart's staple language was still current. The flow of words now on every channel in an age when words are for selling, slandering, not praising or making love (like the two of us going on and on and the phone beside the bed jangling emergency and finally I have to grab it, it might be Leith in trouble, stuck in the storm, but we can't stop so you go on above me and then beaming down mischief you slide down, slowly down while I struggle not to groan or laugh at the man reciting on the line *Mister Allen we're very sorry to call you at nine p.m. so late but we would like you to know our salespeople will be in the neighbourhood tomorrow morning and they'd be delighted to offer you a demonstration of our exciting new model, the Floor-O-Vac, with its superior velocity and suction. At what time would you like your personal demonstration, Mister Allen?*)

You. And every city full of sharks and grifters. Carnivores. Talk-show hosts snickering and strip-malls and derelicts sprawled together for warmth on a hot-air grate off Ste-

Catherine like slabs of cheap meat on a grill. Can't really blame the cynics, can you. The ones who petal themselves shut. A century's worth of gases, ovensmoke, fallout and Agent Orange defoliating the skin, ironizing the atmosphere so foully that the heart's own dialect is alien, unpronounceable.

I'm not saying you were fluent in it, but you tried.

What I am saying and need you to know is that you were right, completely, for that night at least – after all until dawn we were the lone survivors of that Arctic disaster, of the century itself, we could have decreed new meanings, new definitions, any ones we chose. That night my skin *was* flowering, *à fleur de peau*, your body a soft rosetta stone and all night face to face or forming the circle and speaking in tongues we were happy, wide open, we understood those words.

Must be so cold where you are now.

It's been a bad winter this year. February's the dying month in this part of the world – comb the drifts of any churchyard and have a look at the dates, you'll see it's true. People like Leith peer out their half-buried windows in February, the city's grey, another storm socking in and they just say to hell with it, enough. And turn their answering machines to Infinite Record. This year the relatives and older friends have been cashing in at a Bergmanesque pace, my address book a casualty list, I've been on the funeral circuit since late December and last week I would have been there, April, don't doubt me – you can't – but I found out a few days too late. Christ, you always were a lousy driver – always squinting, pushing up your glasses, so short you had to tense your legs straight out and tiptoe the pedals like a small kid on a ten-speed, babbling till a song you loved came on the radio then gasping and groping for the volume, lifting your hands off the wheel and seizing thin air to make a point and snapping your head round at me till I had to burst out *April! April, watch the fucking road!* – us sharing the driving up to Leith's place in a friend's wrecked Pinto while you told me your stories, your dark eyes radared right onto mine instead of using the road as a pretext to look away, as I always had to, *it's dangerous a lot of traffic out there I've got to keep my eyes on, keep my eyes on the.* You know. The black ice, the last road north. Mileage ticking down to 0.

In the end all O's may come down to that – absolute zero, the cold silence of whoever's gone – but you come back to me sometimes and as long as I'm here to wait and listen and call you up from the cold, that other world, you'll keep on coming back. Keep lying back and giving me the garden in the circle of your arms, your lips, your legs. Translating me over and over. Into April.

2 *Who Can Stand*

On our drive home from Montreal after that weekend, April told me about another flowering, a different kind. She talked about her childhood and her family – or what she had come to think of as her family, since her real parents were gone, her mother, a poet, vanished into the west with another man, her father spirited away soon after by a disease called lupus, which had made April think of wolves so that even as a young adult she retained a kind of retinal after-image of her father being jounced down into a wooded ravine on the swarming moonlit backs of a close-running wolfpack.

April and her younger brother Cal had spent the next six years in the old brick house of her father's sister and brother-in-law, in a small town south of Winnipeg, under the sprawling sky of the Gardenlands. Until the summer of the rainstorms when the Red River shouldered up over its banks and drove them and their neighbours to safety in motels and guest houses and the houses of friends, in churches, and, for some of the poorer more transient folks who didn't even have a church, under enormous white marquees set up on the parade ground in Winkler. April and Cal were disappointed that they had to stay in a bleak dank church basement instead of a circus tent and Aunt Mavis and Uncle Fred had to explain in their patient, painstaking way that the truly poor were not to be envied and to do so was to make light of their troubles. And that was wrong. That was why they, Aunt Mavis and Uncle Fred, though relatively poor themselves (but healthy, thank God, and never asking for more than was needful) were doing their best to alleviate those troubles.

Aunt Mavis and Uncle Fred were the kind of devoted, aggressively gentle do-gooders for whom natural disasters are heaven-sent – each giant hailstone plummeting like manna, each act of God a welcome test of their worthiness, their mettle and faith.

Among their nearest neighbours was a plumber and Methodist church warden, Hayden Brawn, who saw the flood as a test not only of his mettle but of his special relationship with the Lord. Repeated advances by the Red Cross, Methodist, Mennonite, and Catholic relief crews, and then by the army itself, had failed to dislodge Brawn and his small family from their three-storey varnished-pine clapboard house, which perched on its grassy knoll amidst the pelting rain and flowing, rising waters like Noah's Ark in the first days of the flood. At last the army instructed Brawn that by Sunday midnight he and his kin would either accompany them peaceably back to shore or be carried to safety by force.

Aunt Mavis and Uncle Fred decided to convince the presiding Colonel Girard that an afternoon visit from familiar, sympathetic neighbours might help Brawn see reason and spare the Colonel the comic opera of a forced evacuation. The wheezing red-eyed Colonel soon beat a retreat before the persistent couple, who as always worked on him slowly, steadily, and in concert. 'Why not then?' he finally wheezed, his blanched weary face a white flag. 'Go ahead, *pourquoi pas*, it's worth a trial.'

What gentle but telling weaponry they had employed to convince the Colonel that children were a necessary part of the scheme, April could not imagine. But she did know that bringing her and Cal was perfectly in keeping with Fred and Mavis's consistent attitude toward 'the orphans', whom they treated with egalitarian forbearance, as if they were a pair of backwoods adults who just needed to be shown the way to the bath, the library, the church, the school, and would soon be able to get by on their own. They were bright, no doubt of it – Aunt Mavis often told them so, though she would caution them not to get too proud, like their lost mother 'the poet lady.' *Think of it – naming a girl-child April when she was born in November! April Persephone. Think of burdening a child with a name like that, then deserting her to boot. At least my brother got to name the boy. Better choice he had in names than choice in bride. But oh, Frederick, that's unfair of me to say, isn't it?*

And Uncle Fred would nod gently and sigh, *Well, dear, I suppose you're right, it is, a little.*

So April soon found herself in a cold camouflaged launch

sloshing with rainwater, Cal on tiptoes in the bow like a tiny tow-headed figurehead while Aunt Mavis and Uncle Fred sat conscientiously amidships, hands folded in their laps, staring straight onward through small, rain-misted, matching wire-frame glasses. April was in the starboard corner of the stern beside a rangy, swankily moustached corporal who grinned a lot as he steered them over the high waters, one hairy fist clutched on the tiller of the outboard engine.

From the embankment to the Brawns' tall, tottery house was a distance of only a few hundred yards but the current was strong and the corporal, never sure of the water's depth, ferried them slowly. 'Look at our place!' Cal shouted from the bow, gaping back over the shoulder of his bulging life-jacket and jabbing a finger into the air. And there it was, a few hundred yards upstream, half the ground floor submerged and the floodwaters sluicing in through the side door and kitchen windows they had left open to ease the pressure. Aunt Mavis had patiently explained that theirs was a brick house and built in the last century, built well, and it would surely be there when the waters drew back. (It wasn't.) The Brawns, on the contrary, were in some danger, even if their house was up on a knoll and so far, to all appearances, not flooded at all.

The corporal opened the throttle to speed them out of the path of a horseless buckboard bobbing straight toward them, no doubt from the Mennonite village upstream.

They approached the Brawn house. Three huge crows lifted slowly off the steep roof and wheeled cawing into the fog. Then Brawn himself, trailed by his dog Beershebah, loomed out of the dark front door and planted himself on the porch, his dark-trousered, black-booted legs set wide apart, hands hidden behind his back. The high stiff collar of his shirt was very white against the beard and suitcoat and tie. As always his upper lip was clean-shaven. Dark stringy hair blowing round his head, huge hands emerging to grip the porch rail, he glowered down at them as if from a pulpit or the deck of a whaler.

'Good day, Hayden!' Uncle Fred called civilly, open hand half raised.

Beershebah rammed his huge black snout through the

railing and yammered at the approaching boat. Brawn nodded, running a speculative thumb along his smooth upper lip. Finally he pushed back off the rail and stood upright, hands again vanishing behind his back. 'Shebah. Enough now. Frederick, Mavis' – he nodded once more – 'what brings you here?'

As the bow of the launch squelched up onto the knoll Brawn leapt into action. Brooding above them he had seemed to command a mortician's rigid dignity, the kind of stillness you can't imagine ever ending, but now, Beershebah yapping again, he brusquely vaulted the porch rail, boots squashing into the muck by the water as he seized the towline and deftly looped it to a post. Face still gravely deadpan, he gripped Cal under the arms and hoisted him kicking out of the bow and over the railing onto the porch. Beershebah snuffled and whined happily as Cal knelt and embraced him. Brawn, growling something about guests always being welcome, tendered a starched arm to Aunt Mavis, helped her over the side then hefted her likewise onto the porch, her long buff skirt dallied up by the air until she found her feet and smoothed it down. When Brawn proffered a hand to Uncle Fred, who was methodically making his own way over the bow, Fred promptly seized the hand and shook it firmly. The two men continued to squeeze hands and lock eyes for longer than was really suitable in the rocking boat on the flooding river – but for less time than they usually did.

April felt strong tickling fingers under her armpits and giggled as the moustached corporal lugged her up to the bow and passed her over. For a moment it seemed she would be torn apart like a wishbone as both Brawn and Uncle Fred reached out for her, but then Uncle Fred seemed to think of something and deferred to Brawn, who lifted her with cold, strong, soap-smelling hands and placed her beside her brother on the porch. '*Isn't this great!*' Cal said under his breath, as if afraid the adventure would end instantly if he were overheard.

The corporal cut the engine and for a moment everyone was silent, listening to the low vast groaning of the floodwaters now lapping at Brawn's bootprints in the mud, washing them away. In the current a few yards behind the stern of the launch, a dead calf floated past. Then a telephone pole.

The corporal reclined in the stern as if relaxing in a punt on a sunny river. He stuck a cigarette into his mouth and winked at Cal, April. The cigarette seemed to adhere to the bottom of his moustache. 'You kids have fun, eh,' he said, lighting up and closing his eyes. 'See yez later.'

In the dark vestibule April and Cal shyly greeted the Brawn children, Ike and Sarah. They were fraternal twins, older and much taller than April but deferential and always scrunched over as if trying politely not to outsize anyone else. Today they only nodded in reply. There was an awkward silence. Ruth Brawn could be heard moving around in the kitchen beyond the hall which funnelled toward them the homely odours of corned beef, turnip, squash and baked apples.

'Your fortune to have come in time for dinner,' Brawn said, squeezing at the knot of his tie. 'Come in.'

Like a duckboard half-sunk in a marsh, the floorboards gave a soft squelching as they followed Beershebah's clicking claws and Brawn's wet boot-prints down the dark hallway through a gauntlet of framed, pinched, yellowing faces: Ruth and Hayden's forebears, then the mutton-chopped, flame-haired Reverend John Brawn glowering down with scandalized outrage as if outlawing all passage into the kitchen with its welter of worldly, illicit pleasures. (Mashed turnip, for one; baked beans and liver and headcheese. April had never gotten used to the wholesome but unpoetic diet of the Gardenland.)

'You've an appetite I trust?'

Aunt Mavis and Uncle Fred traded glances.

'You know how we always enjoy Ruth's cooking,' Aunt Mavis said honestly.

'We'd be delighted to partake,' said Uncle Fred, polishing with handkerchief his misted glasses. 'So long as we're not intruding.'

'We wouldn't want to intrude.'

'But' – Uncle Fred again – 'we would like to have a word or two with you concerning, umm. Well.' He replaced his glasses.

As they entered the big kitchen Ruth Brawn whirled from the woodstove to face them, brow and nose and apron sooted, a feverish, bushwhacked glint in her eyes. Behind her the stove was billowing smoke. Her apron sagged and her body had a baggy, deflated look, as if she'd only just had the twins.

'Hello, Ruth,' said Uncle Fred in his gentlest voice.

Aunt Mavis promptly asked if she could be of assistance while Ruth, slapping loose, wet strands of hair from her eyes as if blackflies were tormenting her, gaped at her neighbours. They might have been fearsome swordbearing angels or drowned men fresh-risen from the flood.

'Ruth ...?'

'She's fine,' Brawn cut in. 'All this bad weather alas. Then uninvited guests.... Not you, you understand. The others. Insisting we do what we know we must not. This house is in no danger.'

'Well, Hayden,' said Uncle Fred.

'The storms,' Aunt Mavis forecast, 'are certain to continue.'

'GOOD,' thundered Brawn, nodding vigorously, beard bunching under his mouth. 'Only a lazy man or a fool hopes for ease in his life. Lord made us for trials. They'll all be found wanting.' He raised one arm dramatically, as if ready to reveal a vast congregation of the judged and the damned; Beershebah cringed and hid behind Cal. All eyes followed Brawn's upraised hand toward the dining room table on the far side of the room.

Ruth glared at her husband momentarily, pushing out the large strong chin that always seemed to hint at powers she gave no other sign of; then she slapped again at her loose hair and turned back to the stove. Ike and Sarah made for the table and began to lay extra settings. Brawn mumbled something to Beershebah and led him through the cellar door. There was a muffled command, then whimpering, then Brawn strode back through the door without the dog and with an extra chair in each hand.

Brawn seated himself at the head of the table, his back to the huge picture window that flanked it: brown floodwaters flowing swiftly, the green roof and red chimney of a house a few hundred yards away where the old shore had been, a dead maple whose stripped branches were festooned with underwear, bedsheets, overalls, as if they'd been hung there to dry.

'Hayden? The curtains?' Ruth said softly from the far end of the table, easing the lid from a platter of corned beef. 'Perhaps our guests would enjoy their dinner more if ... '

'Nonsense!' roared Brawn, yanking off his suitcoat and hitching it to his chair, then tossing his thin black tie over his shoulder just as he had done the last time they had dined here one Sunday a few months before. April and Cal had joked about it ever since, Cal doing likewise each Sunday with his own small tie. But neither child laughed now.

Tie over his shoulder, hair sleeked back as if windblown, Hayden Brawn looked like a circuit preacher galloping on horseback.

'Nonsense,' he said again. 'The children will never forget these days. Or this wonderful event. You must stop being afraid. This house will stand. Shall we eat?'

Sweat stood out on Ruth's brow and pinched upper lip as she brusquely uncovered the mashed potatoes and served them. Brawn eyed her. The rain had started up again. Behind him an upright piano cruised into view and bobbed downstream out of sight. Remembering the piano factory in the next town upriver, wondering if more pianos would be floating past, April felt herself smile, then let a giggle escape her and covered her mouth.

Ruth wondered aloud whether Cal and April might not be a touch more comfortable dining without their life-jackets on. Aunt Mavis swooped in before they could answer and said probably they liked wearing them, it was special. And it was – bizarre and delightful. Now Cal was giggling too.

Beershebah began barking from behind the cellar door.

Brawn, saying grace, had to raise his voice to be heard.

'Actually, Hayden,' said Uncle Fred when grace was over, 'your house – strong as it is, mind you' – he paused and coughed softly into his napkin – 'well ... it may not last forever. It's hard to be certain with these things of course, but with these currents – why, forgive us for pointing this out but even a few brick homes up in Morris ... '

Brawn fisted a forkful of turnip into his mouth and chewed very quickly, as if his teeth were chattering with the damp.

When he spoke his voice seemed hoarser, as if something had gone down the wrong pipe:

'My father built this house.'

'It does seem a very strong house,' Aunt Mavis dabbed at her mouth with her napkin. 'Very strong indeed. Now Cal, may I help you with that gristle?'

'Beautiful, too, I'd hasten to add,' added Uncle Fred.

'But perhaps' – Aunt Mavis smiled fleetingly at Ruth to accept her offer of the gravy boat – 'perhaps under the circumstances, and with your family to consider ... '

Brawn set down his knife and fork and stared at his beef. Ike and Sarah had stopped eating and looked down into their laps, either mimicking their father or awaiting his wrath.

The ceiling right above the table gave a low, sepulchral groan. Behind Brawn's back a camouflaged launch chugged into view, making next to no headway against the current; the three soldiers in the launch were all watching the house, the man in the middle with binoculars.

Brawn looked up as if about to speak. But Uncle Fred preempted him with a gentle, somehow deafening softness: 'After all, Hayden, who can stand?' He shook his head and chuckled modestly, peering down at his spread-open palms and trying, it seemed, to get a glimpse at his watch. His glasses kept misting over with the damp. 'I know you know your scriptures better than any of us here – why, better than anyone, I suppose. You know they assert that none may stand before the will of the Lord. Perhaps, Hayden – or so it seems to us – perhaps the Lord wishes us to make way?'

'Amen,' Ruth said under her breath, pushing out her chin.

The launch was holding steady in the current, directly behind Brawn's trembling head. The man with the binoculars was now on his feet.

'Perhaps,' Aunt Mavis said quickly, 'your stand here might be viewed as, well, more as an act of defiance than as an act of faith?'

Through fogged glasses Uncle Fred studied the mound of turnips he had just drowned in gravy.

'Who can stand, Hayden?'

'If this is God's purging of the land – thank you Ruth, no,

I've plenty now – then perhaps we should all make way and allow His Hand to work unimpeded?'

'His Will be done, Hayden. As in the hymn.'

'This is how Frederick and I have decided to view things.'

'Up to your rooms,' Brawn ordered Ike and Sarah; but Ruth, getting up, said firmly 'No. They're – they should stay here. Hayden, please. It's not safe.'

Brawn's face went overcast and Ruth said, 'If you wish to speak to Fred and Mavis without the rest of us here, then let the children come out to the porch with me.' She reached for the corned beef. Her lower lip began to quiver, then she clenched her jaw and stuck out her chin. 'Please. Isn't there a man waiting out there? Let me take him a dish of food.'

Panicky barking from the cellar door as Ike and Sarah followed Ruth into the hallway.

'May I let him in?' Cal asked, suddenly grave.

A white tool-shed billowed past between the launch and the house. It looked like a tiny, upended chapel.

'I believed,' Brawn said, slowly pushing aside his plate as if clearing room for an arm-wrestle, 'I believed you came as friends.'

'We certainly did!' Aunt Mavis cried.

'We *are* friends,' Uncle Fred said stoutly.

'And' – Aunt Mavis gave it all she had – 'fellow-Christians.'

'Fellow *Protestants!*' Brawn thumped the table, then drew his tie back over his shoulder with the menacing slowness of a man unslinging a rifle. 'So you know a man hasn't the right to force his interpreting of the Lord's Will on another.'

Sweat glinted on the clean-shaven skin above his tight lip.

'Well?'

Uncle Fred, poking at his corned beef as if performing an augury, was lost for words. Aunt Mavis took up the slack.

'You are completely right, Hayden. Of course. We can hardly deny that! But – surely we have the right to share with you our interpretation?'

'And' – Uncle Fred rallying – 'to convey our concern for you and your family.'

Beershebah's paw was groping under the door along with a growing slick of water.

'Look!' Cal cried, 'look at the water! You all right in there Shebah?'

The dog took to yelping at the familiar sound of Cal's voice. Before Aunt Mavis could restrain him, Cal ran to the door. Brawn watched the boy with abruptly daunted, depleted eyes, as if seeing that things were slipping from his hands. When Cal opened the door the black dog streaked past, nails tickering on the floor, and crammed in under his master's chair. A large puddle of water lapped in. April giggled, Cal began to cry.

'At least, Hayden, let us take Ruth and the children when we go?' Uncle Fred eased his chair back from the table and tucked his napkin under his plate. Aunt Mavis was smiling tightly while darting glances at the picture window where a huge bloated sow was sailing past, stiff legs aimed up at the sky.

'Hayden?' Uncle Fred said softly.

Aunt Mavis dabbed at her glasses then smiled right at Brawn. 'And I'm afraid, Hayden, we'll have to, uhh ... push off soon. Frederick and I mean to pitch in with supper tonight at the marquee.'

'The work goes on,' Uncle Fred nodded.

Brawn rose. If he noticed the military launch through the window when he turned to seize his suitcoat off the chair, he gave no sign. He sighed deeply, punching his fists into the arms of his coat and yanking it on, doing up the buttons. There were Popeye-like lumps in the arms where he'd forgotten to roll down his sleeves.

'You may take Ruth and the children to shore,' he muttered. 'And I'd be indebted if you saw them to church – my church. There's room enough for them I'm sure.'

Aunt Mavis shot to her feet and pulled April with her.

'Thank you Hayden. This is a wise decision.'

'As for me I've no intention to leave.'

Uncle Fred bowed his head.

'We respect your decision, Hayden, if that's what it is.'

He offered his hand and Brawn took it. Aunt Mavis was already ushering the excited Cal and April past the stove and up the hallway under the mummified Old Testament grimace of the Reverend John Brawn into the dark vestibule and onward out the door. Uncle Fred followed, then Brawn and the whimpering Beershebah.

They crowded onto the porch. The grey light was dazzling after the sombre hallway and the vestibule. Although the rain had paused the river was still rising and a half-inch of dirty water swashed around their shoes. Ruth was seated severely on the middle bench of the moored launch, her grey-shawled arms like big wings warmly enclosing her pale, moping children. The corporal was still loafing in the stern – an empty plate on the bench beside him – but when Uncle Fred and Hayden Brawn loomed up behind the others he sat up quickly, flicked away his cigarette and yanked the engine to life.

April watched the butt scud away with the current. Farther out on the river, flying lightly with the swell, a pine casket raced along. The corporal shook his head, then crossed himself.

Then laughed.

Brawn's face registered no obvious anger about his family's presence in the launch. If anything he seemed discreetly pleased. With hard, tickling hands he silently hoisted first April then Cal over the porch railing to the corporal, then helped Aunt Mavis and gave Uncle Fred's proffered hand a terse shake goodbye. As the launch pulled away into the current and the returning rain, Brawn rested his big hands on the railing and brooded over them as he had done on their arrival, only now Beershebah, at his heels, was cringing and snuffling at the water rising around his paws. Finally Brawn raised one hand – though he did not wave it – in a gesture that seemed as much blessing as farewell.

'Oh, now, he'll be fine,' Aunt Mavis squeezed April's neck, though April, nodding, was not really worried. And Aunt Mavis added, hugging Cal, 'both of them.'

'HERE COME THE BOATS NOW,' Uncle Fred shouted over the engine, so that his voice sounded like an excited stranger's because Uncle Fred never yelled. 'THERE! THEY KNOW BETTER THAN TO WAIT TILL MIDNIGHT THE WAY IT'S RISING NOW. LOOK!'

And he was right: the launch that had been lurking in the

current behind the house was now trolling round toward the vacant front porch and four other launches had just set out from the embankment the corporal was steering them toward. The small flotilla, with poncho-clad soldiers ranked in the bows, broke apart and passed them in two groups of two on either side. The soldiers saluted and Cal, trying to stand up, saluted back but April pulled him down and laughed and scolded, 'It's him, Callum, the guy behind us, they're saluting each *other*.'

Ike and Sarah's wide-eyed faces peered out from under the shawl on either side of Ruth's stiffly turned back, and now April followed their eyes and looked toward the Brawn house where Hayden had just emerged from the front door, Beershebah yapping beside him, to face the first three soldiers. Right hand raised, he gestured violently, pointing at his own chest, the house, the river, the stocky young men. He loomed over them like a shadow on a wall. They seemed nailed to the spot; they traded glances, hands twitching. Then the middle one drew his truncheon and moved in.

There was a brief sharp scuffle, Beershebah retreating, Brawn's bearded head tilted way back in righteous disdain and his long arms straight out, shoving at the young men as if fending off a horde of demons. But they got to him. They pinned him to the wall. Three more soldiers pitched in and Brawn, as if seeing it was hopeless, went rigid as a child in a tantrum; beard pointing straight up in the air he was lugged like a slab of deadwood across the porch, while two more soldiers came backing out the door dragging Beershebah by the scruff of the neck, the dog's locked legs angled stubbornly before it. As Brawn's stiff body was lowered into the launch April caught a flashed glimpse of the pale vulnerable patch of skin under his beard, never seen before, and as she looked over at Ruth, who had turned and was hugging Ike and Sarah and watching her husband's struggle with a tight grave face, April felt sure Ruth had seen the same thing.

A long time later she would recall how as they came in to the embankment where soldiers and farmers and churchpeople were stacking sandbags under the willows – working together with that sane, stolid cheerfulness she would come to miss when she moved up to the city and then down to Toronto – they intercepted a flock of water lilies uprooted from some flooded pond or swamp. At the sight of them joy, or was it relief, swelled up in her and she laughed: only a few white flowers were left amid the tattered pods but they stood out against the brown deep river so bright and wonderfully comic somehow, bobbing along perky and frantic as a mob of clumsy white chicks charging a toppled feed-pail. Aunt Mavis duly pointed them out but it was unnecessary, they'd all seen them, even Ike and Sarah were briefly cheered up and pointed and pushed out from under their mother's shawl and tried to reach over the side until Ruth yanked them back to safety and the pods jiggled past. Out of view. For a moment April felt herself part of a victory parade, a carnival: it was how everything had been spilled upside down and shaken and all the old rules and routines were swept away, adults building sandcastles on the riverbank, playing soldiers, turning their houses into arks and sailing off into a future where even the most dangerous adventure would end safely, for everyone. And though she saw much later that Hayden's forcible salvation might have torn more than a small chunk from his soul, that Ruth must have had mixed feelings when an hour later the house lifted gently and began sliding away bit by bit without Hayden aboard, and that Aunt Mavis and Uncle Fred must have felt not carnival joy but job satisfaction, for that moment she did feel sure, as a child must, that they were all family and flowering, flowing, the same way. *A fleur de peau.* There in the rain on that river between worlds, where it seemed joy took flesh and dwelt among them.

3 *A Rose in Erebus*

The third flowering comes in solitude – came one time for me in the late eighties when for a while I had a job as the research assistant for a successful, well-known writer. Four years had gone by since I'd graduated in Translation and Journalism and though I'd found a bit of work as a translator, so far I'd failed, in my own eyes, to establish myself as a writer of any kind. While supporting myself on tome-dry legal and clerical translations and a welter of odd jobs pretty much like the ones I'd done to put myself through school (cab driver, bartender, used book store clerk, telephone marketeer) I had managed to land a few writing assignments, but the stuff I knocked off was of such spectacular indistinction that I was rarely offered any more.

I missed the kind of translating I'd done in school. It had spoiled me all right, though not in any material sense; it was the kind of work that not only puts no bread on the table but gives you an appetite for other, still more bankruptive callings, like writing things of your own. And though for a while the excitement of your little projects seems nourishment enough, the question of bread remains, the unpaid bills and rejection slips pile up and race each other toward the roof and on into the smut-brown city sky and in your dreams they seem to ossify into the office towers of Bay Street or Bonaventure or Madison Avenue: the Real World, patiently waiting. So you abandon the kind of work that makes you feel at times like a minor, momentary god – a necromancer breathing over the bones of the dead and stirring them to life – but you remember.

One time I was tested with a brief and until then untranslated poem in Old Norse, a language I could not even swear or ask directions in. As I liked to do I had stayed up late, three in the morning maybe, Toronto quiet and the world tapered down to my desk with its cone of amber light that might have been the light of a lamped helmet in the dark, while my hands – scrabbling through the dictionary or scrawling down words, tense while a meaning bobbed toward the surface – were the hands of a rescuer tearing at ice and scree over an avalanche, a mineshaft, an old grave. Hoping for a miracle. Those Victorian sailors they were digging up in the Arctic that year seemed so lifelike they might have sat up in their coffins and cleared their throats, spoken, let us in on a secret or two – but naturally they kept their own counsel and left all the spadework to us.

I planted a white rose in Erebus, in Erebus under the earth all snow; that was the first line I dug up. Eerie, that moment of exhumation – eerie and beautiful, and addictive, and sad. In the Bergmanesque winter dark of medieval Norway a stranger sat weeping by a fresh grave and tried, with a spell of words, to stir his plague-dead daughter back to life, and six hundred years later in an attic flat in Toronto I was trying to do the same for him and for his daughter, the white rose.... Happily hemmed in by the unabashed jumble and jostling and flagrant colours and rich shameless smells of the noontime streets and alleys of Kensington Market, where I lived, my bizarre nocturnal communions with the dead seemed dreamlike – narcotic reveries – yet I had the scrawled translations to prove they'd taken place and sometimes in a café or a bar I would pull one out and reread, or rework it:

> *I planted a white rose in Erebus,*
> *In Erebus under the earth all snow. My daughter*
> *Why would you go and leave us, rob us*
> *Of our afterlife – you! O see now the water*
> *Of your mother's tears turns to snow*
> *Before it meets the ground; see how grey*
> *Overnight your young father's brow*
> *With grief's frost goes, and ah! how day*
> *Grows dark, and briefer, though April nears ...*

That kind of freedom did spoil me. Everyone should feel their work is a form of magic, of breathing and giving birth, sure, but how many of us ever do? Can? By the mid-eighties I was adrift in a world that everyone kept assuring me was the Real, the One and Only, the World without End Amen.

Between cab-driving and freelance assignments I tried to revisit that other, buried, impractical world by translating obscure and forever unsaleable poems and by writing my own poems and plays, but they were rushed and unfocused and never much good and they languished at the back of my desk buried under rejection slips – the civil, the slanderous, the totally indifferent. Finally, when I heard the successful well-known Writer was looking for someone with languages to help research an 'Encyclopedia of the Arctic', I applied for the job.

It seemed like a good compromise. For one thing I was intrigued by the far north, and then too like a lot of young writers who drudge away years in editing jobs, or publishing houses, I hoped being there in the margins of the literary world would somehow improve me, would do the work for me, as if by osmosis. But my first year, desk-bound in the Writer's stuffy windowless Yonge Street office or salt-mining in the airless shafts of academic libraries in Ottawa and Montreal, left me more than ever at a loss. Drowsy yet restless, I was rapidly turning into one of those bright, bored young people who get locked into the ice of the Real World – unwary explorers – then sit around waiting for it to spring open and free them.

The Writer was always cold. In high summer he would sometimes strip down to a turtleneck and patched old blazer, but in winter he roamed the office hunched up in a tattered greatcoat, muttering grimly and ambushing us with new assignments and checking his watch or the thermostat and muttering some more. He was wizened and wiry, his pale eyes always squinted and his wild shock of grey hair flaring back off his head as if he were standing defiantly in a wind-tunnel or on an exposed Arctic crag. When he called you into his office he would be sitting burrowed into his coat, squinting up at you, his gaunt hands clenching the edge of his desk as if a hurricane were pouring through the door you'd just come through and if he let go it would blast him and his rollered chair backwards over the carpet and out the plate-glass window into space. Hanging on for dear life he would put his head down and growl out the coming week's assignments. Perhaps he was embarrassed, knowing nobody could have kept up? *Backs are against the wall*, he would mutter, *time's running short*. And he would squint up at you with a baleful, impatient glare, grey eyes watering, as if you were the source of the gale-winds he always seemed to be battling.

The only thing I liked about the office was Anne, another research assistant, at work shy, ironic, methodical, after hours buoyant and joyous, generous, warm. We were good to each other for about six months until the Writer dispatched her to Yellowknife where she became a kind of northern correspondent, travelling and conducting interviews and *in situ* research for his sprawling project. And my own research went on bookish and dull.

Anne and I wrote steadily while she was away and talked of moving in together on her return, but when she came back six months later I found in her absence I'd revised her, body and soul, accessorized her, could no longer see her under the collage of editorial changes I'd made. I think she'd done the same to me. So, puzzled and sad – missing each other unbearably even as we lay reunited in bed – we shelved each other like abandoned novels in a stubborn, too-foreign tongue.

Love – I believe this now – requires that you learn to read the lover in her own language, not translate her into yours. I know this now. But Anne, like April, is a lost language, too late to grasp.

It was just after New Year's when Anne and I finally gave up. Suddenly the job, which I'd never liked but had managed to distract myself from, became a labour of loathing; the queasy feeling that set in each morning when the harsh-lit, mirrored elevator lurched upward for the sixteenth floor stayed with me till I left again at five, or six, or seven, rushing out past the plastic sign you used to see in a lot of workplaces in the eighties:

IF YOU DON'T BELIEVE IN THE

RESURRECTION

YOU SHOULD BE HERE AT CLOSING TIME

WHEN THE DEAD

COME BACK TO

LIFE

It was hard, too, working in an office with a woman who still seemed to me like a sort of changeling or impostor – a daily reminder, as I must have been to her, of how our dreams had failed us. Or we our dreams. When after a while she began seeing someone else, and seemed to brighten up, I found myself feeling jealous of something I did not want anyway. And petty. And dull. Afraid that the in-tray out-tray rhythms of my daily routine, like the academic metres of a few years back, were colonizing my brain and body and house-breaking my imagination and reducing me, like so many others before, to a footnote – in my own handwriting.

Then in March the Writer gave me a new assignment that promised more than my recent renderings of – for instance – the minutes of the Danish colonial legislature in wartime Greenland. It involved translating several chapters of the memoirs of Mathieu de Sepourin (1837-1898), the same explorer and biologist whose work I'd encountered years before in my translation course – the man who'd used the phrase *à fleur de peau* so that I'd learned, narrowly, what it meant, and had presumed to teach April.

Working on those strange chapters, written a few years before the author's death, reminded me of April in Montreal, of that time, of how that early translation still haunted me. Over the last year especially I'd been thinking of it. Because I missed April, I supposed, and hadn't heard from her in several years ...? But there was something more. Something about Sepourin's telling of the end of the Franklin expedition whispered to me with fierce intimacy, and urgency, as if I had been there, as if a part of me still was:

What Sir John Franklin could not have surmised upon sailing his commodious, steam-heated ships *Erebus* and *Terror* into a widening channel, which promised to lead him before the Summer's closing direct through the North West Passage and into history, was that the ice of the Peel Strait had not yielded a fraction in centuries, and was not to open again fully in our century; or during his life. In the fifty years since that fateful time, it has parted open but once, very slightly, in the exceptionally warm August of 1872, when I was once again present in the region myself. In the likewise exceptional summer of 1846, then, Sir John Franklin edged eagerly southward into the jagged, widening jaws of the ice; but the fissure was never much to widen, and by September, in a zone of the Arctic so inhospitable to Man that the Eskimaux themselves still shun it, he ran out of time. The singular weather turned; the jaws clamped shut. For almost two years the crews attended the opening of the palaeocrys- tallic ice in which they lay beset; they might have waited a thousand. At length, after Franklin's death aboard the *Erebus* – a ship named for a lightless passage underground, through which the dead of ancient Greece were said to pass en route to Styx River and their tra- verse to the Underworld – the survivors abandoned ship, and commenced, on Easter Eve 1848, their death-march to the south.

Maybe it was my own sense of having sailed hopefully into a job only to find myself locked in; maybe it was something less obvious, more buried. But somehow the new assignment shook me awake and I was back to working late on my own in the clammy basement flat I was then renting, the world again tapered down to a cone of lamplight over a page and my head tilted in hard thought. Or was I just listening with utter atten- tion as the voice of a stranger spoke, first under its breath and then, when I finally cracked the code, like a living voice here in the room beside me? Inside me. Saying what the dead, in translation, always seem to say: *Everything is vanishing. Do not waste your life.*

Doubtless there are those readers who, perusing the following pages, will choose to believe that the singular occurrence I record here was merely a dream; and truly, looking back, it has seemed to me, on more than one occasion, as if such might be the case. Yet I know in my bones it is not. For a dream I cer- tainly did have that night, and it was as different from what occurred on the beach at Starvation Cove, as the night is dis- tinct from the day.

The reader will recall, from the last chapter, that I and other members of our party had been returning from a three-day journey down the west coast of King William Island, where we had been engaged in searching for relics of the Franklin expedition – and, more specifically, for the 'cemented' crypt where many still believe Sir John's logbook must lie – when we discovered on the gravel beach at Starvation Cove, a Narwhal, or 'Sea-Unicorn', which had been washed somehow onto the shore and who, owing to his great girth and unwieldiness, could not return to the sea. The creature was in dire distress, and I have admitted already how my heart was pained to see its whole vast body heaving as it slowly smothered under its own weight. Yet several members of our party, including myself, being by education and vocation Biologists, and having mounted this expedition partly with a view to study the rare and exotic species that abound in the far North, knew well that a fortuitous and singular opportunity of this nature was not to be lost. None of us had ever yet encountered a Narwhal, indeed it had seemed to me until that time to reside in a sort of limbo somewhere between the real creatures that I had studied, be it in field or museum, and those other beings – like the seawoman *Sedna*, whom the Eskimaux thereabouts believe in, and fear, for she is said some times to take on the form of a whale or a shark, and swallow men or pull them down to the bottom of the sea; and our own *Unicorn*, who owes his tusk to the remarkable dentition of the Narwhal – those other beings, I say, who have never existed save in the imaginations of Men. And now we had chanced upon as splendid a specimen as can be supposed to exist. Speckled grey on the dorsal half, and deathly white on the ventral, in length he was, according to the careful measurements of Dr La Tour, 5.3 metres, not including the tusk, which added a full further 2.4 metres to his span; in circumference he varied, according to the degree to which his lungs were inflated or void of oxygen, between 4.4 and 4.9 metres; his weight Dr La Tour estimated to fall between 1,700 and 1,900 kilograms.

The reader will recall that after examining the unhappy creature as thoroughly as our hunger, exhaustion, and the encroaching twilight would allow, we returned to our camp-site, where the cook prepared us a thick potage which we eagerly consumed along with one of our last bottles of wine, to celebrate both our return and our singular discovery.

Now the next day very early we returned to the beach where we found the Narwhal in such reduced estate, I was, I confess, somewhat troubled to see it; and, absurd as this must sound, markedly reluctant to meet its dulled yet still insistent black eye, which swivelled damply in its huge socket under long, disarming lashes, and seemed, like the eyes of a haunting portrait, to seek out my own eyes and thus to impart an ineluctable accusation. My distress being visible to my busy companions, who were carrying out further tests and measurements — lowering arms and lighted scopes into the frantically chuffing blowhole, sketching the beast from all perspectives, draining small quantities of fluid from various parts of its body whilst M. Fouché disappeared under his black silk cope behind his camera and the powder burst in eerie silence — I was roundly taunted as a 'sentimental young man', though I was at that time well into my thirties; however, as I was the youngest among the Biologists and Botanists (as I believe I have mentioned), and given to certain 'Modern' political ideas which my elders found odd, and I dare say unsettling, it was not the first time they had had occasion to air the phrase.

Nevertheless I did contribute what skills I possessed, and by evening when we abandoned the Narwhal, now discernibly near death (his great ribcage ebbing slowly, his pain having seemed to subside in proportion as he yielded to us information which must after all — so I told myself — prove useful to Men, and of little or no use to Narwhals), I felt I was myself again, and relatively untroubled. It having been proposed that we return the next morning, by boat, with axes and our bone-cauldron to strip the flesh from the carcass and render the bones, so that we should be able to return home the next week with the full skeleton for the Musée de Nature in Rheims, I remarked that the animal's evident suffering served no further purpose and that we should free it of its misery before leaving, thus sparing it another night's ordeal; but Dr La Tour insisting that he had still in mind several important experiments and incisions that he wished to carry out, and for which he hoped to have the 'Sea-

Unicorn' still in its living state, I let myself be prevailed upon to leave the beast as it was.

That night, in spite of the long day's work, the good supper and wine, and the late Summer's increasing darkness (which conduced so much better to repose than the ceaseless sunlight of late June), I slept poorly. I slept, indeed, barely at all. My digestion was unimpaired yet the feeling in my bowels was of a kind of indigestion, and kept me awake for some hours, tossing and turning. At length I did sleep, but had a strange dream.

I seemed to be walking along the sea, southwards away from the camp-site towards Starvation Cove. It was very dark, and moonless, as indeed it was outside the tent where I lay dreaming. The sea was calm. The gravel of the shore pained my feet, and I realized I was shoeless. Then I saw it, straight before me, a most uncanny apparition: a woman who bore on her head a crown of burning candles, and who was gliding up the beach in my direction. Over the years I have recounted my dream to several people – to my wife Elise, for one – yet modesty has until now confined me to describing the woman as merely ill-clad; in full truth she was naked. And her skin – how pale it seemed! And her face, I thought, how lovely! – though in truth her face, directly beneath the crown of candles, was lost in deep shadow.

We drew close. Suddenly we stood face to face, so very near that I could feel on my brow the intense heat of the candles, and discern the woman's face, which was indeed lovely, and her eyes, which, however, were beady and bitter, as if they bore me some malice of which I had no inkling. I seemed to see myself inclining forward to kiss her, yet now I felt splayed out upon my chest, icy-cold and repelling me, her spread fingers. In a whisper full of loathing and disgust she explained her rejection of me in four words which I can never cleanse from my mind: *you smell of corpse.*

Abruptly I was alone on the beach, shivering in a cold wind that seemed to echo and re-echo the woman's words – words my dreaming mind took to mean that the Narwhal had just now succumbed, its sufferings finally ended. Yet in the woman's aspersion, and especially in her biting gaze, I had glimpsed and felt something unmistakably personal; as if, indeed, the stench were my own.

Now I saw how an endless line of candles had been planted along the tideline and was guttering in the rising gale, and how the tide itself was sweeping in, very swiftly, how the candles were half-submerged in the cold foam and would soon be overwhelmed and extinguished by waves if not snuffed out by the wind. These imperilled, tiny flames seemed to indicate a trail that I must follow. Now. For now I knew there was little time.

I awakened in the tent. Almost before I knew what I was about I had donned my boots, and, taking care not to disturb Dr La Tour and the others, slipped outside. It was dark, yet not so dark as in my dream; this I took to signify that the dawn, due around four a.m., was no more than an hour off. I took one of the loaded rifles we had leaned together outside the tent as a precaution against Bears. Walking rapidly down to the shore, I proceeded south, obeying an impulse my colleagues, I felt, would not merely hold in disdain but to which they would openly oppose themselves. A faint glow arose behind the bare hills to landward, but the sea remained dark under louring clouds. I broke into a trot, then a run, my breath clouding in the cold morning air; I ran as I had not run in years, and when at length I crested the low cape at the north extremity of Starvation Cove, I at once made out the recumbent bulk of the Narwhal down below me some few hundred metres off, abject as a slug crushed upon cobbles, its grey dorsum flecked with screeching gulls and ravens, the neap tide washing about it like gore, – and at this juncture, to my own surprise, and (why need I pretend otherwise now?) to my great embarrassment, I found myself so stricken I was near weeping.

As I approached the Narwhal at a run, a noisome odour, bilious and fishy, assailed me. Indignantly screeching, the birds dispersed. And now, though I had thought the creature quite defunct, I detected some faint movement of the great torso – oozing now from the many small wounds the scavenging birds had inflicted, and we likewise, in our studies – and I disengaged the safety hasp of my rifle. I had hoped that the Narwhal's grim travails would have ended before my arrival, not only for reasons of humanity, but – shameful to own! – so as to spare me the act I knew I must now, in all good conscience, execute. For clearly the beast was still living. For all that I wished to avoid its baleful gaze I could not refrain from circumambulating its bulk, which involved me in wading the oily and blood-stained tidal shallows around it; and, at length, reaching out to grip the spiral grooves of its tusk to steady myself in the shallows, and as it were for assurance that the creature was real and not the mere product of human fancy or dream, I stood by its great head, and I raised my own head, and I faced it.

The Narwhal's left eye, half-closed, rolled towards me, opening altogether, and the great tusk seemed to quiver awfully in my hand; the eye did not blink and seemed bottomless, as if it stemmed back somehow to the very roots of the Sea. Like a Savage engaged in some cryptic rite of propitiation, I ventured to lean and stroke the feverish lacerated skin of the snout, when the terrible eye, spying me so close, rolled back whitely and the beast sucked in a great breath through its blowhole; then, exhaling a volcanic blast of bloody spume which spattered into the rising tide and over my face and shirtfront, its body quaked out a massive groan and its listless lateral fins shot up momentarily, all of which sufficed to convey how much of life there was yet left to it. Once more, hardly realizing I had moved, I found myself engaged in an act inexplicable, as if my body were dreaming whilst my mind looked on. I had re-engaged the safety hasp and reversed the rifle, digging it like a spade into the low water and gravel beneath the Narwhal's pale ventral flesh, just clear of the fin, and frantically I hefted as if thus to lever it into deeper water. At first my efforts seemed in vain, but then, a small wave washing in around us and buoying the creature slightly, I gave a great heave and felt the body shift to some minute degree. Heartened somewhat, I heaved again, unsure if the stock of the rifle would hold, and endeavoured to time my pushes with the small incoming waves. Now – and here it is that many will class me 'Dreamer' thrice over – it seemed as if the Narwhal, sensing my intentions, or, more likely, feeling himself incline ever so slightly back towards the sea, contributed his own impetus, and with what must have been a dying effort rolled himself to the right, half onto his side, thus exposing the radiant dazzling white of his belly.

Greatly inspired now, panting and sweating with the effort

though my boots were wet through, my feet numb with the cold and my nostrils repelled by the stink of the newly exposed ventral flesh, I once more dug the stock of the rifle under his side and heaved in time with the incoming waves; and now, as a good-sized wave lapped in, I felt the great body shudder and heave and roll over and I cried out with joy, and then with alarm, for my left boot had lapsed suddenly deeper, submerging me to mid-thigh and nearly casting me out into greater depths. Too hastily I retracted my leg for I lost my footing and toppled back into the icy shallows – the Narwhal suddenly afloat and moving slowly yet intently outwards – and there my boot must have brushed the safety hasp, for now, the stock jamming hard into the stones of the shallows, the rifle fired a single round into my guts.

I felt no pain. The bitter cold of the water into which I had fallen had doubtless overwhelmed all other sensations; I rose dizzily and, edging backwards, made my way back up onto the beach. And there I stood, clutching my bleeding side and watching the Sea-Unicorn thrash slowly out from shore, now submerging altogether, now breasting the surface fleetingly – as if, one would like to believe, in farewell – before plunging into the depths of Starvation Cove and invisibly out to sea.

Some minutes later, Dr La Tour and the others, alerted by the rifle's inadvertent report, surrounded me on the beach, shivering where I sat, blood-spattered and bleeding freely from a wound which now pulsated with a gratifying, cleansingly fierce pain; my teeth chattering, I grinned up at them – quite mad, they must have thought, and certainly did think when they learned what I had just accomplished. Yet I was not mad. And my wound, I sensed, was not mortal, was but superficial when compared with the sensation I had enjoyed in the minutes before my colleagues' arrival – a feeling of intense purity and rapture the like of which I had never known until then and never have known again since, be it in company or alone. No. For my life, you see, did not really change after that, and now, when I consider how it might have changed, I weep like a child for the lateness of the hour, for the absence of even the merest scar in the spot where the bullet pierced me; I weep that I have never again encountered her, the woman with the crown of burning candles; I weep for my haste in pulling my leg back out of the sea.

On the beach, too, I wept, but not from pain; indeed, though I should soon have expired of my chill, or bled to death, and knew it, those minutes before my saviours arrived were the happiest of my life.

Late Sunday night, under my miner's lamp, I finished the translation. It was Monday morning, really. I went to bed but I couldn't sleep and a few hours later when I got up and went in to the office I could make no headway on my next assignment. I saw things in the office with altered eyes. Alerted. I'd seen them before, but now I *saw* them: the sleepy insidious evil of the empty routines, the bloodless synthetic surroundings and foul coffee and microwaved Quiksnacks that eroded all our senses, how the office worker trudged toward a desk of duplicate pasteboard towing a mobile coffee I.V. – life-support for the living dead who could no longer muster any of their own, organic energy. For everyone here was perfectly dispensable – interchangeable – and that terrible truth we partied and slept around and fell in love and got raises and changed jobs and ate and cheered on the Blue Jays and the Argos and the Maple Leafs to forget – but which always lingered at the edges of the day, mounting after dark and seeping into dreams – gutted us all of our dignity and strength. Gutted me. Only the Writer showed any vital signs and for the first time I could truly appreciate him, though I did recognize how he thrived on the energy of others – like mine – *and though I can no longer let myself be food for others, Anne, I am, like Sepourin, of a more herbivorous metabolism and I do not relish the idea of making others my food. Anne, everything that dams up the flow of spirit, that deadens particular life, stinks to heaven.*

For a moment she stared up at me, brows furrowed.

'You know it's true,' I urged. 'You've always known it.'

'What are you talking about?' she burst out. 'Workers, the living dead, spirits – my ass. Come on, out of the pulpit, Tobias. And more to the point, get off my desk.' Her face softened. 'Come on, Toby, I'm behind on something here.' As I

turned and crossed the office her voice pursued me. '*Tobias!*
*Are you all right! You better cut all the coffee. I've heard you
get worked up about some nutty ideas before, but this takes
the prize.*'

I sat at my desk and for the first day in almost two years I
wrote something of my own. It was in a voice like Sepourin's,
but even further removed in time. When I left at five, Anne,
still at her desk, looked up at me and said I seemed to be working awfully hard, and was I really all right, she didn't want me
wigging out on her. There were dark heavy crescents under
her eyes. Something clotted in my throat and I leaned over and
kissed her forehead and said goodbye.

Next day I didn't go in to the office. I stayed in my basement
flat, first writing, then seeming to take dictation from a part of
me I could feel stirring back to life – the voice starting out
faint, like someone buried alive and half-conscious, but coming to, the voice growing louder, clearer.... As soon as I
finished the five-page story I started in on a second draft.

Just after lunch, office time, the Writer called me.

'You didn't FAX in sick,' he growled into the phone. 'Sepourin translation was due yesterday. You know that. You know
our deadline's breathing down our neck.' Silence, then a faint
rattle that might have been fingers ticking on a desk or teeth
chattering. 'You surprise me, O'Brien. No. *Disappoint* me.
Your work's been off for a while but it's improved of late, you
seem to have found your feet.'

'Yes,' I said. 'Yes, I have.'

'*Seemed*, O'Brien.'

'I have to go,' I said. 'I'm in the middle of something.'

The faint static coming over the line was like a killing wind
off the tundra. Then finally: 'O'Brien. You still there? Look, if
it's money – you know there's never much of that in books, it's
a job for idealists, a *calling* – but maybe – '

'It's not the money,' I said. 'It's the place.'

'Sure. I know. Too damned cold. *Drafty*. I've done everything I can but it's still – '

'No, not that. I'm sorry. It's the way it smells.'

'It's *what!* Look, Tobias, are you all right? Ms DeMarco
seems worried about your absence, are you sure – '

'I have to go,' I said.

After another windy silence he told me I should go, then, and find myself another boss.

I did. That afternoon, after finishing my second draft faster than anything I'd ever written – as if I was simply remembering something I'd made up a long time ago, then forgotten – I went out to look for a part-time job. I'd never felt happy on a job-hunt before, but now I did. No doubt I'd have to give up my apartment and take a room; that was all right. Everything was. In fact, wonderful. A small café on Baldwin Street needed someone to help in the kitchen and they asked me to come back the next week.

It was unseasonably mild and a warm rain was falling and turning what remained of the snow into slush – an ugly, messy day in some ways, the faces of people cramming past and of commuters frozen at the windows of a stalled TTC bus beige and mournful, etched with wrinkles, yet even this vision of a city locked into the ice couldn't dam the flowing of my mood. I did not worry about whether my story would be published or if others would come so easily or if the café job would bring in enough cash because I sensed, rightly, that I would have leisure enough and reason to worry about those things later on. I let the lay of the street carry me on down Spadina with my coat wide open to the breezes up from the south and when I reached the lake some time later I went out on the spit, off Leslie, hair plastered against my skull as the warm rain beat down against me and seemed now to flow in through my wide-open pores, and through me, and it was good to be alone, for that moment at least needing no one. Seeing no one either as I rushed farther and farther out on the spit that breaks the water and hooks serpentine miles out into Lake Ontario and swings round in front of the downtown, the office towers spiring and clustered in the mist and I was glad to be out here instead, willows, pines and scrub starting to sprout from the rocks and the landfill of the spit and in small coves on the landward side the loosening ice bobbed and buckled in grey thin platelets and the road narrowed and a bridge spanned a thin passage dividing the spit, a foot-path only on the further side and I let it take me on in the sweet mild rain till it narrowed too and only the lake was left to come, free of ice this far out but the heart can't stop, it glides outward over the water or lifts up soaring like geese returning from the underworld as the lakes hatch open and the spit tapers to a fingertip aimed out from the city into open sea, the real world; a spring for the starving. April. That was a moment, an hour, I'll tell you. Ask me any time, I'll tell you.

4 *A Spring for the Starving*

The Map they bore with them is yellowed & begrimed; this Logbook likewise. The Compass & pocket-watch which I retrieved from what remained of Lieutenant Chandler's greatcoat are long past repair. Yet these items – along with a fragment of bone, part perhaps of a knuckle, or a brow – I keep to hand, as if by way of guidance, whilst, from evidence gathered by the private Search Expedition for which I served as Second-in-Command, I strive to recreate the last day of the last survivors of the crews of the HMS *Erebus* & *Terror*, in the Barren Lands north of Great Fish River, Lat. 69° 11′ N, Long. 98° 51′ W, in the early spring of the year 1848.

Over thirteen years past, & a dozen since we found them. Yet I have related the particulars to no one. Even my wife Rachel I have deemed it a mercy to leave in ignorance. I have not seen the other members of our Search Party in all that time, – indeed, I have avoided them, as they have me.

Yet I am haunted still.

There are, let it be owned at once, but the flimsiest grounds for some of my suppositions, not least my charitable vision of what the unhappy Sailors might have seen before them in their last hours. In defence of these pages I shall offer only this: that any extravagance for which I am culpable is to be laid not to incompetence or to Fancy, but rather to Compassion; the Compassion of one who has voyaged long in the Polar Realms & has learned well what such Climes must do to the thickest clan of friends.

In the instant before they spied the Oasis, the Crewmen, I fear, must have loathed each other to the Death. But they had not the strength to kill. It was the protracted climb up the only rise they had met with for days that had elevated their loathing to this last, & homicidal, plateau; yet here the air seemed too thin for strife & they had knelt or sprawled in the snow, panting, feeble & feckless as the pups of a White Bear. In point of fact the April air was not scant & Alpine, merely cold, tho' bitterly so; the rise was a pretty modest one, as in the hills of our own Digby Neck, & covered thinly yet thoroughly with the Snow's silver & chilling Shawl. All round it, under brooding skies of gunbarrel-grey, the level & snow-burdened Barrens recessed boundlessly, as featureless & bewildering as the white & flattened visage of the Sphinx.

Lieutenant Chandler, tasked with leading what remained of the two ship's Crews, had hoped the hill would prove of sufficient eminence to offer a good prospect of the country thereabouts, & some notion of where next to aim. What Chandler had not uttered aloud, but which the Crewmen could not help but sense, was that this climb was a sorry last recourse, & should the circumambient Wilds yield nothing further by way of shelter or Esquimaux settlement, or some fortuitous Bear, or little herd of game, its slight gradient would suffice to deplete their powers to the last, & its low bulk to serve them for a grave-barrow. Chandler, already down on one knee & unwilling in the presence of the Crew to sag further (tho' every fibre of his body seemed to gravitate, quivering, towards the snow), gazed about him at his men strewn over the crest like unburied corpses after a skirmish, & knew the end was upon them. Three Winters beset in the ice had by slow degrees broken the Crew's spirits & Health as the ice itself had destroyed the ships; & the preceding fortnight's Southward march for the Great Fish River had unravelled the last frayed thread that sustained them: their comradeship & fraternity. So that now, upon this windy grave-barrow in the heart of the Barren Lands, they loathed each other enough to kill. But had not the strength.

Chandler's eyesight had been failing for days, – the joint effect of reflected sunlight & malnutrition, as he had confided to Crozier the last of the other Officers, who had hissed back at him: Starvation, you fool. Starvation. And died. – So that now from the crest of the hill Chandler could descry nothing but dismal plains, & snow, besides an object that resembled a Crag or stony outcrop, a mile or so to the South-West. No more than that. Yet as he squinted into the gust, detecting in his ears the first stifled stirrings of the wind-like roar that presaged those collapses he was at constant pains to fend off before the eyes of his men, a precipitous movement caught his eye, – the first sudden motion he had perceived in fortnights, in months, for the Winter seascape and landscape were congealed to utter immobility & offered by way of motion little more than slow monotonous siftings or the steady transport of the Wind; & even when the Crewmen folded in their tracks & perished, one after another, they slumped with a kind of rigid languor as if the force of Gravity itself were rendered numb by the incessant Cold. Likewise had the boreal air invaded and arrested Chandler's pocket-watch & Compass, the Laws embodied by their nimble machinery as it were suspended, whilst the Ships themselves – by far the most advanced our World has yet known – were digested by the ice.

The agent of this unwonted & precipitous movement was Drumwright, a sailor well-regarded for his Hawk's eye & one whom Captain Franklin had often bid up the cordage into the crowsnest at material times; Drumwright who now for days had marched to Death's slowing drum; who, his empty stomach notwithstanding, had been drooling onto the snow since first light a viscous black-green bile; Drumwright who had slept last night with the other men jammed together for warmth in the life-boat which they were employing as a sledge, & at dawn could not raise himself at all, so that having once extracted him from the steely embrace of the unhappy three who had not survived their turn along the outer walls of the boat (& these unfortunates laid side by side on the earth, their bodies perfunctorily covered with a shrouding of snow, whilst a few words were muttered over them, *O Death where is Thy sting, O grave, O grave where ...!*); – Drumwright had then been suffered to remain at rest in the boat, drooling, while the other men strained at the hawsers, & the vessel, bereft of all provender, of use now only for shelter & to bear the vestiges of the Captain's armoire & the grand Piano from which the men still proposed to eke a little firewood, crawled pitifully over the snow. Till noon, by which time so many more men had fallen in their traces that the boat could no longer be pulled, & lay unmoving in the snow, as had Franklin's ships in the Ice. Lieutenant Chandler had then caused the men, staggering, drunken with their own Deaths, to hack up the boat & armoire & Piano & to prepare a great Bonfire, from the heart of which the grinning keys of the Piano leered and mocked them like the teeth of some great, yet inedible, carcass.

The Crew, in an ecstasy of exhaustion, had to a man lapsed to slumber by the wondrous Fire, truly warmed for the first time in months; but when they awakened, to flitting cinders, they were colder than ever, & with no further comfort to be looked for.

Drumwright had then been obliged to join the dwindling Funeral march, dribbling a trail into the snow as he hobbled behind. When Lieutenant Chandler had issued his order to climb the hill, he had not believed Drumwright would ever gain the crest; yet now here he was, upright & eagerly pointing. What was more, he could be heard coughing out a feeble alarum, rousing a handful of other survivors who lamely clustered about him: – a score of men inclining forward in their windblown rags, shielding their ghastly, sunken eyes & pointing whilst keening like a coven of hags upon a moor.

Keening what? Chandler groaned at them, no longer able, he found, to project his voice in any wise. Somehow he rose & hailed them yet again, yet now his voice seemed as if imprisoned within his skull, a paltry thing like a House-fly buzzing in a bottle, or a pebble rattling in a shell. 'What? What?' But they did not hear him, or did not heed; and presently, the Sun peeping somewhat through the clouds, his body & brain shut down, an Aurora Borealis curtained his eyes like a winding-sheet of rainbow hues, & his stout heart ceased to beat where he stood.

Now the gathering sailors glance along the outstretched arm of the drooling Seer till they perceive it too: – where Lieutenant Chandler's enfeebled eyes spied only a crag, they distinguish a little grove of trees, from which a warm steam seems tropically to issue; & they know it for one of the Oases bruited among Arctic mariners for three Centuries, tho' never yet firmly mapped. Yet there it is, a copse of Firs concealing what can only be a bubbling hot-spring and a gentle glade unburdened by snow, – a glade doubtless stocked with berries & Game, surely frequented by Men, the Eskimaux who will lead them out of this wilderness to warmth & to safety...! This magical Island conjured from an ocean of snow by a green granite crag, – a crag caught by a beam of sun through the clouds, the film of ice upon its cliffs caused to steam by this abrupt, fleeting impression of heat. In a part of their minds – their one Mind, now? – all the sailors intuit this must be the case, yet a more powerful, necessitous organ within them denies it. They have seen 'Hoodoos' on the plains of Somerset

Island two summers past, colossal candles of Sandrock rearing vast and vaster in the distance; yet when one finally arrives before them they are no taller than a man. I can attest to this phenomenon, having encountered it myself. And I consider that our common word 'Mirage' designates a process as much as a thing & ought perhaps to be a Verb so as to express the active power of the desideratum whence it springs. Like Atlantis seduced from the Ocean; like the sail of a Halifax whaler, long overdue, fancied in a far-off white-cap. Miraged; for a few moments the Sailors, in the grip of the most common species of madness, & rapture, were Miraged.

There is a Physician now down at Harvard who opines that the opium-sweet sensations of those Federal troops who weather their near-deaths be the product of chemicals in the brain which serve at the last extremity to warm and facilitate the victim's passage into the Polar regions of Death; perhaps then such collective Mirages may be explained in like wise? Ah, explain, explain! Always this drive to discover & explain, as powerful, most probably, as the need for Mirage ... As for me, long home from the Polar wastes and our appalling discoveries there – discoveries which Time can never efface from my memory – I have had enough of such desires, & failures. Enough. Yet I do persist in striving, with the evidence at hand, to envisage how the final end befell, as if by sheer dint of Will I might force Truth to crystallize here beneath my lamp, in my study, on this, the hottest, most sleepless night of the Summer.

So thus it must be that a sterile crag blossomed in the eyes of our Arctic sailors like Eden in the procreative Eye of God; & in that access of mutual invention & discovery the men's loathing for each other melted away, & their kinship flared back with their energy, & they danced on the spot & they held & embraced each other & sang with what voices they had left, like a clump of raggy sweeps or beggars in a Dartmouth alley, who have lucked upon a swag of gold.

'The Lieutenant,' hissed Drumwright, 'he sees it as well, Look!' – but as they limp quickly towards him with open arms, they realize his gaping eyes see nothing. Frozen upright, he stares into the wind. 'We must bring him with us,' cries a sailor. But Drumwright, the Seer, shakes his quivering head: 'No. A sign

must be left for the Others. Searchers. They will surely come.
The Oasis is miles yet. Here – ' And, the others cringing back, he
crooks the Officer's right arm up, level as a musket, & sights the
hand & trigger-finger into the South-West towards the Oasis, –
which even now, alas! is disappearing whilst clouds devour the
Sun & the rising wind blows snow off the waste Plains ... 'Here,
as he'd have wished it,' ordains Drumwright, with maddened
eyes, a black froth beading on his lips. 'A brave man in life. Never
once saw him laying out in the day. Why now?' The others,
nodding and gibbering concurrence, salute in farewell, & at
length they turn, link arms & embark downhill, with new
strength, towards the vanishing Oasis. And nothwithstanding the
driven snow which is swallowing the Mirage with the last of their
hopes, & lives, they are a group again, & happy; hobbling together
like a band of aged team-mates reunited on the playing fields of
their youth.

   This much, at least, I would grant them.

   There was next to no thaw that summer, – the coldest, our
Eskimaux guides assured us, in living memory. When we arrived
the next Spring, Lieutenant Chandler was still at attention upon
the hilltop, half-naked in his gnawed officer's rags, eyes pecked
clean by the Ravens, arm extended over the Barrens towards the
granite headstone that we poor searchers named Cannibal Crag.

5 *The Flower in the Face of God*

She left me another story I can tell, another flowering.

After his ship, torpedoed by an Italian U-boat in the Aegean Sea, has sunk to the bottom with all hands, a British sailor wakes oarless and adrift in a small leaking boat a dozen miles off the Isle of Patmos. He knows the distant, dusty coastline as Patmos because the ship's chaplain pointed clearly and intoned the name just hours before, towards the end of his service for a crewman killed in action. At that time the island was little more than a sulphur-coloured smear far to the east and the Italian U-boat that would soon attack and sink them was still ranging a few knots to the west under the clear, quivering surface of the Aegean.

Patmos. Home, the chaplain emphasized, to many martyrs, many saints, and to St John the Divine, some of whose Revelations the man recited under the hot hallucinogenic sun before the open-ended, flag-draped coffin was tilted and the small swaddled body burst out and slid into the sea.

A sea of glass. A sea of glass, like unto crystal.

The dead man was the sailor's best friend. In the first hours after his death the sailor felt sick to his stomach and head and the sickness had worsened during the long service under the terrible sun. Then soon after came the torpedo. It was heralded by an uncanny rippling sound then someone yelling in the stern but incoherently, the foreign-sounding cries cut short by a baritone roaring as the deck shuddered underfoot and listed aft much faster than the sailor could have thought possible. The rest is hellish, blurred. The lieutenant, screaming, sliding past down the steepening deck straight into the flames and the flames geysering up, whirling in the hold: a chain of underwater explosions, sulphurous and belching. And a hand, outstretched – the sailor gripping a hand. Bluish, cold, trapped when a steel hatchway slammed shut, it stuck out rigid and dead as the steel of the hatchway and yet transmitted a weak but eager vibration, as if the man below were still alive and unwilling to let go. The ship heeled farther. The sailor's grip loosened, snapped, and a hell of spitting flame and water hurtled up to meet him as he plummeted into the sea like his dead, swaddled friend.

Closing his eyes he made no effort to save himself.

Yet somehow, hours later, he remains alive.

Patmos is more now than a sulfurous smudge to the east, but not much more. Beyond it the brooding, jagged mass of the coast of Turkey. A few other islands are visible as well, small baubles of sand-coloured foam afloat on a sea as tranquil and clear as ice – the blue thin ice of that tarn in the moors above Chester the Christmas he and his big sister cycled up there as children, his name being shouted across the hills as he glides out onto the ice of the tarn and his sister, a small silhouette against scudding snowclouds, waves at him from a ridge....

Sunlight scalds down onto his bare head. He senses he is drifting toward the distant Patmos, and safety, but he reckons – numbly – that he must die before landing. Of his wounds, of the sun, of hunger, thirst. The only water in the boat is the low pool of seawater, stained with his own blood, that seeps in through a crack he has not yet found. No food. Not even a nap of canvas to screen his head or prop up as a sail.

But there is no wind.

The sailor lies face down in the boat to shield himself from sunlight direct and reflected and to pinpoint the leak that will otherwise sink him before the next dawn. He has tried bailing with cupped hands but lacks the strength to go on for more than a few minutes. The deep weakness, like the spreading infusion of blood in the water rising on the floor of the boat, is from a deep gash in his forehead just under the hairline; apathetically he has pressed his palm to the wound, but it continues to ooze a hot, half-congealed fluid. Finally he finds the strength to sit up and tear a pocket off his tattered shirt and press it to the gash. This simple act surprises him: until now he hardly cared whether he lived or died but now, it seems, he does. When the bleeding finally slows he peels off the fabric and replaces it with a longer strip, turbaned tightly around his head, the throb in his bound temples spiralling to a migraine.

Behind the boat a faint but discernible pink wake: surely not his own blood? He folds up over a spasm of nausea. For a moment he sees that if he makes himself tiny enough he can curl up and sleep in the cool shadow of his hand. No. He slumps down again, gropes for the leak. *The leak is in my own body and everything is flowing out.* His hand scuttles slowly under the bloodstained water, a crab on the seafloor, starving. To eat the flesh raw. *To suck the sweetness out of the cracked shell and*

The crewman who died was from the coastal part of the same county the sailor came from. On the ship they became great friends. Neither cared much for magazines or chatty hands of poker or the rum-tot banter that sprang up after meals; they were both silent men. They played long quiet games of checkers, chess. In agreeable near-silence they drank together in Gibraltar and Alexandria and went together several times to a brothel in Rabat. The crewman died of wounds sustained after a freak accident: three days ago they were firing at an Italian gunboat off the Isle of Rhodes when a turreted gun swung wildly, its barrel knocking the man overboard. Moments later when they fished him from the sea he was in shock and could not speak – could not say what had happened underwater to leave such strange wounds all over his body. The chaplain and doctor insisted the ship's draught must have sucked him up against the hull under the waterline where it was studded with loosening, rusty rivets, but the lieutenant and some of the older sailors muttered darkly of other things. For twenty-four hours he had hung on, in terrible pain, unable to speak, the sailor in attendance. Then – peering with fierce concentration at the light bulb swinging above his head, as if warding off a presence no one else could see – he died.

No doubt that night's sleepless vigil had contributed to the sailor's 'overreaction' and sickness at the service, and after. And now. *As if they burned. Burned in a mighty*

He finds the leak and with a rusted nail pushes the bloody pocket into the crack. Then rests his head on the thwart on folded, aching arms.

When he wakes the sun is low in the sky and the sea has pumped another finger's-width of water through the leak. The water rising slower now, but rising. Too weak to balance himself over the gunwale he can only add to the bilge in the guts of the boat, tugging open his flies and passing a weak bloody trickle of piss under the thwart. Bleached wood of it like a rib, picked clean. Flesh thinning all of it thawing to a rose a briny flux. Into salt water. The sea –

To starboard something bursts the surface and flares up silver, long and quick as a torpedo and bucks momentarily airborne before plunging back with barely a splashing or a ripple, gone; already the sailor's heart has sunk back down under the burden of his sickness, his dying, but for the split-second when he knew the light for what it was – a dolphin – his heart had leapt and flowered and he had blessed it unawares.

Nothing now inside him or around. Same slow seeping. Patmos with its far-off tombstone cliffs and high beyond them the mountains, their deep treeless folds flooded with evening shadow.

When he wakes from vast billowing dreams full of weird gravities and jittering geometric figures he is too feeble to raise his head. Swallowing is impossible, his throat throttled with dryness. The sun is gone, somewhere behind him, but the last of its light is a cusp of orange cinders on the peaks of the mountains of the Isle of Patmos.

His mother, he reflects, was a pious woman. Surely it would console her to know he died so near a holy place. As for him, who came to hate school and the church and could only tolerate the strictures of the navy because it let him leave home and go to sea – it makes little difference. For he has left those things behind. So he tells himself. A few echoes, perhaps, stirred up by the funeral service for his friend; no more. He would like to go on living – a fraction of him feels this, knows it to be true – but the weary indifferent part is inexorably flattening the other like some gross, inert, bloodless weight crushing the life from something vital.

At dusk a light breeze springs up. Then dies. Everything is still. He slumps back in the boat, hoping the weight of his aching buttocks will slow the leak. Too weak to bail now even a little. He will wake at dawn barely afloat but closer to Patmos or an Allied ship, or he will founder in the night while sleeping. Dreaming.

Somehow these outcomes seem not dissimilar.

He is utterly calm.

Asleep.

Something jolts him up, skull, heart slamming – to stillness, total dark. The splashing that startled him awake is gone. The sea is calm, the moonless sky twittering with autumn stars.

Two clutching hands, palely phosphorescing, glow on the dark wood of the bow. A face appears above them like a grimacing figurehead, but backwards. *Dreaming*, he says aloud – yet a weight in the bow is elevating the stern where he sits, the boat tilting up like his friend's coffin at the end of the service. He shuts his eyes. Opens them: the figure lifting itself over the prow, swinging a pale dripping leg into the boat.

He is impossibly gaunt, hairy, with a drowned man's doughy-swollen, waterlogged skin. Locks of seaweed quiver down from his thick brows and long jetblack hair and beard. His eyes are sombre, sunken as the caves he might have sprung from. A castaway. He must be that – a sailor from another ship whose raft has sunk after weeks at sea, or months, a man who has clung like a limpet to a rock gnawing at lichen and sea-moss and licking the brine from crevices till he is skeletal and demented, his clothes burned away by salt and the sun.

The sailor sits up and peers at the stranger, who squats calmly in the bow facing him. Italian, the sailor thinks. Will he try to harm me. He is certainly stronger, despite his pallor and thinness; I could not have climbed in over the prow.

Who are you then, the sailor croaks out. The man says something in reply. The voice is gentle, unmenacing, the words incomprehensible. Italian? Sounds a touch like the low Greek he has heard in some of the boulevards and bordellos of Alexandria, yet different, richer, more rounded and rolling, less staccato and harsh.

You're Italian then? *Eye-talian*, the sailor pronounces it.

Long teeth shining the man smiles and makes some response. Then inclines his meagre torso forward – sets one bony hand on the middle thwart – and seems to pose some sort of question. For the first time the sailor can make out the man's eyes set in their caverns of shadow: very black and shining with the starved intensity he saw years ago in the eyes of his sister, ill with the Spanish flu', then his friend's eyes a few days back while the flesh candled away down his yellowing cheeks as if before long just the eyes would be left, twin flames flittering in every breeze; guttering; going out. And the same wise, resigned kindness he read in those others – these eyes have it too. The sailor is no longer afraid. *For behold his eyes were as a flame of fire.*

When the stranger opens his upturned palm on the thwart, the sailor covers it with his own.

But now there is something strange. Now it seems the little strength left in the sailor's flesh is starting to drain out of him and into the palm of the stranger, first slowly, then very fast. The stranger continues to eye him firmly and tenderly as a numbness flows up the sailor's arm into his body, his heart and neck – his brain – his last thought the certainty that he was wrong, this man is an enemy, an Italian spy who has drugged him somehow or hypnotized him and will knife or drown or smother him once he slips helpless under the thwart. Ridiculous. And yet the chaplain chanting how the third beast had a face a   *face as a Man:* Beast scudding undersea like a grey torpedo seeking lifeboats   *climb aboard devour you as the whale did jonah as the jerries they do say now with some of their prisoners in the camps in   in the mountains of the*

He surges awake in the drugged half-light of dawn, the sun's first rays clawing the sky and the Devil's hand on the back of his head forcing him down deeper into the salt sewage in the belly of the boat. His own belly. He tries to yell but his throat is dried shut. Tries to crane his head to face his enemy, nightmarewise, but even in panic his strength is useless against those hands. His nose in the sulphurous pool where the last stars are mirrored in strange taunting constellations and then his whole face submerged. Finally his lips bursting open helpless and panting and his mouth and throat are flooded with the foul taste of his own mortality....

But no. The water is cool, springpure, unsalted, it tingles and stings sweetly as it gushes over his chapped, lapping tongue and his palate and into his scorched throat, unsealing it, cleaving a passage so that now the mountain waters are cascading into his mouth and down his throat and the sailor feels his strength flowing back into him and he could fight the bony hand but the need is gone, the weight that was forcing him down is a benign consoling pressure on the back of his head and ready to grip his hair and tug him up to safety should he inhale too much and start drowning.

Now the fingers do gently pull him back as his guts start to gripe and swell with the pressure and the belly of the boat is suddenly dry, the boat riding higher than it has since the sailor first woke aboard it. Moving, too – the boat is moving over the sea with the incredible speed of a torpedo or a corvette.

Finally he lifts his head: the beaming stranger now has oars and is rowing them in towards the island, leaning far forward then smoothly heaving back to drive them almost flying over the sea despite the frailty of his arms, his deathly pallor, those eyes that sag like the martyred eyes of saints in the ikonostases by the chapels in Rhodes. Yet full of power. The man is speaking once more in his rolling unearthly tongue and the sailor is sure he hears the word Patmos, *Patmos*, which sounds like some of the other words the man utters so now the sailor wonders if his language could be a kind of Greek – the dialect of the island perhaps? *His voice as the sound of many waters.* So close now, the cliffs and mountains of Patmos rearing up behind the stranger as he rows them closer with oars he must have plucked from the sea or conjured from the air with his bare hands – miraculous emaciated hands that can turn bilgewater to ambrosia and now ship the oars and dip and snatch from the rising waters a long thrashing flash of silver which quickly stills in his hand. Another flash, then another. Soon, the sailor sees, he will be fed.

The sun lifts over the high ridges of Patmos and the fresh swell kindles around the boat, the red sun a halo behind the head of the man who is urging the sailor to break his fast – so the sailor trusts – who is tendering in cupped hands an ivory fillet which the sailor takes and eats and the flesh is succulent

and sweet and now the stranger is eating too. The sailor's full
strength rushing back to him with a marvellous surge a roaring but the roaring he sees now is the sound of the rising wind
and the breakers battering the cliffs of Patmos only a knot or
so away. How can we land? he says, voice breaking. How – ?
But the haloed head merely nods, the exhausted adoring eyes
blink slowly, urging him to be calm. And he is calm although
the surf's roaring mounts up and the cliffs seem to build above
them and the solar nimbus lifts over the stranger's head and
leaves the face in shadow. And he is calm as the stranger leans
towards him and calmer still as he smells a sweet earthly
scent like sage and basil and samphire that could be blowing
off the cliffs of the Isle of Patmos but seems rather to come
from the stranger, his lips, the open mouth murmuring a
tongue the sailor now understands: words blessing him over
the howl of the cliff-shattering sea *for he sheweth me water*
of life clear as crystal and close, so close, the sweet odour
seeming to rise from the sailor's own body too as if his flesh
were blazing with samphire and basil and sage like unto a cliff-
side in early spring. And he is calm as the stranger leans face-
to-face to kiss the wound weeping on his brow with pure
unprovisional love and heals him as the cliffs crag up over the
boat and the sea grips and sweeps them up straight onto the
eye-teeth of the boulders – calm. *For every mountain and*
island were moved from their places.   grey rockface shuddering towards them they ride the last great landward
swell thin arms a comfort as ribs around a heart's hard beating they smash   *shattering and*

Steel, a grey wall. Rope-ladder spooling over the thwart. A
hand gropes towards him – hands. Lifting him dazed, head
throbbing, up the hull of the ship, aboard. Mouths shaping a
language he can't quite decipher though he knows he knew it
once. And the uniforms. Throat too dry to croak a word, but he
must. My friend, he dredges up, in the boat. Please. The boat.
He saved my. Ah, you must. But the sailors tell him, in words
he now grasps – plain English – the boat is empty. Must have
fallen out. Sorry, but it's so. You were alone.

The lip of a canteen breaching his broken mouth and he
drinks and though he is too weak, his throat too dry, still he

does, he must babble his story and the chaplain's aide there on the deck of the HMCS *Fort Garry* searching ten knots off the coast of Patmos cradled the feverish head in his hands and leaned over and caught the words carried on the foul, dying breath of the sailor. The chaplain's aide was April's uncle Fred and when April was nine years old he told her the story as a Christian parable, and ten years later, the two of us wandering hand in hand by the docks near the frozen port of Montreal, she told me.

6 Persephone

O of her open lips out of time so widening the skull crowning through like a bulb a bubble the world mouthed and mothered out of winter dark and the word her lips forming made flesh. A friend and her husband had me there with the midwives, asked me to film it and though I didn't want to watch through a frame – I was tired of frames and pages and I knew this would be the real translation, from nothing into life, and daylight – still I understood the desire, I told them sure, this a few weeks after you had died and me thinking it could have been you, April, been us. So I filmed things as well as I could for the full two hours not realizing it was miked so a day later playing it back they heard my voice bumbling on and on, this incredulous breathless mumbled colour-commentary *oh god I can't believe this   holy shit I can't believe it's coming out of her   oh god would you   a girl is it   look –*

And they had a good laugh. Then replayed it: my friend finally forcing out the difficult red bud of her son's head (Leith, I'd have named him if she'd asked) and squeezing tears from her eyes, of both kinds, circles inside circles, *o god   can't believe.* She reaching to feel. April, full circle, home from the underworld: I'd lay the living word in your hands. And hear how it cries. O.

7 With April to Patmos

You might have gone some day with April to Patmos. To the last flowering, the one that comes to old couples after long drought. Say the two of you never split up after a year and a half in Toronto, say she never died ten years later in a used Mazda driving home from her fiancee's place in Vermont, in the Green Mountains, hitting a run of black ice at dusk.... Instead a few more fast-paced years together in Toronto before you evacuate to somewhere else, some smaller, calmer, decaffeinated place like Burlington Vermont, St John's or Kingston or out over the mountains to Victoria – somewhere you settle down and raise a family and stick together for years in the drowsy, undistracted way some couples manage. Couples who think of themselves as happy, and sometimes are. Couples not tugged and torn to pieces by the intense centrifugal pressures of the Big City. And your differences? The ones that uncoupled the two of you as surely as rush hours in the subway, five in the afternoon when your body is tired yet excited and you're trapped underground in cars shuddering with strangers who jostle on, cheeks flushed, scan the ads just above your head as if reading the Personals, meet your eyes in passing so a volt of high current shoots through you but they're always turning away too soon and leaving at Union or Rosedale or Castle Frank and slipping away over the platform; all the shadow-paths your life might have followed mapping themselves onto your face as wrinkles of frustration, fatigue.

Could it be you? You?

And your differences – what about *them*. Look, it was a match made in Vaudeville, Molly Bloom meets Raskolnikov, exciting while the sparks flew but once they caught and the framework of your lives went up in smoke....

Anyway, in the underworld there's no looking back.

Yet now, somehow, you see yourself growing happily-ever-after-old with April who after all was warm and brilliant and seismic with sudden joys, and beautiful (and yes, all too often, bitchy and selfish and impractical and you with your own hard flaws so finally when there was nothing left for the two of you to murder in argument you went your own roads). Yet now, one day in late middle age, daughter and son finally grown and evicted, the two of you fly to Athens and board the ferry for Aeghina, the Cyclades, and Patmos. For her, a summer holiday (but from what? – as hard to think of April at any one job for more than a few months as to think of her settled down and married. But let it go). For you, a chance to take in the sights and drink cold beer in the evening while finishing a few stubborn translations and writing a travel piece or two. Patmos is a happy compromise – what any long-term couple fumbles for all the time – since April is a lover of dancing and music, any music, and the steep coast of Patmos is spattered with towns like rockfalls of ivory limestone and every town has its own taverna with music, with dancing, noon until night.

And you? I think you may have become one of those intense, skeletal eccentrics with trimmed beard and beak-sharp nose and eyes of a bright, neurotic ferocity – the kind of man who's up each dawn to stride intensely, guidebook in hand, through cathedrals and ruins and buried galleries, and till evening and the beer he has walked all day to earn he puts off the beach and *kafeneion* where his wife loiters, guiltless, and which he once preferred himself.

After the ferry from the Cyclades drops you on barren Patmos, you and April divide your days. In the warm stippled shade of a taverna's vine-roofed garden she taps her fingers on the table by her cup of Greek coffee or bira while the bouzouki and santouri skitter, the cook and waiter dance away their break and Mr Apostolakis, the fat, sweating proprietor of the Agios Yiannis Café, sways with arms extended and head way back, a black wooden chair and then a table – a whole table, Toby, you've got to see it! – balanced between his teeth, his strong white teeth. How they shine against the black wood of the table! Suddenly it's evening, dark and hot inside the taverna, Mr A's teeth more than ever shining, his dog Charybdis snarling and cornering the cowed mandolinist. In the back corner by the cellar stairs two pleasant, elderly New Yorkers, in an orgasm of touristic fervour, begin to hurl their plates and glasses onto the floor, into the empty fireplace, down the repercussing stairwell! In a flashing of white teeth and black wood Mr Apostolakis swings his balanced burden down with a thud and begins cursing in Greek and bellowing in broken English, No! *skata!* SKATA! if you would PLEASE! Too late – the beaming old couple have already atomized the last sideplate and are now jettisoning their cutlery. It will take the apoplectic Mr Apostolakis some time to cool their ardour and give them to understand that one only demolishes plates and glasses in *some* tavernas, at *certain* times....

And you: in the balding ascetic hills far above these Dionysian high jinks, for the second day in a row: wandering along ancient paths among shrines and ruins and ikonostases, the dry tang of broom, basil and desert-cedar censering the hot thin air. The concentrated sun turning your light jacket into a hair-shirt, the shuddering heat collecting in your shoes till your feet are stigmatized with blisters. This time you will make it all the way across the island to the thousand-year-old monastery near the caves where St John the Divine, having starved for visions or stuffed himself with psychedelic mushrooms, composed his Book of Revelations. You would be walking there faster – because you're a lean terse unswerving man and because the history and magic of the island are things you can only translate into real terms by exploring, measuring, seeing – but something slows you down. Fatigue, partly, but it's not just the heat. You round a hook in the trail: a cluster of buildings that must be the monastery fans out far below you at the base of a long ravine that sheers downward two thousand feet to the level of the sea. *A fleur de mer.* The buildings are white as bone and the sunlit sea is green and then sapphire where it deepens and across the straits the edge of Asia with its seven lost churches is mountainous, deserted and grey.

April. Seeing the monastery and the Aegean and the coast of Asia you remember something you had almost forgotten because it happened in the dead of night, last night – a dream? – and now your dour weathered face, the face of some Byzantine martyr, softens, blessed with a kind of second youth like a face on a church ceiling lovingly restored with brushes and gentle washes. How you and April retired early, by local standards, tired from the trip, indulging the cozy drowsiness of long-time couples no longer rocked and racked by the mating-dance pressures of the desperately single. Pleasant, in some ways, yet sometimes that drowsiness seems an oppression, you blame your wife for infecting you and if only, you know, if only you were alone or with someone new....

You both felt that way last night – frustrated – April because the dust settling in her body these last few years has been churned to a sand-storm by the zithering music and the whirling young couples in Mr A's taverna, on holiday, on honeymoon, and she alone, and you wishing there could have been someone else up there in the high shrill air of the mountains to pause with you at an ikonostasis and look out over the sunburnt slopes toward the Aegean and squeeze your hand in understanding.

Both of you soon asleep, disgruntled, barely touching on the too-small bed in the fanless room. She dreams of a windowed coffin, its glass walls so misted with breath that whoever lies breathing inside cannot be seen. You are dreaming in another language, as you often do, but no language you have ever worked with or heard. Nothing to see at first, only words sounding in your ears like wind in the dark. She dreams of green shoots and stems cracking like fingers through the misted glass of the coffin. The coffin is a tiny greenhouse. But there is someone inside. You are reading in the same strange language from a thick volume bound in red leather, your own voice translating the beautiful cursive script into sounds you cannot quite decipher. A face appears against the misted glass like a face rising out of water. Then two hands, pressed to the glass, on either side of the face. You have taken the author of the book, who as you scanned the words was peering over your shoulder, and you fold him up in the book and drop the book into a flowing rockpool in a crevice high over the sea. The book sinks and for a few moments bubbles gurgle up in the pool. Then stop.

You're awake. Too dark to read the time. Beside you the uncanny, almost physical silence of somebody else awake and listening, as if to the sea outside, which is calm. Lying on her back, whoever she is, the only light a faint glinting from her eyes.

Your fingers brush together as if by chance and suddenly without conscious motion you're crushed in each other's arms, squeezing each other as if to fuse the skin and mesh your ribs together like fingers and you would do all that, no question, if you had the strength, you might crush each other to death. You almost do have the strength – you feel three decades younger, her nipples tight against the slack skin of your chest your mouths mashed together your teeth grinding hard. Hardness of her pubic bone in the dark then heat and softness as you find each other and plunge together, groaning, like a blind couple, new to each other each time – so you've heard. But something more than the dark has stripped away years and the dry terracing of dailiness like dust gathering under a loveless bed: you're as strange to each other now as the ones you dreamed of following off subway cars in Union Station thirty-five years back, yet more than ever you're the sum of yourselves, more than ever unmistakable. Her orgasm and yours – together, as it seldom works out – have the shared force to shatter the small contracting room that habit has bricked in around you, so after long drought you lie together in a pasture under the planets with smells of lavender and dung and lilac and flowering almond wreathing you in the dark.

All this comes back to you as you stand at the trail-hook high over the sea and look down at the monastery. You start walking down the path through the ravine and then find yourself trotting, running, letting the slope reel you downward as the damp earth-smells of the valley rise pulsing to meet you. Your body feels like last night again, young; on the verge of a knowledge too long put off. Now the colour of the sea seems to change and deepen as you scramble down the switchback trail and the air grows rich and damp and green and sweat-hot as you gulp it in and it's only when you're almost down among the buildings that you see you must have made a wrong turn, somewhere way back, this is not the monastery, that long white building with the orange tree growing from its roof and swaying in the wind like a bangled dancer is – it must be – the Agios Yiannis Café. You hurry ahead over the culvert past the yapping Charybdis toward the rising music and wafting erotic smells of onion and basil and grape-leaves and garlic and burst into the shaded garden and there she is, at her table in the corner as you brush the damp grey hair from your eyes (*O agape*, they are singing, *agape mou*) her glasses slipping down her nose as she lowers her cup her open mouth spreading to a rapt stunned smile and Mr Apostolakis turns from the old New Yorkers he's teaching to dance and grabs and pirouettes you and shakes his grinning head and wheezes into your ear, *Ach, philo mou. You will stand here all day like a fool! Look, she is waiting! Dance!*

The Patrons

for Vanny

LUCK. He knew he'd been lucky to get off so early, in time for the two-thirty-five to Montreal. And – there was no way out of it – the midnight bus back. Plenty of work would be there for him in the morning, the other dishwasher only worked night-shifts and the busboys never had time for washing once the Place Paris filled up. Tomorrow, Sunday, the restaurant would open early and serve its popular brunch and by seven a.m. Ravuth would be back under the ancient Hobart, dredging handfuls of clammy rice and slushy diced vegetables from the guts of the machine, trying to hose down a disaster of crammed clattering bus tubs.

It would be a long shift. He would try to catch a few hours' sleep on the night bus home.

Ravuth picked his way north through a labyrinth of side streets toward the depot. Until a week before he'd gotten around on a child's ten-speed, but it had been stolen from back of the rooming house where he lived and the next police auction was not until fall, so for now he was on foot. Hurrying through a narrow chasm of wartime tenements – garden-less, tilted – his echoed footfalls rapping off clapboard and concrete, a sound like flesh being slapped. Crack of gunshots. A girl slouched in a warped doorway in cut-off jeans and high-heeled pumps, a baby in the crook of her arm. Somehow she was like those others silhouetted in doorways in the huts of burning villages, watching him and his brother Dara and their mother pass with a stream of refugees that was swelling river-like as they neared Khlong Yai and the Gulf of Thailand. There were said to be boats there, waiting for them. Ravuth was twelve and his brother sixteen.

He reached the depot and went in. It was good to get out of the heat. He was badly out of breath – too much smoking the last while. Last long while. He blamed the extra shifts. He blamed his life here. He blamed, in quiet moments, himself.

In a cramped toilet at the back of the depot he pummelled his face with cold water.

Outside in the queue, people looked shabby, slumped, as if they'd been lined up since dawn. When he had asked Mr Lennon, manager of the Place Paris, if he could leave a bit early to be sure for the bus, the man had laughed and said *Of course, Ravuth, but I want you to promise me that after I give you your next raise you'll start taking the train. Nobody takes the bus if they can help it, eh? We want you fresh for tomorrow!*

As he remembered Mr Lennon's words, Ravuth found himself nodding and smiling in mechanical agreement, just as he'd done at the time. A clenched old woman at the back of the queue eyed him. He stamped his cigarette into the diesel rainbow at his feet.

Some time after the bus passed the outskirts of Brockville, Ravuth fell asleep over the copy of *Canadian Art* he had bought three days ago when his brother's letter arrived. The magazine was tough going. He began to dream in a simpler English – that Dara had become famous for his work and the small Montreal gallery he was on his way to visit was besieged by critics and reporters and affluent patrons, that Dara retired to a private cottage in those low mountains north of Montreal where he could work comfortably on his paintings and sculpture. And though Ravuth knew next to nothing about art – even traditional Cambodian art – his brother invited him to stay for as long as he wished and in that way they were finally reconciled, five years after their clash in Vancouver, their mother sick and Ravuth working at three jobs to support them while Dara, the child prodigy of Pursat – the spoiled older brother with his gift for moulding faces from the clay of the Cardamom Mountains, for painting the landscape with the same brilliant pigments it was made of – toyed with foreign materials and sold little and worked part time as a busboy and would do nothing more. Their mother dying through a cold wet Vancouver winter. Dara leaving after her death for Montreal. And Ravuth going east as well but only as far as Banff so he would not have to see Dara, whom he blamed for her death as much as he blamed the strangeness of the Canadian sky, its low clouds laden with invisible contagions. Though for her death – in times of stillness, broken sleep – he blamed himself too.

Ravuth woke suddenly in Cornwall. He caught the fermented smells of wild rice and veal and prawns that always clung to his skin, his clothing. Taking his day-pack into the toilet he changed his shoes and shirt and smoked a cigarette, and after finishing he sat awhile on the lidded toilet. The cigarette smoke killed the smell. Ravuth liked it in the tiny rumbling cubicle and would have stayed there, gladly, for the rest of the trip.

The Montreal terminus was crammed and jostling with pushy, purposeful weekend crowds. Ravuth had promised to call Dara on arrival to get directions to the gallery but now he decided not to, not yet, since he hadn't known if he would get off in time for the early bus and he'd predicted a later arrival. He paused by a line of payphones. Hands clenched deep in his pockets he thought of their reunion: five-thirty now and the show opened at eight.

When a big schoolkid with high-tops and a Walkman barged up and grabbed the nearest phone Ravuth turned for the exit.

The sidewalks were busy along Ste-Catherine. Many of the restaurants had removable windows so their well-dressed patrons – gesturing, pouting, shrugging emphatically – could eat in the open air. The food reminded Ravuth of his appetite and he dug in his back pocket for his cigarettes, lit one, kept walking. Watchful and tense. Through the empty centre of Pursat after the looting: windows and doors along the main streets shattered, staved in, the tables in the gutted tea-houses charred and empty.

On Ste-Catherine there were no cheap Cambodian restaurants.

It was after six. Ravuth stood on the corner of Atwater and

Ste-Catherine scanning the intersection for a phone. Surely dinner with Dara was a better idea, it was foolish of him to put things off, to feel this way.

A hand on his shoulder.

'Ravuth!'

'Yeah you're right, it is Ravi. Ravi Shankar.'

Two faces pressed in on him, inches away. A whiff of liquor and something else – cologne.

'Ravuth, old man, what are you doing here!'

He knew the faces from somewhere. The lean one young but seedy, with caved-in bristling cheeks, eyes bloodshot and pink-edged as if squinting into a bitter wind, the other one plump, double-chinned as an aging landlord – Ravuth's landlord, Mr Givner, a kind old man – but these flushed cheeks were young and lineless, a baby's unblinking blue eyes goggling from behind tiny wire-frame glasses.

'It's Stephen, Ravuth, Stephen Earle – I know, I know, the hair's a-going, but the signature – still yours truly. Just the same. And here – my old accomplice after the fact, Richard. A.K.A. Rick. Rick Slessor? We toiled at your side out in Banff, three years ago. At the hotel? You must remember.'

A corner of Rick Slessor's tight mouth rose. 'We're the ones kept bringing you those dishes,' he said.

And Ravuth remembered. He nodded and grinned and shook Stephen's proffered hand. 'I'm very sorry,' he said. 'I did not recognize you without your bow ties.'

Stephen gave an infectious high-tenor laugh and fingered the roll of flesh over his collar. His white shirt was done up to the top but he had no tie, which Ravuth found strange. He wore a huge loose double-breasted blazer and baggy grey flannels that rumpled over his black loafers, elephantine, like the lowered pants and shoes Ravuth glimpsed in stalls at the Place Paris when cleaning the men's.

'Ravuth,' he beamed, 'you haven't changed a fraction. That's how we picked you out. We saw you from the other side of the street.'

Stephen's hand was plump and soft but his handshake was very firm. Ravuth tried to escape by relaxing his own grip but his hand simply crumpled and Stephen, plainly unaware of the discomfort, continued to clamp and mangle the smaller hand with bluff, barging goodwill.

'Okay enough,' Rick snapped. 'Time.' He'd dug his hands deep into his jeans pockets. Under the false shoulders of his leather jacket he was hunched up, as if chilled by a bitter breeze only he could feel.

'Time,' he said. 'I need a drink.'

'You see, Ravuth, Richard and I are en route to meet some old college cronies at a bistro much better than the place *we* worked' – he liberated Ravuth's hand and squeezed his thin shoulder – 'and we'd be delighted if you'd join us.'

Rick glanced at Stephen, then down at his own boots.

'The more the merrier, yes Richard? Ravuth, it's on us.'

Rick blinked and turned his face away. Belched. That boozy smell again. 'Well hey,' he finally said. 'Why not. No telling anyway if the others.... Anyway, shit. We unloaded enough dishes on you at Banff eh?' He looked up, managed a cadaverous smile. Now Ravuth recalled him well – he'd been thin at Banff, too, but with a simmering, hair-trigger intensity, his features sharp, movements keyed-up and quick and irritable. Every morning he smelled of liquor. Always giving the dishwashers curt dark warning glances as he dumped his overloaded trays.

'You see, Ravuth, I've come to take Richard out to B.C. tomorrow, to the Kootenays, helicopter skiing. To cheer him up. He's had a, well, a difficult time of late, haven't you Richard?' – he slapped his friend on the back, Rick's eyes reddening as if he would belch again – 'and we feel like a night on the town. Lay in some provisions for the trip, yes Richard? Ravuth, you're perfectly free to come along.'

Ravuth glanced at his watch. 'I – well, I would like to eat with you, but I can't stay over one hour. At eight o'clock tonight my brother has his first show of painting and sculpture, that's why I am here. I suppose I can get to the show after we eat?'

'Ravuth, if the service is just as brisk as when I lived here, there's no question about that. Besides, we have a car.'

'An hour, *sans doute*,' Rick said, twisting his mouth round the French.

* * *

The restaurant was busy but Stephen flagged down the maître d' and got them a spot right away. In Banff too he had marched up to the Hobart bantering and gesturing with the same elaborate, theatrical self-assurance, as if certain of the world's goodwill, and though at first the other dishwashers had made fun of him, before long they all missed him on his days off – the high-pitched laugh, the corny banter, the crisp fastidious stacking of dishes on his trays. He and Rick were partners in the dining room. *Tweedledim and Tweedletum*, the others had called them, and Ravuth had not understood.

Ravuth needed to smoke now but the table was non-smoking.

When after thirty minutes the expected friends had still not shown, Stephen, intoxicated with his own good-natured conversation, ordered another bottle of Beaujolais. The menu was in French and though Ravuth told them he remembered enough from his schooldays (*in Pursat*, he wanted to tell them, *in Cambodia*) to choose and order for himself, Stephen begged him not to worry. '*Mais je peux parler beaucoup,*' Ravuth declared with an uncharacteristic flourish, light-headed from the wine he had drunk, his stomach empty.

'*Mais oui, Ravuth,*' Rick said, breaking a long silence. '*Bien sûr.*' And he leaned way over the table as if to add more, as if taking Ravuth into his confidence. 'Ra-*voot*' – he said slowly, breathing the name in the French way and scanning Ravuth's face with bruised, boxer's eyes that seemed both intense and totally vacant. Ravuth, trying to smile, thought of the old Belgian priest who had taught them French in grade-school and frightened them with his long yellow teeth and huge beard.

Suddenly Rick settled back in his chair and regarded Ravuth with a strange smile. Drunk, but deliberate. '*Ton français est top-notch, la,*' he said with a phony twang and Ravuth knew when an accent was being mocked. A couple, plainly French, glared from the next table. Stephen turned to them and shrugged with a sheepish grin.

'Now, now, Richard.'

'So he's an *artiste,* your brother,' Rick went on, tilting his glass as if to pour the dregs onto the tablecloth. 'Any good?'

'When he was younger he was very good,' Ravuth said. 'In our part of the country he was famous. But when we were in the camp in Thailand he could not work, and when we came to Vancouver no one would buy his painting or sculpture. Then some people became interested in our country, and his work now became very popular. But I have not seen it in five years because in Vancouver we split apart, we had a – type of disagreement.'

'A falling out,' Stephen supplied, emptying the bottle into Ravuth's glass.

'Over a beautiful woman no doubt,' Rick said.

For a moment Ravuth was confused. He did not like to talk about the incident and was surprised he had let himself mention it. The wine was making him say, and feel, too much. 'Well – yes. My mother *was* beautiful, but on the boats she became very sick, and in Vancouver she died. My brother was not helping to take care of her when she was sick. We had very little money. My brother would not take another job ... '

'Well you have to expect that sort of thing from artists,' Rick said. 'Where did you say you're from again? Thailand?'

'We *are* very sorry about your news, Ravuth – your mother. That's very sad. If it's any comfort, we do understand how artists can be. At McGill we had a friend named – well, he called himself Speed. Not to mention "friend". Forever sponging drinks and borrowing money and never giving it back, yes Richard? Not that – '

'Must've thought you were loaded,' Rick snapped. 'Where the fuck's that waiter?'

'He was intended to come tonight?' Ravuth asked.

'*He* was the rich one,' Stephen was chiding Rick. 'Had he not been, I would have had no.... It's the *posturing* that I ... '

'A falling out,' Rick told Ravuth. 'You know how it goes.'

The waiter rushed up with steaming plates and Stephen's face cleared with boyish abruptness. Rick, eyeing the waiter, pointed at the empty bottle. Stephen had gotten for himself and Ravuth a kind of pilaf much like one of the dishes the

Place Paris served. Ravuth had tried it before. When he worked, to save money, he ate anything good the customers left on their plates.

Rick had ordered a fish of some kind. It seemed scruffy and dried out, dwarfed by the mounds of wild rice and broccoli around it. For what seemed a long time Rick stared down at the plate as if hypnotized by the gelatinous open eye.

'Richard?' Stephen said, leaning toward his friend. He looked over at Ravuth and winked. 'Bit of a difficult time of late. He'll be all right, though. Yes, Richard?'

Once Rick started to eat he seemed to feel better. He stopped belching and drank less wine. Stephen, deeply flushed, pushed away his plate, as if conscientiously refusing to eat more – though there was no more, like Ravuth he had quickly finished the delicious pilaf. Leaning back in his chair he removed his spotless spectacles and polished them with a handkerchief.

'I do miss this city. At college Rick and I used to go out all the time, with friends. You know, Ravuth, in a single week here you can virtually tour the globe – gastronomically speaking, I mean. In my view that's important, too – such wonderful diversity. I think it instills tolerance. *Respect*. One can only hate what one does not know.'

Tongue sluggish with wine, Ravuth started to respond. 'Well – '

'To know her is to hate her,' Rick said.

'Now, Richard, it's going to be all right. Truly.'

'Son of a *bitch*. Quit not pouring me more wine. You're the one can't hold the stuff.'

The French couple were glaring again. Others too. Ravuth checked his watch: seven-thirty.

'Richard, really.'

Ravuth grinned down nervously at his plate. Then Rick laughed and he saw it had all been a joke. Stephen sat back and furtively fumbled with his belt loop, cutting himself more slack – then the waiter was there with the bill and he and Rick tensed like two guerrillas before a raid. They locked eyes for a moment and then pounced, their fingers darting, scuffling for the twitching slip. Stephen prevailed. He raised the bill above the table like a captured flag.

'Fuck, Steve, come on. You're paying for the whole trip, for once let me – '

'It's perfectly all right,' Stephen said. 'There's no shame in it. I've been lucky for a few years, you haven't. After you graduate you can buy *me* a few dinners, and I'll hold you to it too.' He looked over. 'You see, Ravuth, there's no work to be had here these days – just as in Kingston I'm sure – so Richard has had a difficult few years.'

'Richard and wife,' Rick said, scraping at the skeleton on his plate.

'So like his good friend before him he's decided to enter law school. In the fall.'

Rick said nothing. He was watching his own hand form a fist in front of his eyes as if he would punch himself, then he relaxed the fingers and with the other hand plucked off his wedding ring and jammed it into the mouth of the fish. Then pinched the mouth closed. A cusp of silver still gleamed from inside, like a broken hook.

There was a silence.

'Hey hey,' Rick finally said, emptying the wine bottle into their glasses, 'another dead soldier. I got a feeling casualties are going to be heavy tonight.'

'Gastronomical,' Stephen quipped, trying to laugh but coughing instead. 'But then we *have* to celebrate, our Richard here is making a new start.'

'She is. Not me. Drink up, Ra-*voot*.'

'I suppose we really should be on our way,' Stephen said.

'Your friends?' Ravuth said.

'Fuck them,' Rick snapped. 'Some friends. She's got custody of them all.'

Stephen rose wearily and signalled the waiter with a mournful smile. Then reached down and eased the ring from the fish's mouth with a calm, accustomed look.

'Not to worry, Ravuth – bottoms up and we'll give you a lift.'

'Do you know this address?' Ravuth asked from the back seat, tendering a slip of paper to Rick. Stephen was driving. It was a new car, smooth and powerful, its leather upholstery smelling cool and sumptuous like the deep armchairs Ravuth dusted in the Place Paris bar.

'Yeah. But it's a ways from here. What do you say we make another pitstop along the way, Steve.'

In the rearview mirror Stephen's pale eyebrows puckered. Then his hand swept a handkerchief over his forehead. Back of the small spectacles his pink eyes kept blinking, as if he could hardly focus on the road.

'I wonder, Richard – perhaps you need a bit of a break? I'm afraid I've overindulged a bit myself, probably shouldn't be driving. Why don't we drop off Ravuth then go have a Scotch up at my uncle's – '

'*Fuck* man would you just watch the – just pull the fuck over, all right? You're driving like an asshole.'

'Richard *please* don't touch the wheel.'

'Yeah, don't want to write off the old man's car, eh. Look, just pull over. Now, okay? I need a drink. Fuck, Steve, I hurt all over, you understand? Arse to elbow, pain. Just pull the fuck over, we'll have a quick one at the Roma.'

Ravuth saw Stephen's eyes glance at him in the mirror. It was almost eight and Ravuth was more than a little drunk already. On the rare occasions when he had had more than the one beer Mr Lennon would give him after his night shift, he had noticed how strongly it affected him. It always had. He liked the feeling but now he knew how important it was that he get to the gallery for the opening of the show. It would be good to see his brother again – good to begin the forgetting. As for Stephen and Rick, well, his people had a saying: the strongest drink cannot bind men the way common blood binds them. He was afraid of offending Stephen – Rick – but in his mind he kept reading Dara's words: *Kyom saum taus, I am sorry. Let's forget what happened, we are family, when all is said. I have friends here in Montreal and they would like to meet you. How few people must speak Khmer in your tiny city! Please come to see what I've been doing since Vancouver....*

The car screeched, fishtailed to a stop at a red light.

'I'm sorry,' Ravuth started, 'but – '

'*I'm* sorry,' Stephen said breathlessly. 'Is everyone ...?'

Rick, who had already thrown open his door and leapt out, turned and craned his head back into the car. 'You two just sit here all night and practise your etiquette, I'm going into the Roma for a beer.' He slammed the door and weaved away among the stopped cars.

'I'm afraid we'll have to join him, Ravuth,' Stephen sighed, flicking on his signal. 'Can't leave him alone now.'

The turn signal ticked on the dash. The light changed.

'Just a few minutes,' Stephen said.

When they found Rick he had nine drinks on the table in front of him: three bourbons, three Scotches, three beers, with an empty glass beside Stephen's beer. A set for each of them, Rick explained. Drink up. Ravuth thought he heard Stephen sigh but it was too dim in the bar to read his expression. They sat down.

'What's up, Ravi.' Rick downed his bourbon. 'Dishwasher's wrist or something?'

'My watch,' Ravuth mumbled. 'I am sorry, I was checking the time.'

'Yeah, I noticed. Come on, kill her. *La nuit est jeune.*'

Ravuth drank his bourbon in a gulp, as did Stephen.

'On to the next,' Rick said hoarsely. He opened his mouth wide and threw his head back, a silver filling gleaming from the molars. Then he tilted his shot glass above his head and let the liquor spill straight in.

'Same old Richard,' Stephen chuckled down at his own shot glass and shook his head. 'Really, you know, I shouldn't.... You promise you'll leave after this one?'

Rick said nothing. After a moment Stephen, mumbling to himself, snatched up his Scotch and shot it down.

'You too, Ra-voot. Kill her. That's the way. Can I bum one of those?'

'Here's-to-law-school,' Stephen blurted, pouring beer into his glass too quickly and lifting it in a toast and watching, red eyes wide, as it foamed over and cascaded onto the table. Rick clacked his bottle against the foaming glass.

'Law!'

'A new start, Rich. And here – to old times. And Ravuth – to old friends regained.'

Ravuth conscientiously raised and gulped his beer, then let Rick light his cigarette after he had tried it himself with no luck. He wondered if Stephen's face and eyes could really be as red as they looked or if he was seeing everything through a fiery fog, the same one churning in his head and his guts. He liked Stephen and always had; the manners of a good guest dictated that he stay and finish his beer. Though there was something else, another reason glimpsed in flickers like a man in camouflage bent double and loping in the distance along a line of trees; lit up by a burst of fire. *Let him wait – let Dara wait.*

A man had appeared back of the bar and Rick was pointing at him as if he were a witness in a stand. 'Yeah, you. Right. I sentence us to another round.'

Instantly, it seemed, more whiskies and beer. Ravuth could not recall finishing his first beer. He read the label on the fresh one: LAURENTIDE. Head weightless, spiralling free, his body levitating as monks in the Cardamom Mountains were said to do for weeks on end. But he had to go soon, no question of that. Almost nine by his watch. One more drink and he would.

He was talking. Of mountains. *Do you remember the mountains.*

'The skiing for sure,' Rick said, draining his Scotch. 'The beach.' He gazed away over Ravuth's shoulder with a softened, ruthful look, as if spying an old flame. 'Beach at Lake Anne. Used to go between shifts, catch some sleep, swim. Introduced me to Gail there, eh Stephen?'

Stephen seemed not to hear. He was hunched low over the table, slowly mopping the spilled beer with his handkerchief. Perhaps he had spilled his whisky too: both shot glasses were empty. He was groaning.

'Oh fuck here we go. Never could hold up your end, eh Steve?'

'Are you feel fine?' Ravuth stuttered, wanting to reach out. Stephen's groans grew soft and clogged, his mopping slowed, his face settled into the soaked handkerchief.

After a few seconds Rick grabbed his friend's thin hair and

tugged him upright. The red face and small spectacles were glazed and shining.

'Looks like I pay for this one, eh. Don't sweat it, Ravi, he'll be fine. Got anything you can throw in the pot?'

'Pardon? Oh, of course, I – '

'Good. Here's our share, go pay the man the rest and come help me get Daddy's boy here into the car.'

As Ravuth lurched back toward the table, trying and failing to calculate how much cash he had left, he saw Rick perched over Stephen who was sprawled in his chair, limbs splayed, double chin bulging out over his collar. He looked like a big dead bullfrog. Rick had grabbed napkins from some other table and was clumsily swabbing his friend's glasses and beer-sopped shirt. In the murky light the wetness was like blood: his father's friend Dr Chhoum crumpled up on the ground against the wall of a schoolhouse in Pursat, head lolling over the pulpy crimson cave in his stout, white-smocked chest. It was the school Ravuth's father had taught at for years. Been led away from, forever. Ravuth, falling, felt a hand on his wrist, steadying him, helping him up: the waiter on one side, Rick on the other. He watched one of the hands and his own wrist as if both belonged to strangers. Thick whitening knuckles freed the wrist. A watch showed. It was almost ten.

Almost ten o'clock.

They were outside the Roma, it was dark now and the chrome and polished hood of Stephen's car gleamed in the street-lights like some factory-new machine. Ravuth kept reaching out to help Rick and the waiter, who were lugging Stephen to the car, but somehow he could not catch up, always weaving a step or two behind. 'I am afraid I am very drunk,' he called out, his accent so thick he wondered if they had understood. But Rick laughed as he and the waiter fed Stephen into the back seat. 'Just like in Banff eh Ravuth? Had us some great times eh?'

'Please, a taxi,' Ravuth told the waiter.

'In the car, Ravi. I'll take you.'

The waiter shrugged and walked away.

'Old times' sake,' Rick snapped. 'Come on. Come *on*.'

Numbly Ravuth nodded and slumped in, puzzled because he

could not remember doing anything like this with Rick and Stephen, no, in Banff as at the Place Paris the waiters had not fraternized with the kitchen help.

Rick slammed the door behind him.

They were hurtling up a steep, sinuous road lined with houses so big they hemmed in the road like a gorge. The gallery must be around here, Ravuth decided, it looks like the right area. There was a mechanical whirring above his head. He raised his hands protectively and cringed, awaiting the shadow of a helicopter, and then it seemed he was back under the roaring Hobart filling the racks with dirty dishes, glasses, cutlery.

He glanced up: a sunroof sliding open. He shuddered, laughed. Some time in the course of the evening he must have mentioned his plan to save for a second-hand car because now Rick was advising him how in summertime you just had to have the sunroof option. *Summertime*, Rick sang hoarsely, *and the living is easy. Livin' is easy, cotton is high.*

Rick would have a good car himself before long. For now Gail had their car. Gail and her pepsi architect. Piece of shit anyway, they'd been broke for two years before she. Always bailing out at the hard part, women. Eh? Hadn't Ravuth said his own wife fucked off on him in Vancouver? For a painter or something? Ravuth gaped up into a framed vista of passing treetops, telephone wires and clustered stars. He fought off a wave of dizziness.

'I know it's getting late Ravi but you really ought to see the place right, before your bus.' Rick looked over at him and Ravuth could only watch as the car cruised blindly for the guard-rail on a sheer corner. At the last moment Rick looked back, braked, leaned hard and steered them round.

'*Fucking bitch*,' he said under his breath. 'Bitch of a road, eh? Eh, Ravuth?' Rick laughed and again the filling gleamed in his mouth. 'See there are two mountains, Ravuth. We'll give you the full tour. Then we'd better get sleeping beauty here back to his uncle's castle – right near the summit. *Le sommet.* Come in for a nightcap then I'll get you to the bus.'

'The gallery!' Ravuth heard himself cry.

'Whatever. Hey – easy does it, eh?'

They pitched squealing round a sharp corner and barely missed another car coming down the mountain. Now Ravuth felt sick. 'It is rude for me,' he managed, 'yet really I must go. Now.'

'Fucking *bitch*,' Rick hissed, smacking the wheel with the heel of his palm. Had he not heard Ravuth? But it was hard to hear a thing with the engine geared so low and the wind gushing in through the sunroof. Ten thirty-five. Overhead the stars were reeling giddily, sniping in and out of their steel frame in those strange constellations he had never grown used to. Dara would be worried now. *Let him worry.* And angry. *Yes.* And hurt.

'It is rude for me, I am sorry, but really – '

The car had stopped. Ravuth was helped out and led to a chest-high cement wall overlooking a galaxy of lights. Through blurred eyes it seemed to him the whole city was burning. He remembered seeing from a hilltop two days' walk from Khlong Yai the campfires of the Khmer Rouge a few hours off to the northeast, and before sunrise their group had risen famished and walked in a single day all the way to the sea.

Rick was pointing out the landmarks of what he kept calling *our city, yeah, used to go there all the time. Meet me at the rooftop bar when she got off. Quit drinking though.* GOOD *for her, eh. Remember her from Banff, Ravi?* But Ravuth could not answer: in the lights crawling over distant bridges he saw the long convoys of tanks and trucks and jeeps and carriers that had followed them out of the northeast and through towns and villages on fire, the fields, the whole countryside burning.

– when for a while you were the fucking light in her eyes.

Ravuth was vomiting over the stone wall. The scalding stream over his tongue seemed endless. Finally the retching slowed and he straightened up and sputtered, 'I am sorry, sorry,' and Rick gripped his trembling arm and pulled him upright.

'You all right Ravi? Yeah. You'll be fine. Good to spew it out, eh.' He laughed. 'Hey, Mount Royal was a volcano once, you know that? Eh? Fuck, just look at you, guess I'll be closing the joint alone again.'

The lights of the city looped and weaved, assuming enigmatic, ominous patterns, seeming to relay warnings in a language Ravuth no longer grasped. His tongue was burning, his temples throbbed. Then a smell he knew cut through the bitter thickness in his nose and throat.

'If it's all the same I just pinched these from your back pocket Ravi. Here. You must be dying for one now. I was.'

Ravuth inhaled gratefully, nodding.

'Come on, we'll get you cleaned up. Won't believe this uncle's place – and he's away. Get Steve happening again and make a night of it.' Ravuth was in the car, the car moving. Rick, reckless again, was humming and mumbling as he drove. Ravuth closed his eyes so as not to see his watch. Tears seared his heavy eyelids and flowed over. He felt the car swerve and brake continually, as if lost and frantic in a labyrinth of backstreets, time ticking down.

They stopped.

'Buckingham Palace, Ravi. Come on, give me a hand with the crown prince.'

As he got out of the car Ravuth noticed he felt a bit stronger and could stand without help. His stomach had settled. The fresh air of the mountain seemed to have cleared his head.

'You have been very kind,' he said. 'Thank you. But now really I will go.'

'Not before we get him inside.'

'Of course. But then – '

'Then get you cleaned up a bit, Ravi, you look right off the boat. Clean up and have a Red Eye. Beer and tomato juice, does wonders for the gut. Here, take his arm.'

Stephen was half-conscious now and made some effort to move. At the front door he fumbled in his pocket, gave Rick the key. They helped him inside. Rick groped for the light-switch and found it: the front hall was broad and spacious, brightly lit, yet Ravuth felt the first stirrings of a claustrophobic panic. They led Stephen past a Persian-carpeted stairway into an elegant den that looked like the bar of the Place Paris. An ornate clock hung on the wall above the fireplace. Still too far to make out the time. But late. *Kyom saum taus* – I am sorry, sorry. Rick helped the moaning Stephen to an armchair then opened a polished mahogany cabinet: in his hands a decanter, three crystal glasses.

The clock chimed harshly, 11:15.

'I must leave,' Ravuth said. 'Now. No. Thank you. No more to drink. Please tell me where is the gallery and I will go myself.'

'Ravi, take it *easy*, all right?' Rick poured out three glasses. 'Cousin's show must be over now anyway. And it's too far, you'd never make it now. Sit down have a drink and talk to me. Swear to God, Ravi, that's the problem with the world these days, such a big fucking hurry no one ever wants to talk. Or *listen*. Got to pay for it like she did. But they just pretend to care. That your problem too Ravi? You a bad listener?'

'No. I am sorry, no, I – '

Rick's look stopped him. Stephen raised his head and opened his eyes, then belched and slumped again, drooling. Ravuth looked away as a reek of vomit filled the room.

'Hey, Ravi? Ra-*voot*! Look at me. Yeah – now let me make myself clear, okay? We've stood you dinner and wine, then drinks, showed you around town, we've given you the tour, Ravi, the *full fucking tour* – we're trying to be decent hosts Ravi, just loosen up and enjoy yourself, okay? You with me?' Suddenly the gaunt face softened pathetically. 'I'm just not into it, Ravuth. Sitting up all night, Steve here dribbling puke. Man, it's babysitting. Fuck. *Fucking* baby, Mr Chancre, she's got one in the oven, you with me? Everything's *dead*. It's like a fucking wake! Up all night with the body!'

He seized his drink and shot it down.

'There. Just what the doctor, eh. She listened to him too.'

He filled two glasses and lurched toward Ravuth.

'Can't have a round for one, can you?'

'Bus goes at twelve,' Ravuth mumbled, backing out of the room.

'*Fuck* the bus, man, I'll drive you in the morning. Old times' sake, Ravi, you worked with her too didn't you? That summer?'

'I can't, I'm sorry.'

'No – no you wouldn't remember, would you, Ravi. Because you're just like all the rest. Aren't you. You don't look, you don't *listen.*'

'Sorry,' Ravuth whispered – 'goodbye!' And he turned and rushed up the hall and seized at the doorknob. But it would not turn. He felt paralysed as in the recurring dream where the moving lights of the Khmer Rouge columns advanced up a dark valley toward the hill where he stood alone, deserted by his mother and Dara, trembling and helpless to cry out or flee. He struggled to escape. The knob turned with a crack and the door swung in and he stumbled backward, crashing into something – someone – a sound of glass breaking below.

He spun round: Rick leering meanly, the carpet at his feet stained and glinting with shattered crystal. Ravuth turned and pushed through the door but Rick grabbed him from behind.

'Asshole,' Rick breathed in his ear. 'Ungrateful little. Fuck, look what you've done.'

Ravuth twisted round and lashed out, his open hand mashing back Rick's nose, blood spraying over the leather jacket – but the bigger man wrestled him close and forced him back inside, hugging him, grunting as he dragged him away from the door toward the staircase. Ravuth's head was shoved between two balusters. Fists sunk into his belly, thumped his chest. There was little pain. He did not feel himself fall, yet now he lay on the carpet under a crossfire of voices.

Paki. Fucking gook.

Richard! Richard, what have you done!

Get up man. Quit pretending you're hurt.

Ravuth – are you all right? Ravuth!

Fuck, can't you see he hit me! Go back to your nap while I clean up the hundred-buck glasses he just wrote off.

Ravuth? Richard – stop!

Get the fuck up, man, you're not hurt. GET UP!

Arms lifting him through a door. The voices arguing all around him now, as if floating in the air. *Fuck, get your hands off me Steve. Just leave me put out the trash here.* He smelled a garden, flowers a few inches from his face. Then a trace of vomit as a hand softly gripped his arm, pulled him upright. 'Ravuth?' *Just leave it, man!* 'No!' *Leave him!* 'Ravuth?' He broke Stephen's weak grasp and ran blindly.

Ravuth! Ravuth, come back!

Ravuth ...!

He was running down the mountain. Hobbling, often falling. He bled from his right hand and from his forehead. His watch was gone. He had left the street and cut through a lampless park, down a steep path undulating between hedges, trees, the blood drying on his hands and in his hair, down his neck.

He came out of the woods onto a busy street. Several cabs whipped past him. Then one pulled up.

'*Merde, mon ami, qu'est-ce que tu as?* Eh? What happen to you?'

Ravuth gave the driver the address of the gallery and told him he had to be there by 11:30. The man shrugged – it was almost midnight now. 'Anyway,' he said, 'you couldn't afford. It's in Repentigny, from here half an hour.'

Ravuth swore under his breath, bitterly. He asked what it cost to the bus station. The man said he would take him to the hospital for free. 'No,' Ravuth said, 'the bus. Please. The bus station by twelve. I will lose my job.'

'Do what I can,' the driver said, accelerating, pitching them into late Saturday night traffic and charging through cross-streets as the stoplights turned amber, red, and the horns of other cars shrieked and faded out behind them. Ravuth gazed up at the buildings along the streets. Sallow light seeped from a few windows above all-night groceries, cafés, boutiques and restaurants but most of the windows were dark. Then he saw a shadow behind blinds – a small man, it seemed, in motion-less, mournful silhouette. He wanted to mistake it for his brother. The light went off and the man vanished.

'Here is the bus station now,' the driver cried, caught up in the excitement of the task. 'You see, just past the lights.' But Ravuth told him to stop.

'Now,' he cried, 'here!' The man jammed on the brakes. He spun round in his seat and Ravuth, half out of the cab, mum-bled thanks and tossed over his last few bills. He weaved between fenders of parked cars to a phone booth. For a few sec-onds the cab stayed put with a lane of traffic honking behind

it, the driver hunched over the wheel and peering out at the
booth – then the back door was yanked shut and the cab
screeched away.

A couple of quarters. Ravuth put one in the slot but it
rattled through the machine and came out. He tried again and
got a dial tone. Fumbling in his pocket he found the paper slip
with Dara's number: his fingers had stained it with blood but
it was legible. He dialled the number and heard it ring like
some faint, far-off alarm. After twenty rings he gave up.

He was running up the sidewalk, weaving, stumbling like a
drunk, alarming the few passersby until he crossed against a
light and the pain cut fierce and deep under his ribs as he
climbed the fence around the bus station lot.

The driver had just pulled shut the door when he reached
the bus. It had to be the right one, he would lose his job. He
tried to yell but his voice was drowned out by the jet-like
rumble of the engine and he slapped open-palmed on the
ridged steel of the door till it was stained pink with the
shadow of his hands.

The door swung open and he clambered aboard. A tired
driver in a captain's hat stared at him and said nothing.

As the bus yawed and shuddered from the station Ravuth
slumped into a pair of seats near the back. The few other passengers were already sprawled unconscious, mouths gaping, as
in that bus that once rolled down out of the Cardamom Mountains into the heart of Pursat, its driver barely alive, the passengers all folded dead and bloody in their seats after a guerrilla raid. His brother had been there when the bus, like the
ghost of a bus, had glided to a halt, and he had told the whole
family how he had rushed aboard with other bystanders to
help the driver out into the street and to rescue any survivors.
There were no survivors. Ravuth got up and went into the toilet and locked the door. Sitting on the closed lid he let his head
sag forward to rest against the metal wall and the dull, dis-
torted image of his face. The whole trip he would stay that
way, aboard but invisible, a ghost passenger, and tomorrow
when he called Dara – for he would call him, *kom prakan
kyom*, forgive me, *you must, all is paid back between us, the
slate clean* – the first anxious, breathless rasping of his voice

would sound like a dying man's last words: the dead calling long-distance from Vancouver or Pursat, the distances growing longer by the hour, and the year and the faces melting into the mind's mass-grave, but somehow it seems there is time, still time, and two survivors, and tomorrow, before work, you will call.

Everything White is Closed

A Christmas sermon, Chiang Mai

A GREYING, SUNBURNT American missionary stopped us in the fruit market and invited us for a drink. He drove us across the bridge to a slick Hawaiian-style tavern whose patio jutted far out over the brown drowsy current of the river. Everywhere there were Christmas decorations – winking lights, stuffed stockings, dangling sprigs of mock mistletoe – and the patio was filled with merry expatriates: tourists and others, our host confided, affiliated with either the church or the drug trade.

The missionary was from Connecticut. His voice was soft and shaky and a bit too fast, fuelled, it seemed, by expatriate loneliness. His pinched face had the unwholesome, mottled redness of an old apple core. Explaining that he did not drink, he ordered a round of lemonades and began to tell us about his struggles in the primitive regions to the north. Some progress was being made, he reassured us, but it was impossible to cite precise figures – the natives were so courteous they often feigned conversion simply to avoid disappointing the missionary, whose visits they seemed to enjoy. He liked the visits too, he said, despite his ultimate lack of success – if 'success' was the right word! And after all it was quite the same for all the others. Recidivism, he said. Like … falling off the wagon. *Any* church quoting precise figures for its sphere of influence was not being altogether honest. Not really. (The province, he explained, had been split up and allotted like a pie.)

The work did not get easier. The Buddhists were a frustrating opposition. But it was *tolerance*, not antagonism, that made them so formidable. Because, you see – he looked down into the slow current, eyes wistful, troubled – because like mystics or secular humanists they sincerely believe that different religions follow various paths to the same goal. A humane doctrine, of course, but. Well.

The missionary cleared his throat.

The worst of it was, he confessed, he *liked* them.

He sighed and excused himself and walked with brittle stiffness toward the washroom, brushing past an elf on his way and then a very thin, sweat-stained Santa Claus who had just shuffled out of the kitchen. *Very* thin. Face shadowed in the baggy, sagging hood, a huge plastic candy-cane sickled over his shoulder, he looked like the Grim Reaper in holiday disguise.

The festive elf turned out to be a waitress. She placed three pink lemonades on the table and wished us a Muddy Christmas. We sat awhile watching the condensation form and flow down our glasses, but the missionary did not come back. Finally a blond, balding man in mirrored Vuarnets, his sportshirt unbuttoned to the paunch, swayed up and took a seat. The extra drink, I thought.

He was Canadian. He'd been in Thailand a couple of years. He worked for buddies in Vancouver and Frisco and though he wasn't at liberty to give us the full lowdown he didn't mind letting us know it was exciting, even dangerous.

Before we could say anything he seized our host's lemonade and took a reckless gulp. Then scowled at the glass. 'Hey, you're not missionaries are you?'

We told him no. We both looked over at the men's room: the Grim Reaper was rapping on the door with his giant candy-cane, calling out something in polite, high-pitched Thai, then pushing open the door and vanishing inside.

'Place is crawling with them,' the man said. 'And this stuff you're drinking … '

'Lemonade,' I said. 'I take it you're interested in harder stuff.'

For a second he eyed us, then leaned over the table. At close range I saw the fretwork of wrinkles radiating from the edge of his Vuarnets. A gold cross, hidden till then in a jungle of rust-coloured chest hair, swung forward and dangled over his drink.

'You two seem pretty bright,' he said. 'But if you're thinking of getting into the trade I'd advise you to be careful. I'm through with it myself. I'm ready to settle down. I'll be looking for a Thai wife' – he gazed out at the river and pursed his lips – 'no offence meant to you Miss, but Thai women, well, they know how a man likes to be treated.'

In his mirrored lenses I saw my wife frown down at her glass.

'Sure, I can tell what you're thinking but the fact of it is I'll take good care of her too. I've saved up enough to go into business here in Chiang Mai. Carpets, probably, or lacquer work. You can take my word as coin, there's good money to be made. Can't see it in the streets, I know, but it's there.' I looked away, over at the men's room, then out at the river where a duck was bobbing downstream with her chicks in tow. Behind her, two jaws like a pair of huge rusted scissors broke surface, silently snapped closed, eased back out of view. Not a ripple left on the water. Unaware that one of her chicks was gone, the mother bobbed downstream out of sight.

My wife left the table for the women's. The man grinned and shrugged and leaned even closer, as if to smuggle me some rare, unobtainable stash of wisdom. When he whispered I could smell his breath, ingratiating and sweet like a whiff of lemon candy.

'A poor man will work for anything,' he said. 'I see she can't handle the hard goods, maybe you can. Eh? Well, there she be. The bottom line. Welcome to the world, chief. Got to live in her like she is.' He sat back and jerked up his glass as if in a toast, then leered, shook his head violently and sprayed the bitter liquid out over the railing into the river. I stood up and backed from the table as the pink pulp spattered and spread over the water and floated off.

'Hey not so fast, man. Take it easy eh? Where you off to? Sit down, it's Christmas, I'm buying. *Hey!*'

I paused by the washrooms, rapped hard on the door of the women's. The door of the men's opened instead. The Grim Reaper stood there appraising me, black eyes bright inside his baggy hood. Then in a soft high exasperated voice: 'Could you please now give me assistance! It's the Father again. It's better once he stopped the gin, but he locks himself in the toilet still. Stays there.' From behind him a stream of muffled words like the rambling regrets of a man in a confessional. And from the patio behind me the dealer's voice, bitter now, lonely: *Where else you figure on going today, chief? Nowhere else, it's Christmas. Everything white is closed.*

End of the Festival

A brief supplement to the Berlitz guide

THERE HAD BEEN ANOTHER power failure and though it was not yet dusk, torches had been lit and set up all along the narrow streets. Far too narrow, the visitor thought as a small car swerved past with horn screaming. He clenched his hands but kept his mouth shut. These streets, his guidebook told him, had not been made for cars.

As if to punctuate his thought the small car, festooned with orange petals and smeared with thick red streaks like some exotically marked animal, screeched to a halt a few steps ahead before a crowd of pedestrians and livestock. Its horn blared wildly but the dense knot of drovers and animals, children and their vividly costumed parents ignored or did not notice it over the noise they themselves were making: somewhere in the crowd drums were being beaten, cymbals rattled, and a high-pitched ecstatic chanting repercussed between the wood buildings. From upper windows a shower of orange petals poured down.

The visitor sensed some kind of disturbance ahead. Heard shouting, screams, and a bull, lean and black, broke snorting from the crowd in front of the car. For a second it was airborne trying to leap clear and then its hoofs clopped sharply on the car's hood and smacked and shattered the windshield, the bull's body sliding over the roof and then off, legs scrabbling, into the dust. The car horn kept bleating, frantic. The bull struggled and tried to stand but it was too late, young men were surrounding it and two tall bearded men in bloodstained smocks loomed out of the crowd. One held a long butcher's knife and the other an axe.

The visitor rushed forward to watch but the crowd had shifted, swarming around him, separating him from the fallen bull. He saw the axe-blade catch and reflect the pale torchlight as it swung over and down into the crowd. The horn of the small car continued to scream as if malfunctioning, then for a moment the bull's furious roaring rose and swallowed it.

Soon both sounds stammered and died out.

The people around him took up a chant with a strange, accelerating tempo and when enough of them had moved along he was able to see the fallen bull butchered. The actions of the bearded men were quick and skilful. The windows of the small car, now silent and abandoned, were spattered with fresh blood.

On the ninth day of the Dasai Festival everyone in Nepal eats meat. The tourist will see animals slaughtered everywhere, on the steps of small temples, under shrines, in alleys paved festively with orange petals.... Orange seamed with red. The carcasses and severed heads of goats dyed an eerie, mysterious orange. Odour of blood. Blood surging in the gutters, Kathmandu a single body intricately veined, all arteries flowing inward to Durbar Square. The body's core, the city's heart, the guidebook used terms like that. *The cultural and spiritual hub of the country. On the ninth and last day of the Dasai Festival everyone in Nepal eats meat.*

He had read that the main ceremonial slaughter would occur in Durbar Square just after dark and he was hurrying – trying to hurry – along the main streets that led into it. Half the city was doing the same. The streets were clotted with pedestrians and skittish bawling livestock that seemed to sense in the air something menacing, inevitable. He saw the snouts of cattle lifted above the crowd, sniffing the breeze, their eyes rolling back so that the whites gleamed. Perhaps they knew the scent of keepers about to turn on them.

The streets were too narrow, they had not been made for cars. But the excited locals dodged them with a blithe agility as if the machines were insubstantial, the harmless figments of a far-off culture unconnected to their own. Their indifference and casual immunity to accident, like *their utter absorption in the ambient culture* (the guidebook again), struck him at every turn and reminded him of his strangeness. His own reactions to the traffic were automatic. As a horn blurted close by he felt himself springing sideways into a shop wall, bruising his shoulder and soaking his shoes in a puddle of warm blood;

driven along by the crowd to an intersection whose traffic light had failed with the city's power, he found himself slowing, stopping by instinct – awaiting a signal like a conditioned dog.

To the Nepalis the traffic lights meant little or nothing. Orange was the colour of Dasai, it was an invitation to unrestraint, not a symbol of caution. According to his guidebook the government's efforts to modernize the country kept running up against this stubborn, immovable, perfectly good-natured passivity. Tomorrow, the guidebook guaranteed, things would be done as they always had.

Swept into the intersection by the crowd he caught from off toward Durbar Square the sounds of massed drumming and chanting. People flowed over and around a traffic island on which a single policeman, politely ignored, looked on, smiling, and with a bow accepted from an old woman a necklace or orange flowers.

The crowd was becoming too dense, the speeding traffic dangerous, so the visitor turned down an alley and tried to follow a tortuous series of back streets. Their pattern obeyed no logic he understood. His maps could not help him. The streets were not squarely laid out but diverging, veering, doubling back and stopping dead and three times he had to turn back and retrace his way. But he was not lost – the drumming and chanting from Durbar Square were guiding him on and in several streets he overtook mobs of revellers blaring trumpets, tin horns, whistles, flutes.

He squeezed past them, hurrying.

It was almost dark.

He came onto a street wide enough for cars and just avoided a taxi that roared out of nowhere. For a second his gut fisted with shock, fear, anger, but they were soon swallowed by a fresh excitement, the air now bated, charged with a natural current, a wireless power that sparked all his senses. Sounds from the square grew louder: cymbals and massed sitars played at a quickening rhythm and beneath them like a ground-bass ran the rumble of a gathered crowd. The night (dusk was drawing brightness from torches all along the street) added its own impetus. Its chill was reviving, its darkness promised anonymity. This is why he had come. Why he had chosen to walk and not take a taxi as the guidebook urged: to feel the spirit of another culture first-hand, to lose himself, to be infected and absorbed. To feel the drumbeats beating inside him.

Almost running he reached a line of orange-streaked cars, parked or abandoned, under the awning of a book shop. The doors facing the street lolled open and blood leaked like oil from the base of the doors and the chassis into a running gutter. In the front and back seats of the cars slaughtered goats had been laid.

Laughing, three young men squatted on the fenders of the nearest car, eating meat from skewers and sharing a half-empty jug of clear liquor. They eyed him. One of them called out a kind of explanation in polite, slurred English and he smiled and assured them he understood, he'd read about this, the festival was old but featured a remarkable new rite: animals slaughtered and placed in vehicles as an offering to ensure road saftey.

How quickly things become custom here, he thought, unsure if the words were his own or an echo of something he'd recently read – in the guidebook, perhaps, or some brochure. *The Nepalis accept nothing from the West without making it their own. Initiating, assimilating everything into the old system. Fixed in their ways and indifferent to ours. Passionately apathetic.*

In the full ecstasy of the festival he found himself admiring both their indifference and devotion, for suddenly it was clear to him how this frantic annuality forged a sense of connection and membership his own world no longer afforded – and could not disrupt or break into here. Even in his enthusiasm he saw he was excluded – a car loudly demanding passage of oblivious pedestrians. But these were not cars.

He rushed on. The sitars were somewhere close ahead, their sound skirling and imperative. A confused bellowing of animals and from a window high above him a rain of petals, blood-red. For a moment he thought they were the festival-flowers made scarlet by the torchlight but catching bits in his hand and pulling others from his hair he made out their colour, felt their stickiness and knew their smell. Blood. Shreds of blood-soaked tissue surely used in preparing the night's meal. *On the ninth day of the Dasai Festival.*

A child stood in the street blocking his way. She was thin and dirty but so beautiful that for a moment the constant chatter in his brain, the ticking of names, those echoes of the guidebook, stopped. Her huge eyes peered up at him. He smiled at her, riffled her hair. She was very thin. She watched him. She smiled at last and warmth flooded into his chest and he wanted to lead her from the busy street, protect her. Be careful, he told her, please, thinking *traffic, crowds* – and with the words his sense of purpose rushed back. Now he wondered if she were begging. There were so many beggars here. He dug in his pocket for a bill but she scampered off and made way for him as if sensing his fresh impatience; he shot her a smile, waved briefly, slid back into the surge.

Seconds later when he glanced back the beautiful child was gone, swallowed by the crowds that were thickening as they neared Durbar Square. Above the nodding, jostling heads to his left a line of carcasses dangled from the high windows of a butcher shop – goats, he thought, or sheep. On either side of them torches guttered and flared and the flesh gleamed and twisted in the breeze as on a spit. He seemed to hear in the crowd's roaring the sound of his own breath. A sense of intoxication was brewing inside him, that feeling of consummate egoless licence he had heard and read of and sometimes even feigned but never really seen or experienced.

He was gripped from behind. He spun round and a young Nepali man draped an orange petal-necklace over his head. He could see and feel how some of the petals had ripped free and clung to his hair and beard. Another stranger shoved in smiling and offered him a drink and as he took the bottle the man vanished into the crowd.

He drank. The clear liquor scorched his throat and made his head spin. *Rakshi*, a word from the guidebook now alive, on fire, inside him. Other words crowded into his brain, vital terms in Nepali, the names of Hindu deities, the repeated word *Dasai*. His eyes clouded. He could not think clearly. He felt himself swept up and on by the growing movement, he gave in to its swell. A wave passed through the crowd and as strangers crammed up against him he clutched the *rakshi* and the guidebook was torn from his other hand. From nearby the sitars screeched in a weird staccato like a car trying to start. The drumming had grown more frenzied, its bass beat thundered in his belly and chest as if his heart, surging with adrenalin, were about to break down. But the crowds reassured him. He was nearing the city core he'd seen only on working days when it was half-empty, profaned by lunching clerks and loud lumbering tourists and tourguides and cops and post-card hawkers. Now everybody in the city would be there. One body. Here. He could smell the blood. He brushed a falling petal from his eye.

This is why he had to come.

To be pierced by the spirit of the festival, and swallowed, to lose himself, to merge, to feel the drumbeats beating inside him. *On the ninth day of the Dasai Festival everybody in Nepal.* He rounded a corner into a broad street and Durbar Square leapt into view, a carnival of bonfires and faces swaying, saris and banners and upraised hands gleaming in the rusty torchlight. For a moment on the upper tier of the middle temple he saw a grey bull kneel under a hovering blade, and he stopped; he did not see the cab till its shape filled the corner of his eye, a flash of careering orange, and struck him.

Downing's Fast

Love of knowledge is a hunger for life.
Daily bread is no answer.

– Ralph Downing, from *The Early Essays*

Somewhere out beyond
                    all ideas
        of right doing
                    & wrong doing
    there is a field —

                    I'll meet you there

YEARS AFTER FIRST reading these lines of a long-dead Anatolian poet – reading them through tear-startled eyes – Ralph Downing started out toward the office for the last time. He was now what he had once referred to as *another fairly routine man, noosed in necktie and four-piece grey-flannel straitjacket, his schedule a five-day forty-hour malaise beginning each morning at nine sharp.* Though those mornings could hardly be called beginnings. They were points on the wheel. For years Ralph Downing's activities had clocked an almost unbroken circle, though he did enjoy a brief respite each Christmas (which he usually spent at home) and a month-long summer holiday (when he liked to vacation in the Thousand Islands).

His month-long summer holiday was due to increase by a week in another year, and by another week five years after that.

The office that wolfed down such a large proportion of the

pie-graph of Ralph Downing's life was the Canadian adminis-
trative branch of a large international firm. This firm special-
ized in the manufacture of ovens, toasters, food processors,
blenders, crockpots, garberators, battery-powered rolling-pins,
dinner-roll warming-bins, microwaves and countless other
domestic indispensables, *all ideal for the working woman.*
(Downing was responsible for promoting its newest devices
throughout Canada.)

Although divorced, Downing was a decent family man; his
ex-wife lived in a distant city with their daughters but he vis-
ited whenever he could, taking the girls for occasional weekends and nearly a week every Christmas. He would send his
alimony and child support payments punctually and often
enclosed more than officially required – especially around
birthdays and holidays. Although Downing had had a few
insignificant flings since the divorce (and, to be honest, before
it) his relationship with his ex-wife remained amicable, and
over an after-office pint or two he could boast to colleagues
(most of whom were also divorced) that Penelope was one of
his 'very closest friends.' The boys'd drink to that. But Downing would shake his balding head and slap assorted sharkskin
shoulders with affable finality if another round were proposed,
for since those first, subversive stabs of angina and his doctor's
warnings, he had become more moderate, cautious.

Not much of a story to begin with. Common enough
though, even universal in some ways. Lay away the pin-
striped suit (Downing's suit was actually herringbone, cut
tastefully in a subdued expensive grey), cancel the polished
shoes and brand-new briefcase webbed delicately and smelling
sumptuous as the interior of a new car – write these off and
suppose a wide-brimmed straw hat, loose linen trousers or
skirts and sunburnt shoulders and you find yourself among
thousands of dark labourers, stooped in a flooded network of
ricefields – cornfields, milletfields, canefields – you find red-
jawed fishermen in ice-rimed slickers, forearms ridged and
thick as hawsers heaving in nets full of slithering fish. Their
hours vary (and their powers, man, their powers) but they
work a set circumference of time, a set locus of soil or saltwa-
ter, and there is no escaping the gleaming nets and the steel-

silver millions thriving onto the deck and dying, or the table in a hut by the paddies where a candle lights a simple meal of rice, some fish with spices, the bed where you'll lapse exhausted for eight brief hours till hushed voices wake you to a simple meal of rice, some fish with spices, and the path *somewhere out beyond* back into a network of steaming paddies....

Always the need for a full plate, though it has never been enough. Always the need for a bamboo mat or a hammock and something to summon you out of it at dawn. In the mountains of Anatolia they tell the story of a farmer who one morning refused to get out of bed: the farmer, in need of a respite from the immemorial routine, announced that he was tired and could no longer work; he expected to be waited upon till he was ready to return to the fields, and his family, fearing he was gravely ill, were methodically compliant. They brought him nourishing meals of goat and fresh river-trout and barley-bread, they offered up great tumblers of wine, lager and *raki*. And yet, oddly, he began to lose weight. The anxious wife insisted he eat an extra meal daily and the puzzled farmer, who actually felt fine and could not understand the weight loss, readily agreed. Soon he was eating more than his wife and husky sons together and still he went on dwindling. He ate a whole roast spitted lamb crammed with garlic and peppered figs, yet almost overnight his arms grew thin and brittle as the walking stick he was now forced to use on the rare occasions when he did rise. He wolfed down numberless loaves of barley-bread and pillar-like stacks of pita: his ribs bulged out through his skin like steel hoops on a rotten cask. And his usually ascetic sexual appetites had grown abruptly omnivorous; his wife, toiling to satisfy his needs, began to look as dazed and gnawed-down as did he. Finally, in the midst of a vast casserole which the whole family had helped prepare and was now watching him dispatch, the sprig-thin farmer sagged back into his pillows, raised one thin arm, belched operatically, and expired.

Unhappily the Anatolian peasants who handed down this remarkable fable append no moral for our edification. Even Professor Sarah Dawkins, from whom Downing first heard it during his undergraduate years, refused to draw any drift-net conclusions. Modern medical science could no doubt offer a resonant term, a sturdy diagnosis of the farmer's disorder, but surely it is more tempting to see it as somehow metaphorical. Is the tale chiefly didactic, a piece of feudal propaganda designed to keep the peasants in the fields? Or perhaps the Sunday offering of a priest cautioning his horny flock against sensual excess? For a part of us is always asking would there ever be enough. The forty-hour work week (or fifty, or sixty) effectively insulates the self from the senses – from the real life we're too ground down to lead. Or too afraid. Or, for a man like Ralph, too numbed:

Monday saves us. Tuesday is an excuse. Wednesday is the week's fulcrum, tottering with chores. Saturday and Sunday are carrots that reward us and carbo-load us for the coming week, and the morning after, another Monday, is unpleasant but at least not very real. And if one Monday you refused to get up and were promised all you could eat....

But Downing would not have done anything like that – at any rate not after his chaotic, often unhappy days as a student. And he never did get around to asking his doctor-friend Hans what kind of disease could have prompted such outlandish symptoms. Over their after-office pint Hans would have drawn on his pipe and speculated. He should certainly have come up with something.

2.

BETTER HOMES AND GARDENS' 'NEWFANGLED' QUICK-BREAD

    3 cups white flour
    1 cup 'one-minute' oats
    1 tbsp. baking soda
    1 cup 'fresh' milk (or use powdered milk) soured with
        vinegar (or use buttermilk)
    2 eggs (or use instant egg powder)
    Half-cup white sugar (or use saccharine, aspartame,
        honey, or other substitute)

In a large bowl mix the flour, oats and sugar together, then add the soda. In another bowl combine the soured milk and egg. Mix all the ingredients and fold together till you have a thick paste. Briefly knead paste on a bread-board (or use DoughMaster EasyKnead Electric Kneader) and place in the microwave for 90 seconds.

Eat immediately.

3.

'But even the seasons are temporary: the cycles we consider most permanent are, like those we invent for ourselves, subject to change ... ' (At this point I looked up and saw that only Ralph Downing was listening to me, taking notes. *Somewhere*, I thought, *out beyond all ideas ...*) 'During the last ice age, then, the summer our distant ancestors conceived, in their inarticulate way, as predestined and perennial finally failed one year to arrive. Ugh, they must have said, scratching themselves and shivering, It's too damned cold. As they fled south to Florida or died. And in three or four billion years (there is some disagreement in the scientific community about the date) the solar and terrestrial cycles we now consider eternal will break down forever, and everything will die.

'Now class, if we accept this unsettling forecast surely it grows harder to take comfort in the synthetic regularity of work, the cooked-up punctuation of mealtimes, the punctual flipping over of calendar leaves decorated with scenes of Lake Huron sunsets or the wavering amber grainfields of China; harder to find strength for the annual famines of Lent and Av and Ramadan and other religious ordeals; harder to place faith in the transient order and precision of language, which – take this down please – "*in the hands of a master of exposition is an intricate, prodigiously specific instrument of communication, and in the mouth of a major poet a conduit to the unconscious & the seething, insurgent (sic) imagination.*"

Downing's handwriting was abysmal and even now this editor finds it difficult to decipher and transcribe. (This editor has been reading Downing's scattered, eccentric essays on and off for years. His death frees her to publish them.)

And this:

One Monday morning at 8:30 on the dot, Ralph Downing started out toward the office for the last time. He walked, trying to remember to swing his arms (fitting exercise into his morning routine, in hopes that by feigning the climb-every-mountain keenness of students and cheerful, dynamic sit-com career-women he would shake awake the Rip Van Winkling youngster in himself). Instead he aroused the memory of a teacher he'd had back in college. Professor Sarah Dawkins had taught philosophy (as well as editing collections of essays) and hers was the only humanities course Downing had ever much attended. Dawkins had given the erratic Downing an A+ for his unorthodox work, and one time she said to him in her characteristically forthright way, 'Ralph, I like you. You have a clear and simple way of looking at the world. A world that smirks and snickers while you persist in smiling, laughing. Stay simple, Ralph. Stay out of fashion, stay in love. Keep writing. Some day write a book about your way of looking at the world.'

This was years ago, of course, and I can't be sure I've remembered the exact words. But that hardly matters. A good scholar seldom says exactly what is in her mind – her heart. And perhaps, after all, in the muffled world we've professed and tutored and booked into being, it *is* necessary to distance oneself from people and events in order to perceive them clearly. Downing would not have made a good scholar. I knew this to be true and yet I did hope he would write his book – though I realized elements of the academic community (what a risible contradiction in terms) would demolish it if it ever were published. Because it would deal in unfashionable earnest with that silent, roaring edge where things come into being and die. Because it would tug fiercely at the tweedy legs of tranced theorists floating off into ethers of abstraction and it would pull them back down to earth, *somewhere out beyond all ideas* – to sweet, spontaneous earth, that perfect edge. Because it would force them to stare down, like Gloucester, into the writhing belly of the world: and see. See or lose sight forever. For aye. *Four eyes!* Because it would have to be written in a new dialect. A kind of poetry, Ralph once said, a kind of concrete incantation, that's the only wake-up call the truth understands. Make it dance. Make it dance all night. And maybe the whole thing could never be written anyway but would have to be acted out.

In the flesh.

Professor Dawkins had a fleeting vision of a philosophical road-show that would star the young Downing and which she would M.C. *Step right up, folks. Step right up.*

Downing entered the park and began to cut across the grass as he always did when the ground was dry. There was a time when he would have felt the grass even through the soles of his shoes. Or so he'd once written. Now smells from an invisibly tended garden reminded him of the 'power-lunch' he was to have at one; a smattering of small round silver flowers vibrant in the breeze put him in mind of a current project involving ballbearings. That battery-powered rolling pin, or was it the DoughMaster Electric Kneader – real time savers-both. Then it struck him that these small silver flowers, whose name he knew he knew but could not quite summon up, would not always have resembled ballbearings. Because he'd been thinking of Sarah Dawkins, he supposed. Sarah.

He left the grass for the sidewalk at the far side of the park and sped up. *There is a field.*

Dawkins. Dear Professor Dawkins. *Shit,* he couldn't write that. SARAH. *In reply to your letter of the fifth I've got to admit that, in the commonly accepted sense of the phrase, I've 'sold out'. My uncle has arranged for me to have a job as {&c &c} and I won't be returning to school to work with you next year. Though you warned me about the 'lulling monotony' and (I think you put it) 'stultifying hardship, stultifying ease' of a regular job and income I'm afraid 'the academy' has come to terrify me even more (not you but the other things, the competitive, coercive things – I know you understand) and so my decision is made. I realize it's fashionable in academic circles (what a contradiction in terms!) to see the 'real world' as the Great Whore or slavering Philistine, but I feel confident that I can continue to live my philosophy in the gullet of the Beast – while raising real cash I can use to make a difference & do good. Maybe this is the best way to prove it can work. After all it's too easy to be a saint in seclusion, a sage in an ivory tower. The only way to prove it, this. Wish me luck.*

I want to thank you for the interest you showed in me and those ideas as no other professor ever did and gave me low marks as I told you before. {I} will visit in future.

ps: it occurs to me this will seem a little cold.
Don't ever think I could forget everything.

Love, R.D.

4.

From *The Early Essays:*

Fast food has become the most important form of 'nutrition' in our society. I guess there are plenty of reasons for it – what disease has a single cause? – but I feel it's mainly because people think artificial food is somehow safer. I sense people these days will do almost anything to avoid absorbing real things.

5.

Caught by the omniscient narrator in an act of glaring hypocrisy, Downing is seen extracting an instant breakfast, then a loaf of quick-bread, from his microwave. The loaf is a failure. He forgets to eat the breakfast. So little time!

6.

The traffic was always heavy at this hour. Downing was forced to wait a few seconds before crossing the busy street west of the park. On the far side he began striding through the buildings of his old campus but this morning, instead of staring at the pavement ten paces ahead, planning his day and the next day and evening and the next and the next, and planning, like so many of us, everything up to and including his funeral details – noosing up each and every loose end, worrying, scurrying, his brain a gerbil on the Wheel of

Worry – he looked up and around at the looming old lime-stone towers. There was the humanities hall. Thick vines of ivy had completed their squid-like, rapacious embrace of the whale-grey east wall, so that now only the windows could be seen.

Fact: Downing had been an excellent promotions manager. Had been praised for his imagination and initiative. Had himself been promoted almost annually for the first six years of his employment after starting as a minor clerk.

Fact: Downing read widely (non-fiction) and borrowed smartly for his promotional campaigns. Though his most remarkable policy as an undergraduate had been to refine his reading to raw essentials (Rumi, Shakespeare, Whitman, Sappho, Dickinson, the various scriptures – most of which his peers had not read) and, instead, weather permitting, to stage genial debates with puzzled companions, to compose dialogues with dead saints, heretics, zealots, helots, poets, profs and prophets, philosophers and other fruitcakes, *all ye who pitch your mansion on the precipice* – and to scribble bad poetry and stumble, laden with wine (what else?), through the local woods. And to spend nights with Sarah Dawkins.

There is a field

Fact: Downing's marriage to another woman, much younger than Sarah Dawkins, had spoiled after fourteen years because 'he had changed.' Conventional explanation. Upheld however by the court. Visiting rights to comprise three visits monthly, none to exceed thirty-six hours in duration.

Fact: When after almost twenty years he had paid his old professor a visit, she'd seemed not to recognize him. 'Poor old Sarah must be going senile.' Conventional explanation. In this case incorrect. Dr. Hans's considered diagnosis was Alzheimer's disease, incipient but certain to progress rapidly. Yes, two more pints here please and a packet of chips.

'Poor Sarah, she must be losing it.' She really hadn't known who he was! At first. Well, old four-eyes Downing wore contacts now. Or was it his grey herringbone suit? At college he'd dressed like a cross between Whitman and a whirling dervish. But no. People expect your attire to change with age. You get accustomed to the necktie. Fifty years on the gallows of habit. Perhaps Doc Dawkins was peering this very instant through the double-paned storm of her glass window on level five of the humanities hall, two dark probing eyes whorled below with indigo, her small head steadily shaking the way certain old folks' heads will do, as if the world has become a daily reminder of how much they've lost and they must constantly deny and gainsay everything they see. *No. No. I must be dreaming.*

No —

But if she were there she would see only Downing's grey herringbone back, borne away in the rushing stream of students roaring through the stone canyons of the co-ed residence *somewhere out beyond* the college art gallery and on toward the lake and their morning classes. It was 8:50. On the pavement by the gallery Downing felt himself glare at his watch (as many of the students were doing) and looking up was surprised to see Sarah Dawkins standing motionless ten feet away.

– Sarah, he said. He managed.

The old woman did not reply. He noticed her eyes were still very clear, acute.

– Sarah. Sarah, you must remember me.

The old woman did not, apparently, as she would not confirm this allegation in words. She did seem to be weeping though.

7.

Divorce granted by the court, 16 August 1985.

'Because you have changed.'

But when?

Impossible to say. Looking back over a lifetime, class, consider the salient patterns the vital episodes and occasions and then admit *not here nor here, norhere; norhere.* Nowhere. We betray ourselves slowly, act by act, at an insidious, anaesthetizing pace. I can remember the feeling of loving my office, its snugness, the smell of the desk, the shelves full of familiar reading, and much later I remember hating it for its smothering air, the stacks of unanswered correspondence, the impudent lopsided leer of books I had not read and would never get round to. But when the last twinges of affection yielded to pangs of dislike I cannot say.

Language, they say, is a labyrinth. A maze where the gerbil runs. Like the library of a great university there are a million aisles and stacks and cracks and niches where the past can be discreetly shelved, a thousand limestone wings and abutments behind which pivotal incidents or the shadow of another self can hide. Are hidden; were hidden; have been would be will be hidden. I was never like that at all, I haven't changed. I haven't lost a thing, the leaves of grass are still there surging under my naked heels and there is time, still time: *I'll meet you there.*

Yes, you will need to know this. But not for the exam.

Love, take this down:

Grammar is the greatest disguise. Though we need it, though it has its own stiff beauty. Trust poets, but only when they're new at the trade or have grown seasoned and reborn.

And yet

8.

Before you, Sarah, I did have one good teacher. Last year. He said one time that whenever good friends ate together it was in 'the church of the holy restaurant'.

Everyone thought that was a laugh.

I laughed too, but from the belly.

9.

Downing fidgeted while Sarah burned, like Rome, with her tears. He stole a glance at his watch: 8:51. As a young man he'd been a promoter of tears – *they make each face a rivered country where nothing is frozen, everything flows* he'd written messily in one of his most successful 'essays'. (In the margin there had been a red checkmark and an avidly scrawled *yes*: Sarah.)

Who continued to weep, a sentimental old woman. But Sarah that was years ago. I'm sorry that your husband was a sad, stymied man who belittled your life's work and was swallowed completely by his own – but that is not my fault. For that much, at least, I'm not to blame. I could hardly have stayed with you. Think of us together now! You're an old woman – *old*. Weeping among the undergraduates, shamelessly. I wish you would stop now, Sarah.

Sarah? Please. Stop it. Please.

For Christ's sake Sarah get a HOLD.

It was 8:53. Downing had not been late for years. A brisk purposeful nod to an acquaintance or a subtle eyes-averted circumvention, nothing personal you understand, was the best insurance against being late. (*The tyranny of appointments keeps us from penetrating the skins of passersby.* Another red checkmark – two.)

Sarah Dawkins kept on weeping. Because of his hypocrisy? Hardly. Time makes hypocrites of us all. And everyone knows the Wheel World can't won on sidewalk conversation and sentimental philosophy. Always the need for food, for sleep. *A field*. Rice paddies in the sun.

– I'm sorry, Sarah, I'll be late, he said, brushing past her. For a second it really seemed his hand might edge out and seize hers, but the sallow, papery folding of her skin seen at close quarters stopped him. For a moment he thought he caught the rich dense scent of her hair – the same, the same. But he had to hurry. He'd be late.

– You had something, she said softly. She diagnosed? Her keen eyes peered from deep sockets encircled by a network of wrinkles. They were a few inches from Downing's eyes. They seemed to have a life of their own, like two remote faces pressed against abbey casements, consumptive poets peering from garret windows in a romantic myth, impossible to live ...

– I've got to go Sarah. I'm sorry.

And Downing did go then, though glancing back at the bent woman as he rushed off he was startled by tears, tears in his own eyes, then a sudden numbness in the arms, a pain around the heart. *Angina* – it sounded like some far-off, exotic country, a land of high dusty plains ringed with monasteries and

remote, snowy mountains, monks filing among ruins and bar-
rows in the high shrill air.... Stress-related, the pain. The tears
too, a function of stress. Always they came unexpectedly, a
sudden upwelling from some mysterious spring he'd thought
long dry – that he'd bricked up gradually as he discovered how
peaceful life could be without insoluble questions and frantic,
fruitless mental endeavour. Each year another brick. An old
story, without beginning or end. Who can say when the last
trickle dried? Doc Dawkins, wiping tears from her eyes: *The
unexamined life is not worth living.* That rusty old saw. Anyone could see it was a joke, the melodramatic motto of neuro-
paths and tenured snakeoilers hoping to inject more sanguine
souls with the venom of their angst. And yet these tears. A
sudden hunger. Regular meals had always been soothing.
When one ended there was another on deck. It was 8:58. The
pain stabbed once, twice, unbearably, and Downing felt a part
of himself fall – but here, here was the office tower. Yet he
found himself walking past it and ignoring the curious stare of
the secretary he usually met each morning at the front door
but now brushed by on the sidewalk. At 9:03 he crossed Division St (though Division St should not be here) and turned
onto Union (though Union, too ...) and started downhill
towards the lake. He'd never done this sort of thing before. He
felt irresponsible, exhilarated, a nine-year old skipping math,
and his body felt younger now too, the angina relenting, the
word itself now sounding earthy, warm, and carnal. He felt
good. A generous wave suffused him and he hoped Sarah was
all right too. He sensed however it was too late to turn back
and find out.

Six after nine, he was really late now. The lakefront was
deserted save for a few students scattered on the grass sun-
bathing. *When the day is sunny and hot a true philosopher
walks outdoors. Remember the stoa. A philosopher is a 'lover
of knowledge' and should let the sun have knowledge of him.
Grace consists in the breaking of skin —*

Three checkmarks here, an almost illegible *Yes.*

By 9:25 or so Downing had found a trail leading into pine
woods along the water. This was just past the federal peni-
tentiary that juts out into the lake. *Placing a prison on the*

*waterfront, in sight of a beach where the affluent student
body sunbathes, seems to me a gratuitous insult with endless sadistic implications. With unconscious sensitivity the
architects left out windows.*

The forest was dark and cool, deserted. It was almost ten
when Ralph found his trail crooking sharply to the left
where it really ought not to go. Though he'd never actually
been here he'd seen enough maps of the region to know the
lakeshore didn't veer or end so soon, but there it was: the
shore turned south and receded into a brilliant shimmering
light that fused water and sky to a single mass. For as far as
he could see, headlands of emerald and indigo ranged out
like reaching fingers. The coast had grown rocky. Leaving
the shore his trail became thinner, a mere trampling of grass
and weeds, an animal track. He found himself climbing from
the shore into open country, a moor of dwarf pines and
wavering yellow grass glistening like cornfields in a stiff
wind. The sun was hot on the pines and on the yellow grass.
He removed his suitcoat and remembered to rest it on an
esker by the trail so he could pick it up when he returned;
he walked on, his faint track moving briefly inland then
curving back to follow the cliffs and capes over the sea, for
looking east he saw the lake had fanned impossibly into a
wide expanse of water churned by cool onshore winds and
traversed an hour offshore by a whale who arched his slick
black spine filled the air with a creamy, sexual spume and
vanished deftly. The going along these cliffs was rough for
his shoes slipped and twisted on the stones so he removed
them and found it easier to go barefoot though the naked
feet stung and bled a little, pierced he supposed, by the kni-
fesharp gravel. Coming down the stones turned gradually to
sand, as a young child he glided down dunes in sprays of
white scudding into a small cove where the sea breathed
and expired continuous over salt and pebbled flotsam, it was
hot, the high sun severed in generous shafts the green was
bloodwarm with the light and he stripped and started to
wade and found a fluted seafloor wavering underfoot heard
music as water seeped through his open pores and long
bones up to his chest now swimming

and found himself both under and above his head arcing
up to the left he did a slow stroke now steady breathing as
he crossed the lake once to Garden Island near the ferry like
a dolphin vaulting so the passengers ran to the rail and
pointed and waved as a young man in Sarah's class he performed his creed and when he did not come and swam
instead she understood and met him one evening on wolfe
island with food and wine making love in a field behind a
disused church she taught him how as his face breached up
through a haze of water he saw mountains reared and sleev-
ing themselves in snow clear as a blank page as skin as
water a spectral element sweeps through him in rippling
waves with numbness and then in the forest with sarah he
called how the snow drifted through us it seemed your tears
ran down through dying foliage melting now and beneath
him the sea's fingers reached in reeds from what depths
what silence twining at his balls ah sarah his ankles and
toes & grew briefly into his   growing hair through years I
have left you nearing an island where we'll meet the far east
side of the brain *somewhere out beyond right doing and
wrong doing there is a feast and we're swallowed,
swallowed*   still swimming the seafloor rose up in sand
to meet him he walked from the water or on it onto banks
where a meal was laid there were sandbrown loaves steaming in light bottles of redwine jewelled in the glass chilled &
beaded even then he could taste them like summer the sun
was nearly gone behind the far capes & light was longing
like the world over sand into crowded forest above where
maybe

By the gallery a small crowd of students gathered and turned
over the body of Ralph Downing. One of them backed off a
few steps and threw up in a tulip bed. A jogger in black
tights raced off to find help.

– But I'm afraid we're – I'm afraid it's too late, said
another of the students: a thin blond man in a medical
school jacket.

Professor Dawkins peered between shoulders. She seemed

to be crying. What could have happened, she said.

– It looks like he's had a severe myocardial – a heart attack. Bad. A really bad one. I'm afraid I can't risk any kind of resuscitation, I might injure him more.

Professor Dawkins insisted he try anyway, but the student said softly that his hands were tied. He pleaded inexperience and muttered something about lawsuits. Dawkins knelt beside the body and continued to weep. Please, she said. Please.

– I'm afraid we'll have to wait for the ambulance, the student said, tendering his hand toward the old woman's trembling shoulder and stopping just short. Try not to worry. There's still time after the heart stops.

– Yes?

a crowded forest above where maybe I find her & maybe

ten thousand fields of rice gleaming like fishscales in the sun

Heart & Arrow

... for it does seem to us that time moves onward, forward, like water, yet the very timepieces we wear and use deny that notion: the hands of the watch are always moving yet go nowhere; the pendulum dandles back and forth, but always in the same locus.... It may be that time moves, in the eye of God, as in the mind of a drunk man: whirling, in fits and starts, in all directions at once – and in none.

– JEAN HAUTEVILLE, *The Physics of Time*

Now, in his thirties, Merrick spends little time at bars, but as he tells his big sister Laurel near the end of her 'fortieth-birthday bash,' at ten he was a genuine regular.

'What do you mean a *regular?*' Her smudged eyes, blue and shrewd, squint out at him through the big beige-rimmed glasses he still isn't used to seeing her wear. He looks down smiling, rubbing the blond stubble of a beard that Sheila, his girlfriend back in Toronto, has urged him to grow so he'll look older, more hireable.

'Downstairs,' he says shrugging. 'At Mom and Dad's.'

'Well I don't remember going there. And in high school believe me I did the full tour.'

'I mean the bar in our basement, Laurel. Our own bar.'

'Oh. *Oh* – you mean Mom and *Dad's.*'

'That's the place.'

She lowers her lined puffy face and studies him over the top of her glasses, faint red eyebrows arched, the way their mother used to do when she was sober, serious. 'Merr. You're not telling me *you* – look, does Sheila know this? – you drank their booze when you were little? You?'

'Hey, that's what I'm telling you.' Merrick clinks his rye against her spritzer and forges a coy wink and his whole manner, he can't help seeing, is lifted from somewhere else – maybe one of those ear-splitting, strobe-lit TV beer ads where a scrum of college All-Stars flex and guzzle and crack wise along a bar? He can't be sure. But he does know how much he hates the note of glibness that keeps breezing into his voice – the keynote of so much that he reads these days and almost every party he endures. A note he sometimes picks up and sings in tune with, ashamed of himself the whole time.

Yet at one time his only shame was solitude, exclusion. A time when he'd have given the hand he earns his bread with, marks with – he's a physics teacher now – to sing along with the crowd, to be allowed to, to be let in. But not just any crowd. Contemptuous of the herd of his grade-school peers, it was Laurel's tough crowd he aspired to, and, somewhere beyond them (through them, really) the grown-up world of his parents' parties.

Guests are shambling out now, halting and awkward, stooping over to embrace Laurel as if she can't get up herself, as if she's aged thirty years with the birthday. And – it's unsaid but hangs smokelike in the smokeless, lamplit den – the break-up last month. *Call us if we can do something,* a friend offers, *I know it'll be fine.* And after all it was Laurel's choice and she and Gavin really may 'link up again', the boys, in their teens, are pretty stable for their age, and her career in the civil service is going better than she could have planned.

'The black sheep that made good,' Merrick toasts her – then, out of character, he kills his rye in one go. Trouble of his own these days, he's broke and even part-time teaching is impossible to find. Funny how things turn out – when they were children it was Merrick who showed all the promise, at least in school.

And now he reminds her of that ironic reversal, to encourage her, he thinks, to cheer her up. Or is it to punish her instead? And what is it pushing him to guide her back down that long-demolished stairway into their childhood rec-room, the basement bar where he first tried to drown his childhood self and play the hardened, hard-drinking Grownup while she, in her early teens, already seemed set to inherit the only earth that really mattered then: a grotty, feral frontier of contraband cigarettes and mickeys, skipped classes, first lays in junior high, stubbornly slack jaws flip with swear words, roach-clips, chewing gum, the lyrics of hard rock standards by Black Sabbath and Led Zeppelin and BTO. *Stoners*, they were called, nobody sure if that honorific referred to the state they were always said to be in or the flooded limestone quarry where they hung out and smoked up and chugged beer and threw themselves naked off the cliffs.

Merrick knows he can't hold back, he has to talk his sister back down that basement stairway and on a particular day besides. He starts to speak in his best teacher's voice – low, soft, even, implacable – and pours them both another glass.

That afternoon he had been sitting as usual on one of the two high stools that faced the bar: a kidney-shaped counter of fake marble, brown buttoned vinyl down the front, set at the head of a dim, low, half-finished rec-room. Their father had worked episodically two summers before to finish the basement and then, after a brief bender of late-summer use, both parents had drifted back upstairs where they'd wintered and entertained their friends at the much larger bar in their lamplit, fire-warmed family room. No surprise they'd never come back – the baseboard heaters that Father had installed never did quite work, his light fixtures were few and ill-placed and even in June the light leaking down from the leaf-clogged window-wells was dull and sullen, the air stagnant, chilled. A Bogart poster and a faded Group of Seven print did little to primp up the cheap panelling behind the bar; in the dimness and still-ness the print – of a full moon and stars reflected in a northern lake – had a sombre, ominous quality, as if the water had just smoothed out over a violent drowning. Merrick tried hard not to look at it. Like Bogart in the poster he brooded down into his glass or slouched over cue-in-hand at the pool table where the coloured balls glowed in strange, static constellations, like the solar system in Mr Leung's model at school.

Merrick liked the muted dimness of the rec-room, especially after school, where the sunlight of the playground and the classroom's crisp lighting would always bring back into sharp relief the smallness and weakness of his grade. And him too. Alone at recess he would fight his way up a drainpipe onto the school's flat gravelled roof and stand shielding his eyes, squinting out fiercely over the sprawling development past the limestone quarry until his eye was snagged and drawn downward by a fluttering toy-fort flag, a lean smokestack fuming darkly, an aerial like the empty, angular husk of a huge praying mantis. Laurel's school. And out beyond it the switchblade glinting of the river, the scarred and furrowed hills.

Laurel was not there, in school. She was hidden away in other, darker basements, doing things that made her parents and her principal and teachers 'grey with worry'. Carrying on. Without a thought for her family. Unaware, it seemed, of the little brother who still worshipped her and whom she'd played with happily a few years before. (All the toys they'd shared were buried in a crawl space under the basement stairs and sometimes during a long 'binge' Merrick would make for that space, lurching and weaving with fierce concentration, and he would remove their old toys and sit playing with them in the sallow light from inside, a freakish silhouette with his small hunched shoulders dwarfed by his father's hulking fedora. Sometimes for the rest of the day he would forget all about the dingy bar, the apprenticeship he sensed awaiting him there with dwindling patience.)

He did not get drunk – not really. He did go through the dark cabinets under the sink behind the bar and shook into lacquered bowls the stale, exotic snacks abandoned there – peanuts mummified in mysterious coatings, shrimp wafers and candied ginger, marzipan, macadamias, milk chocolate truffles in delicate shells of fluted foil – and then, playing bartender, he would set up on the 'marble' bartop a clique of bottles and pour doses of gin or white rum or vodka into shotglasses that gleamed icily in the underground light, as exotic and imposing in their way as the tubes and scopes and beakers in Mr Leung's spotless lab or the implements and whole rite of Anglican Eucharist, which he now took with his parents each Sunday and Laurel now spurned, so he was caught between idols, the adult and the teen, not knowing which to follow, which to betray.

On his first visits to the bar he did not use any mixes

because a grown-up should take his drink the way his parents did, always, *straight up* – but once he got to be a regular he gave in and started groping under the sink for the sticky old bottles of mix forgotten there. He dug out a few half-empty specimens of Pepsi and 7-Up and Canada Dry, but they were too flat and besides that they were for kids. The pina colada mix, its gluey cap sporting a skirt of bark shavings, warned him off with a rancid stink. But the citrus cordial was still good, and, mixed with water and the faintest ration of price-less four-centuries-old Tanqueray, it made a drink that tasted like lemonade just before it goes off. Sipping slowly he could get it down. His 'Bloody Marys' were best: a splash of white rum and water diluted with enough grenadine to stain the lake at the Stoner's Quarry a bloodshot red. A spoonful of sugar. He could easily kill two, slumped and rumpled as Bogart on the corner of the bar, a cigarillo dangling from his sneer, his father's vast FBI Ray-Bans held on with a pipecleaner tied round the back.

His parents would not be impressed, he knew. In his guts he knew it and he was always afraid, hearing them up in the family room as supper-time neared, the murmur and slur of their voices strained down to him through the ceiling – his mother's voice especially. Often rising with that blurred, abruptly outraged inflection he had come to associate with her second hour of drink. His father's footsteps growing louder – choppier – each time he rose to replenish them. To Merrick it always seemed – especially after his second Bloody Mary when his guts and small fists unclamped and his veins flooded with sluggish warmth and he thought of himself as 'gloriously drunk' – that those footsteps splashed huge shadows across the ceiling, down the panelled walls, over the rec-room's grey linoleum floor. Red shadows. He knew that made no sense. He knew that Mr Leung, who liked and encouraged him in science class, would be disappointed he could think such childish things.

The afternoon Laurel came down to the rec-room Merrick was slouching as always on the corner stool by the bar. He had on his father's Ray-Bans and huge red Shriner's fez and was sucking smokelessly on an old dried-up cigar, drinking hard, he told himself, to forget. It had been a long day at school and he had picked a fight and lost it then picked another and won but had not much cared and even Mr Leung was curt with him, impatient, it seemed, with his crisp familiarities – the way he answered questions like one learned colleague responding tolerantly to the engaging, if imperfect, lecture of another. Shouting now, a crashing of footsteps from close above and big shadows seeming to lunge over the dark walls and ceiling, as had happened before when Laurel came home after staying out overnight without calling – but this time she'd been gone several nights and the shouting was louder. And louder. Now, hearing feet on the basement stairway instead of the usual shoot-out of slammed doors, Merrick leapt off the stool and over the bar and in a riot of blind groping – the big fez lidding down over his shades – he grabbed at the bottles he'd lined up and clunked them back under the sink with his rancid snacks. And his glass. His Bloody Mary. His third one, for the first time ever a third round and it *had* made him awkward and dizzy and he knew he was making too much noise, like that time before when another intruder had come down: his mother, her slippers spatting and weaving down the steps and over the tiles by the crawl space and on into the rec-room towards the bar, and her son. But not hearing any noise he made. With her stumbling and her tears – standing at the bar choking, sputtering, turning back for the stairs – she was making too much of her own.

Some day, Merrick hoped, she and Father would be able to join him at the bar. For a round. It would be good to see more of them. But not now. The footfalls were lighter, faster: Laurel. For a long time he'd been hoping this would happen, hoping Laurel would come down and surprise him in the romantic, reckless, manly act of drinking alone. Hurting himself in private, hurting himself by the glass. And taking it. And taking it. Laurel, he'd wanted to say, come down to the rec-room and I'll fix you a drink, you don't need to stay out late with those friends of yours – but he'd been afraid she might laugh at him, or disbelieve him, or even turn him in to their parents. But if she just happened on him now, how different things would seem. *Merry, I had no idea you were so cool ... shit, you don't have to sit here all alone if you don't want.*

But he'd hidden himself and the bottles and it was too late to present the unforgettable scene he'd long planned. Time only for this: grip the last of his Bloody Mary and leap up back of the bar to toast her, let her see him as he was – a man. He froze. Caught a glimpse of her and froze. Ducked down. Like their mother she was crying but in a different way – no quiet, drawn, depleted sadness but a violent wheezing, long red curls shaking over her freckled face, her eyes bruised with smeared mascara.

Laurel turned and walked stiffly towards the crawl space and Merrick had to crane his head out around the bar to watch her open the low door, kneel down, squeeze in. He couldn't guess what she might want in there with the jumbled remains of her dolls and stuffed animals, their board games and science kits and hockey cards and Lego; he snatched his drink down off the bar and drained it. The pounding in his head seemed to come from elsewhere as if his parents, drunk again, were stumbling around upstairs with a gang of their friends in search of the drinks they'd set down somewhere and forgotten. Laurel, still on hands and knees, came backwards out of the dark space and shoved the door shut, turned round, lurched up, her old pink skipping rope clenched in a fist.

She wasn't crying now. But her face was so pale. She stood on tiptoes and struggled to knot one end of the rope to the brass hook screwed in the ceiling for a spider plant which had died last year in the chilly dimness and been removed. Laurel came towards the bar. Merrick pulled in his head. He heard a stool being dragged over the floor, then a faint wet sob, more a hiccup. He peeped round again: Laurel was trying to balance her bare feet on the middle rung of the stool as she stood wobbling, the seat's edge squeezing the backs of her thighs, her arms raised, hands fumbling with the rope. Merrick felt choked as if by the tie he liked to wear Sundays but could never quite knot before church so that Father, surly, his blue eyes sunken small and red, had to be summoned to help.

Summon him now, he thought. Both of them.

But Laurel pulled back – she settled back on the chair and wept weakly, and Merrick let out his breath, yet he was still afraid of startling her so he waited – a minute, two minutes –

the time seeming to stretch into hours, the way a ten-foot drop will deepen to a thousand when you're trying to do it, *jump* – and now he saw himself back in the brutal sunlight up on the edge of the quarry where his sister and friends always went to chug beer and smoke up and hurl themselves off the cliffs into the water. A month before: he'd followed her and her crowd up to the edge, again, telling himself it was to watch over her in secret but really hoping they would notice him and ask him over for a drink. Hunched sunglassed and sweating in the tall grass he'd spied her and the others sprawling in the unseasonably warm sun on the clifftop, a portable radio and a two-four of Export in the gravel among them. The Band was playing 'Stage Fright'. Some of the stoners dozed and sunbathed, Laurel and her lithe wiry boyfriend, who had a tan though it was only May, sat face to face, legs twined, on an open sleeping bag sharing a cigarette and a beer, Laurel gently reaching her hands along the boy's sideburned face and inching up the bandana wreathed hippie-style around his long hair. Kissing his open lips. Merrick's face burning as the boy's dark hand slid into Laurel's bikini top.

One of the stoners, his skinny chest tattooed, sat up in mock umbrage, ripped off his mirrored John Lennons and in a pinched, spinsterly voice scolded them both to go get a suite at the Lord Elgin if they could not help behaving in that way. And another boy, working off a beer-cap with the blade of his knife: *They just need a cool dip.*

They were all up now, ready to throw Laurel and her boyfriend over the edge, but the two of them raised their hands in cheerful surrender and got up stretching like lean limber animals and daring each other to go first. When the tattooed boy with the granny shades, his bangs so long they seemed to part round his nose, bent and clinched the boyfriend round the waist as if to trundle him over, Laurel coolly stripped out of her bikini and with a shout sped away towards the cliff. In motion that way – naked, running – she was a stranger to Merrick, without a face or a name. As she moved he felt flushed and anxious and then as she leapt out into space he was afraid. His last glimpse of her was a sunburst of long red curls splayed up by the breeze and gravity. Gone. The others hurried towards the edge of the cliff and stopped – leaned over – yelled – and a faint splash came back in answer.

Laurel's boyfriend jumped a few moments later, also naked, so for a moment as he turned from the cliff and slipped out of his tight cutoffs Merrick saw his dense black pubic hair and long, half-swollen penis – larger, he realized with a shock, than his father's glimpsed in the bath.

Merrick stumbled out of the grass after the boyfriend had jumped.

Who's the kid with the monster shades, a girl said.

Where? snapped the tattooed boy. Merrick couldn't see it, the tattoo, clearly. He took off his glasses. *Oh fuck, it's Laurel's kid brother again.*

Tell him to beat it, the girl said.

Tell him herself, the tattooed boy said, gesturing with his bottle at the cliff where Laurel was just appearing, head and shoulders and small high breasts seeming to levitate over the cliff's edge; she must have been climbing a steep path. Her bare skin still dripped, glowed with the freezing water, the ice only a few weeks gone. The tattooed boy whistled and Laurel blushed and rolled her eyes and flitted over to her things and dressed with great speed as if the bikini could warm her.

Your kid brother, he said, smirking.

Laurel, fumbling behind her back, looked up with smudged startled eyes and frowned. Then blushed again. *What are you doing here, Merrick?*

Don't know, he mumbled. Then lied: *Came to jump I guess.*

Don't be an asshole, the other girl said. *Don't be stupid.*

Be in shit, said the tattooed boy. *If he got hurt …*

His sister stared at him a moment. Shaking her head, she rolled her eyes long-sufferingly the way she always did with their parents and then fastened her eyes on the cliff, frowning, till finally, looking down at the gravel, she shrugged, or shuddered, and made a lopsided smile. *If he really wants to, he can try.*

Be in shit.

Kid can hardly walk, Lor, he's hardly out of diapers.

Shut up, Janet, Laurel told her. *Just shut the fuck up OK?*

Must be a hundred feet down, the tattooed boy leered, then cocked an eyebrow over one mirrored lens as if Merrick were a moron incapable of decoding such gradeschool irony.

Laurel's boyfriend appeared on the lip of the cliff, wet headband high on his forehead, sinewy torso clenched up and shaking with cold, his penis wizened now, puny as a child's.

That your kid brother again Lor!

I can do it, Merrick brought out, spitting dryly. *No shit. I can.*

Someone gave a hoot of derision or excitement and the radio's volume shot up: it was The Who, 'I Can See For Miles.'

Let me try.

Laurel, frowning slightly, put out her hand. ok, *Merr – come on. Don't listen to those guys. It's fun, I'll show you.*

And she did. She led him to the cliff-edge and told him what to do and she told him again, then again, with dwindling patience, as he stood there a full hour stripped to his underwear sweating and trembling, eyes trained on his watch to avoid seeing the water far below as his big chance ticked away and the stoners sauntered up beside him and teased or encouraged him and one after another, with some hesitation, leapt. Laurel said it was just forty feet down to the water, tops, all you had to do was tuck in your arms and go straight down but to Merrick the drop seemed endless, sickening as that film he had seen at school: the camera in a jet fighter skimming low and fast over the desert towards the edge of the Grand Canyon till the drop shudders into view and in a flash the earth's floor sheers away and the abyss explodes underneath you and your breath is gone, your guts, and you're plummeting till the lifecord jerks taut and your parachute hangs you in mid-air – a jolt like the slap on a newborn's back – and you breathe. Even the toughest of Laurel's gang were a bit scared. It took most of them a minute or two and two or three good chugs of beer to muster the courage for each jump and when they did jump their arms would start gangling, windmilling like third-graders on a trampoline – though when they surfaced they were themselves again, cured, aged, by the waters, the way liquor could age you, absolve you of childhood – the tattooed boy coolly tossing his head to flick the wet bangs from his eyes.

After an hour they went back to their beer and Top-40 countdown and left Merrick on the edge of the cliff, teeth rattling, loose shale stabbing into his soles. In the distance past the city the river was a long quivering blade carving up the sandbars and beyond it the hills seemed to fold and crumple under waves of rising heat. Down on the water Merrick's shadow was scrawny. It seemed to move like an hour-hand as the sun burning his shoulders and head crossed the sky behind him and started to fall. *Mellow yellow*, the tattooed boy was echoing the radio, a jeer in his voice – but if Merrick couldn't jump he could not back away either, though Laurel, feet slung over the edge where she sat digging red fingernails into a beer label, was now trying to talk him out of it, telling him it was cool, the cliff was bigger for him than it was for them cause he was still so small, right? Shit, he was the brain on relativity.

Her brow and mouth began to pucker, harden. She grabbed their father's sunglasses from the ground and rammed them on. Merrick choked back a welling in his throat. For a few years they had hardly exchanged a word and now she was making this overture, offering him this chance, and he knew he could not shame them both and let her down.

But he could not jump.

Laurel shot up and tilted her beer back and drained it and hurled the bottle out across the quarry. It shattered, sparkling, on the far rocks. *Maybe you should be heading home, kid.* And as he nodded gravely and half turned, knowing his last chance was lost, a stone flipped, jabbing sharply under his heel and he lost balance, lurched forward and back and he would have to fall and that knowledge braced him with a kind of helpless courage; as Laurel reached out to help him he pushed off with his feet, skinny arms flapping, and he was airborne – motionless it seemed – then gravity was roaring up through his bowels and belly and throat and the ice-blue eye of the water was flashing dead for him. He whipped and lashed his arms for balance and kicked at the air but at the last moment he wobbled off-kilter, yelled and smacked the water at an angle not quite belly-flat but it was bad enough and when the roaring, the wild kaleidoscope of ice-green fragments wound down, to a stillness, he felt the sun's heat on his eyelids and heard high above him the mewing of a gull. Lips were being pressed to his and breath flowed into him in waves, he coughed wetly and heard Laurel behind him, close by, panting, then something eclipsed the sun and he opened his eyes: the tattooed boy's granny shades goggled down at him through long bracketing wings of hair, his sunken chest a few inches away as he tried to nurse Merrick with a bottle of Ex. Drinking the warm beer Merrick eyed his chest-tattoo: a conventional pierced, bleeding-heart design except the black thin arrow was tipped at both ends.

You all right? Shit, kid, that was some belly flop. You cool?

He nodded. *Yes.* Because he had done it. Even if Laurel, they told him, had had to dive in after and fish him in to shore because he was too shocked by the impact and the icy cold to swim.... And later as she walked him home she'd actually let him know how proud she was – maybe in part, he guessed, so he wouldn't tell Mother what had happened, how he'd wrenched his neck and ankle and lost his watch and nearly drowned? As if he would. *At first I thought you just slipped, then I realized you were really jumping. But it looked so strange. Like there was somebody behind you pushing and you were trying not to go off the edge but this invisible man was pushing you. And the way your arms were flapping! Fuck, Merr, I'm sorry to – I'm glad you're all right.* As she let out another, thinner laugh, draping an arm over his shoulder, he felt a smile surge up inside him and burst into light like a man surfacing from far down after a perfect dive, his arms raised, lungs gobbling the air in rapture and relief.

But that hour turned out to be an interlude, a singularity, not a fresh start, and in the weeks that followed he saw Laurel less than ever before. As if that day had meant little to her and the ripples caused by his jump, which to him had seemed seismic (he was the first in his school to do it, ever), were for her soon overwhelmed by the tides and churnings of some greater storm.

When Laurel leapt off the barstool it seemed some invisible thing had shoved her because the set of her face and body and even the last twitch before the fall all seemed to be resisting it – yet she did fall and when the rope jerked her up short with a tight shuddering bounce her legs started scissoring wildly, a child in a tantrum, she trying to kick away the stool or to climb back on. The stool toppled over with a crash. There was an echoing crash upstairs, shadows seeming to lunge over the ceiling and walls. Laurel's hands clutched spastically at the pink rope tightening round her neck and her pale face reddened, smeared eyes bugged out, the jumprope strained to its quivering limit.

For seconds he'd been frozen like up on the cliff but now again something shoved him out of the grip of fear or whatever it was that held him, and he moved. He was halfway across to her, crying out her name *Oh Laurel, Laurel please* when he realized the rope was still stretching like a piece of red licorice pulled apart, his sister slowly descending to the floor.

The glass slipped from his hand and smashed at his feet. Their mother's voice yelling down to him from the head of the stairs. Laurel lighting on her toes and clawing at the licorice still squeezing her neck and glaring as he threw himself at her and gripped her round the belly to lift her, to ease the choking, and a vision came back of the two of them in the quarry: underwater, tightly twinned, Laurel buoying him up through tunnels of green light till they breach in a shock of sunlight and spray, he gulps at the air, she tows him coughing back in to shore.... Merrick heard her gasp, he looked up and she was glowering down as if to say *Let go of me you moron, get this stupid jump-rope off my neck.*

Their mother looming before them, a drink in one hand, pawing at her glasses with the other as if to clear a lens and discredit this hellish scene: her delinquent daughter half-hanged by the broken barstool and her sunglassed ten-year-old a drunkard, cut open, kneeling in glass like shards of broken ice and clutching the girl as if he had just hauled her up out of a hole in the frozen river.

Their mother crossed herself, drained her glass, bit her fist and began to shake.

The last guests are gone and Merrick and Laurel clean up. She's quiet now, tired it seems, and sad. Partly it's Gavin. For fifteen years he's been a part of their small galaxy of family and friends, a satellite of stable orbit, and now suddenly his orbit has changed and carried him off in a way that violates all the old logic, old laws.

Merrick is thinking of things in this way because of his own teaching and because talk of that day at the quarry has reminded him of something the whole school believed then. Mr Leung notwithstanding, it was a well-known fact that the quarry had been gouged out thousands of years before by a meteorite: a great flaming boulder billowing clouds of smoke had catapulted through the atmosphere and stamped itself into the limestone, leaving behind a crater of scorched cliffs, a deep blue-green eye of water that had rushed in, steaming, from the river two miles off.

'But you must have known it wasn't true before the rest of us,' Laurel tells him, looking drawn and cross in the kitchen's guttering fluorescent light. Almost three a.m. They stand over the sink washing up, the clack of glass and the slopping of water a bland, comforting counterpoint to the hard talk they've been having.

'I mean, you always were a smart kid for your age. Always such a hurry to grow up.'

'Sure,' he says, trying to gauge her tone, 'so I knew it wasn't a meteorite. Fine. I knew that and a lot more. But where did it get me? All those facts, I mean. The *hurry*.' He looks down into the ticking suds, embarrassed; the words, churned up by this talk of the past and only half-applicable to his life now, have sounded self-pitying, hollow. Pre-emptive. As if reminding her of his own troubles might disarm the anger he sees in her curt, careless stabs at drying.

Her voice softens a little. 'You'll find something soon though, I'm sure you will. And Sheila's work's secure, I'll bet.'

'No shortage of work these days for addiction counsellors.'

'Anyway it's a recession, you said yourself a lot of the colleges –'

'I'm doing fine,' he says. 'Listen, I'm sorry.'

'It's three in the morning, you don't usually drink, you're entitled to feel a bit sorry for yourself.' She doesn't sound convinced.

'Not just that. I mean for bringing up what happened. But

I've been, you can see I've been mulling it over for years and I guess – '

'It's all right.' She shoves her towel-wrapped fingers into the last glass to swab it dry. 'I just wish we remembered things the same. I remember the hospital after, and the shrinks, and you and Dad coming to visit – you brought me grownup books every time, remember? instead of magazines? – but going down to the basement, the rope – I haven't blocked any of that out, Merrick, it's just clearer all the time.' She swabs harder now, insistent, the glass getting streaked and cloudy with specks of lint. 'And you weren't there, Merrick. You really were not. You think I could have forgotten that?'

She grinds the dirty glass into the crammed dishrack.

'Fuck, none of you were ever there, that was the whole problem.'

'Laurel – '

'You came down with Mom at the end. Just when I was pulling it off. You both just – stood there, gawking, then she screamed and ran over and she held me. For once in her fucking life.'

'But I was there the whole time. I was right there! People remember things differently when – '

'They remember things *wrong*,' she cries with something of her old fire, and back of her new glasses her eyes roll like a teenager's.

'Laurel, listen, you don't – '

'And I *was* lying when I said I knew you'd jumped, not slipped. On the cliff. You're grown up now, you can handle it. It's a small thing anyway. But I knew you slipped all along, I just wanted to make you feel better.'

He pulls the plug and the sink gives a throttled gargling and goes empty faster than any sink he's ever seen. A spattered, sudsy jumble of cutlery breaks surface, bones on the floor of a drained lake. (When he was in high school a construction firm had finally drained the quarry, revealing oil drums, dumpsters, gutted TVs, bicycles, a dozen cars, thousands of beer bottles and the weed-green skeleton of an unknown man. They'd built a shopping mall over the top and turned the pit into an underground carpark, where Merrick, in town last spring for an unsuccessful interview, parked and bought flowers for his parents' grave.)

'Mine's always plugged,' he says, putting his watch back on.

'What?'

'My sink.'

After a few seconds she turns to him, glasses fogged over.

'I'm sorry I said those things. I didn't mean it, Merr, I'm sorry, I'm just so wiped out these days, and ... '

'Forget it,' he shrugs.

'The kids tell me I'm biting everyone's head off.'

Briskly, lightly, so as not to embarrass her, he puts his hands on her stooped shoulders and kisses the dulled freckles on her cheek. The hair at her temples, once fire-coloured, is cooled to grey now, ashen. Or is that tempered to steel? She's wearing their mother's old Sunday earrings, small crosses of white gold.

'Laurel?' – he speaks softly, hugs her and rubs her bowed back as it begins to quiver, then shake – 'it's all right, Lor. Go ahead, I don't mind. Go get some rest.' She pulls her head back from his shoulder so he can see her face: she's laughing, really, though her eyes are full.

'It did look so damn funny when you went off, you know. With that stupid hat on your head and those big shades ... '

As Merrick puts the last of the glasses away – checking each by raising it to the light, as if focussing a small telescope on some heavenly body – he notices the set is incomplete, two missing, and he starts up the narrow hallway towards the living room to find them. A ragged, bereft, somehow elderly snoring already ripples from Laurel's room. He pauses, socks aglow, by the grinning full-moon night-light between his nephews' doors and thinks of Sheila, how good it will be to get back to their place in Toronto tomorrow night and make love and sleep beside her again and how bad it will be the next day when they start fighting again about family, how she wants one urgently and he's still afraid. 'There's no work out there,' he'll say again, though they both know that's not really it. As she tells him again in her best counsellor's voice that a fear of children is a fear of growing up.

Maybe the glasses are in one of the boys' rooms – but he won't stumble in and wake them the way his own parents used to do, searching for their lost drinks how many years back. Like Laurel he *is* different from them, he has learned something, there is, he believes, some progress in time. He'll go on up the hall into the living room and check there, then out the sliding doors into the cool yard the way his parents did more and more in their last years, searching, so Merrick still has dreams of one or both of them shambling like sleepwalkers hours out from the house and the city and a long way past all houses, hours over sifting dunes, along the moonlit beach and wading out to vanish at a bend in the river – or silhouetted, hand in hand, on the cliffs above the drop.

Root-Fires

Seven scenes for an Easter play

Gib & his father Evan came out of the forest
towing the two young pines they had dug from the soil.
Breath bloomed & hovered above them in the chill
grey air. Alongside a pool
sky-blue with snowmelt, in a fold between hills
they laid the two trees down. Gib traced
I *his father's gaze up the higher hill, west*
to where a black pine, much bigger than the others
they'd rooted up, wind-contorted, faced
down out of thistle & dead brown grass. His father's
big, still-powerful body crutched
on a spade. Against the grizzled fringe of his hair
his bald scalp his face burning, flushed –

Shouldn't we take a rest now? Father? (Gib's own strained breaths clouding the air.) Your heart.

His father turning away.

Besides, she'll have the meal ready by now. And these trees –

They'll be fine half an hour. Too far back to the road now. We'll take out the big tree, I'll drag it and you'll drag the two small ones back the same time. Replant them together.

Evan's face goes even redder as he speaks. Tired. Having jostled Gib up before dawn and in the hours since then pulling six small pines from the forest and hauling them over the hilly fields back to the house, replanting them by the road. A bristling wall. His mother's plan. Gib thinks he understands why she must want, now, to shut out the world. He feels his own face reddening as he glares at his father's stocky, planted form, dressed for the first time Gib can recall in rough workman's clothes: a thick red-and-black-tartaned flannel shirt, patched corduroys, the stained eroded workboots Evan must have bought when he came home from Korea and opened his lumberyard in the city. By the time Gib was born, Evan had long since found others to wrestle with the merchandise and he'd sat among the clerks and secretaries of a tidy office (Gib had seen the old photos) in tailored wool suits that always seemed too small, his shoulders taxing and chafing at the fabric, the vest-buttons over his belly stretched taut....

Evan coughs and starts up the hill towards the tree, spade rifled over his shoulder. Gib waits a second or two, then follows. His legs are tired and the cowboy boots he's worn comfortably at school wobble and twist on the wet, rocky slope. Just a few years back he might have bounded up this hill – in the off-season his coach made them train that way – but in the last two years at law school his physique (his father's physique, really) has sagged and softened and though bigger than ever seems somehow depleted, worn down.

Another reason for his father to feel disappointed.

From the top of the hill the house can be seen. Evan had it built two years ago in the most mundane, graceless suburban style – a squat sprawling grey-brick thing, bluntly out of place in this country of deserted fields marked by a few chapels and the odd red-brick, gabled farm-house. Gib knows his father must have grown up in a house like that – and in the shadow of such chapels – a half-hour's drive up the escarpment near Milton, but a few years back when he asked to go see it, his father told him he was too busy.

Evan rammed his spade into clay by the pine
his work boot driving the dull blade deeper. Gib –
through a curtain of needles, bristling – watched
then did the same. His soft, blistering hands scorched
on the spade's shaft & handle, the bone
2 *& sinews of his forearms ached, a fisted*
tightness clenched his eyes from the night's wasted
broken sleep. Working in silence the two men
carved out a circle round the tree. A cold, slow
drizzle fell as Gib took in
his father's laboured breathing & the low
grunts when his spade hit roots or stone.

It's rooted in there pretty deep, Gib calls out, looking for his father's face through the boughs. The wind up here, I guess, and the summers being so dry.

His father coughs, swears under his breath. Gib, through the boughs, can just glimpse the top of his head. Still flushed. He adds, I guess you did a lot of work like this with your father when you were a boy?

More silence. Gib stops, abruptly drained of breath, and braces his folded hands and chin on the handle of his spade.

His father plods out from back of the tree, high forehead glazed with rain and sweat. Staring down at Gib's work: Got to get in deeper under the roots. Can't pull her out like this. And he bends and jabs his spade into the loose turf Gib has been working.

Tired?

Hungry, Gib admits. Out of shape, too.

I can see that. You should play hockey again. Autumn when you go back. Evan kneels in the wet grass and with his big hands – red and raw, like Gib's – pries from between roots a grey, head-sized stone.

I'm not going back to law school, Father. I told you, I can't.

Evan twists from the waist and with both hands heaves the stone as far as he can. As he struggles to his feet Gib fights off the urge to reach out and help him.

I'm sorry, it's just – I'm just not cut out for it. I'll have to go into something else.

You're not thinking carpentry again? Or *drama*? Evan grips his spade and snorts. Go back to school get your degree and in ten years you'll thank me for not being soft.

I can't go back. I'm not cut out for it.

Evan drives his spade into the ground and presses down with his boot. He darts a glance at the idle head of Gib's spade. Presses harder. Gib knows his father will say nothing – just keep on struggling, his silence a verdict – till Gib is shamed into joining in.

You could go back for exams, Evan mutters, jerking a spade-ful of earth over his shoulder. There's time. They start next week you said.

I'm too far behind as it is.

You could try.

Father, I'm too far behind, I'm *finished*. And I can't go back into Commerce, either.

Evan had shipped him to Western with high expectations. He would earn a B.Comm. and maybe an MBA and come back to Toronto and take over the business. Gib already knew the yard well from working there summers since he was fourteen, and Evan was ready to take some time off, retire, give up work as he'd given up tobacco – at the doctors' urging. But the yard had been slow for a few years and in the fall of '83, when Gib started school, things got a lot worse. By the next fall Evan decided to cut his losses, sell the yard while he still could; Gib struggled through two more semesters of Commerce before bowing out.

Gib. Dig here, this way.

Pardon?

Over here, I said. You're daydreaming.

Gib obeys, digging where he's told, but his thoughts remain on school. How at his father's insistence and after a summer of argument (he and Evan all the time; he and his business-school girlfriend till finally they broke up) he'd thrown himself into law school – and barely got through his first year. How by reading week of second year the situation was hopeless and all his hard trying for his father's sake undermined by what he'd learned on his trip home at Christmas. About his father. So at Easter he came home again – he came back – to the house in the country where he slept in a guest room bristling with Evan's sport trophies and war medals, racked rifles, files, triumphantly fat old account books – and he brought back no books of his own.

They dig together in silence, shoving spades deeper under the snarled, extensive roots. The rain has stopped but a wind has come on. Its chill seeps into Gib through his damp jean jacket and whips into his eyes some of the red, thinning hair he's lately let grow.

And I *am* thinking of carpentry again, or drama. His spade jams on a rock and his left hand slides down the shaft, catching splinters. He winces and adds sharply, Maybe even sculpture.

Evan on his knees again jabbing the spade with sharp hard

strokes into the earth. Like a bayonet. He was decorated in Korea, Gib knows, for helping his platoon defend a small barren hill against 'enemy columns pouring down from the north' – but he'd never told Gib what he'd done. It always was like that, his real life hidden, housed away, seeming to fan out as heat and a dense feral scent from some internal – what? A kind of hearth, maybe – a furnace, maybe, stoked with slow-burning anger. A root-fire. Channelled sometimes, pouring out at the eyes – eyes Gib has lately begun to dream of, nights – and sometimes leaping from his throat in curt staccato eruptions. *No. Won't let you waste your life. Your own damned good. You will go back.*

It's for children, playing with wood. Fine when you were a boy but you're a man now, you'll be wanting a real job.

A real job, Gib says, crouching down for leverage.

A real job. And I won't help out if you take a course – grunting as his spade cuts a root and plunges into soil – in cabinet-making.

Gib squeezes both hands on the handle, ramming his spade into earth, hauling back as if pulling on an oar and repeating the action over and over. *You say it was fine when I was a boy but it was never all right,* he thinks – out loud? – recalling the scrap wood his father brought home for the fireplace years ago, how Gib carved faces and figurines and pared small houses, small towns of houses, and excelled in Woodworking class at school. And Drama as well – till his father discouraged that too.

It was never all right. You never liked it.

Didn't say a word.

You didn't have to, I could feel it. I always could.

You got everything figured out now, don't you?

Sure, Gib grunts, shoving hard. The smart-ass college kid.

Evan lets the spade slip from his grasp. Still kneeling he splays a big hand on either thigh and glares into the excavation.

Back-talking now to your mother and me. All the time.

Not to her.

To her too.

Yeah, well at least *I* –

He stops. The pain flaring in his hands makes his heart thud, breath quicken. Around him a raw dank odour of wet soil.

Evan's eyes bore into him.

That's enough now, Gib, you understand?

Gib stabs his spade into earth, wincing.

Guess it's a bad thing these days, a man wanting to see his boy has a good job, some money. Some *respect*. Those back-to-the-land types twenty years ago found what it's like trying to make a living out here. All of them running back to Bay Street for their watch and chain soon as they found some bigshot developer to buy them out. You got to understand this about the world, Gib, there's no future now working with your hands. Forty years ago I saw it and it's truer than ever. But you been so protected you don't see it. And by the time you do it'll be too late.

I'll be damned if I'm going to stand here watching you ruin your life for some – whim.

Gib looks at his father – gapes at him – unable to recall ever hearing him say so much at one time. That last time, maybe, when they fought over law school.

It's not a *whim*, Gib finally says. And I'm not going to ruin my life. There's a lot of work these days for –

There's no work these days for anybody but the man wearing the white collar.

You were working with your hands at first.

Not for long. It was a way out. Your uncle Bryce stayed on the farm the way I was meant to and look what happened to him.

Expropriated when they built the 401 – Gib has heard the story many times before. When Evan made his case for Commerce. When Evan made his case for Law.

And I'll be damned if I'm going to support you to prance around some stage or lay back in some – artist's studio on Queen Street and carve naked ladies.

Gib glares down at his father's head. Bowed to the earth, as if praying. Flushed: glowing from beneath. When settlers like his grandfather had cleared this land they'd burned off the stumps of oaks, maples and pines, and sometimes the root-fires had smouldered years under the ground.

I'm not asking for anyone's support, he wants to say, but the sentence dries in his throat. He shivers as a wet gust slaps him. From the sky to the northwest above and beyond the house, more rain clouds closing in.

See if we can pull her out now, Evan says, tottering to his feet. He plods back around the tree and moments later the boughs begin to shudder and beads of cold water come flashing off the needle-tips. *Get under with the spade and pry.* Evan's muffled order. Gib almost smiles – the voice seems to come from inside the shaking tree.

Get under and I'll pull from here.

> *Gib slid both spades under the wickering*
> *of snarled roots packed with earth & fell to his knees*
> *between them. Wincing*
> *he gripped the handles & at the shock of pain*
3 *his heart bolted his face burned. The branches began*
> *to shudder away as the crown of the tree inclined*
> *stiffly back. With all his weight & strength, Gib*
> *leaned*
> *on the spades &*
> *pumped down with quick strong strokes &*
> *through the wood he felt the clay as it cracked*
> *open, the dumb, dogged resistance of sinews, the shock*
> *of release as a root snapped free.*

Pry, his father shouts.

I am. *Damn it,* Gib breathes, *damn you.* I am! The wind gusts and spits fresh rain in his face – his eyes – and Gib swears again, this time out loud. A taproot cracks and the tree lurches over another ten degrees. Gib's strength is giving out the way it used to when his coach in Triple A made them skate short bursts back and forth over the same crumbling strip of ice until their knees shook and buckled and their lungs ached with every breath. Evan would always be there, too, face clouded in cigarette smoke back of the glass by the penalty box – watching every practice. Never praising him for goals or chiding him for slips like the other, more audible parents but just squinting down, his stern, demanding silence veiling him like the smoke, the steel-rimmed glass – another remove from Gib. Gib's hands were tougher then, calloused, accustomed to gripping the wood shaft of his hockey sticks through the long winter months – and fighting bare-fisted when he had to. *He's got to learn,* Gib once heard Evan tell his mother when she objected to his driving him up to the rink Sunday morning, early, before church, for some extra drills.

The tree shudders over a bit farther but a few roots hold. God damn it, his father growls and Gib thinks *He's going to kill himself. He's going to kill himself and it'll be his own fault.*

For a moment Gib stops pressing on the spades and lets his head hang down. Feels wind, cold rain on the crown of his head, plastering flat the thinning hair.

What are you doing! Evan cries. *We've almost got her.*

Gib stiffens, clutches the handles again and pushes hard. A gust of wind thorned with hail slaps and stings his skin and brings blood rushing to his cheeks like an open hand – his father's hand two years before, in the new guest room, on a mid-August day. The day they clashed over law school. It was far from the first time Evan had struck his son but it was the first time Gib had struck back, instantly, powerfully lashing out, though later he saw that in the split-second his fist had taken to reach Evan's chest it had loosed from a dense knot to a flabby, ineffectual clump of fingers. But Gib was big and, like his father, brute-strong, and the muted blow was enough to knock the old man stumbling back into the filing cabinet and a shelf full of trophies – his son's and his own.

Gib was ordered to leave the house at once. Two days later, contrite, he'd come home and promised to go to law school.

> *Gib giving up on the two spades to grip both hands back*
> *on one. Throttling the handle with cold fingers, knuckles*
> *white. Small tattered*
> *clouds of his father's breath blew past, the pine buckled*
> *back & forth & each time further – a crack*
> 4 *rifling the air & Gib shot flying head-*
> *first into barbed lower branches*

swearing, the spade's hard handle & the shattered
shaft in his hands. Evan called out again. A scraping
a low sepulchral thud as the shaking
pine settled back in. Gib wriggling free of branches,
needles – caught in his hair & stinging his head –

Silence a moment – then Evan stalks out from back of the pine and stands looking down at Gib and the broken spade, looming over him as he does in Gib's boyhood memories – an unappeasable giant, a guardian, invincible – a God of straps and sermons and Old Testament justice.

How did you break it? Are you ... Gib?

I'm fine. He sets down the useless shaft. It just broke.

Well, take the other. We've almost got her.

Gib looks down. Blood-smeared, the fractured shaft lies in the soil like a bone. Father? Why don't we just – go back to the house for a while. You look tired. I know you're not supposed to work this way – pausing to let the words sink in – the way your health is now.

Evan's eyes are vague. He stands, head tilted slightly, as if tracking the inner progress of some sly, persistent pain. But then Gib hears it too: from the distance, for the first time in hours, a car. The smell of needles in his hair and by his face turns bitter and wintry. Christmas day too there were only a few cars on the road and in his chair between the television and the fresh-cut, sparsely decorated tree, Evan sat listening to each one approach, pass, and drive off. But at five in the afternoon, the snowy fields already dark, one had eased into their driveway, its high-beams strafing like search-lights through the windows of the house.

Gib had never really seen his father look pale before. His mother was at the counter scraping bread-stuffing from the turkey onto a dish while Gib hovered by the table halfway between her and Evan, wanting to help with the food but afraid it would shame his father. Then as the high-beams blanched his mother's face she'd set down the dish and the scraper.

The other shovel, his father says, voice raised over the wind.

No, Gib mutters. *No.* (The purposeful slam of a car door,

the rap of the knocker, the front door shoved open before anyone could move.)

What? What's wrong with you? Here, give me the spade,
you go round and pull.

The sound of the car grows louder now, wind bearing it
clearly. Brushing by his father and rounding the tree, Gib
scans the road past the house and catches a fleck of pale red
dipping behind a hill.

Pull now, Evan hollers, *I'm getting under with the spade.
Still stuff down here.*

(In the doorway, face hidden, silhouetted by the headlights
still glaring from the driveway behind her but clearly slim,
young – a woman not much older than Gib. His mother eyeing
Gib blankly then looking down and rubbing her hands over
her apron, hard. Then, very slowly, as if asleep, tilting the
heaped-up dish against the garbage pail so the stuffing slid
steaming in. *Claire,* his father moving toward the woman,
voice menacing and heavy but all the anger seeming somehow
staged, his stride brisk and clumsy as if he were rushing,
flustered, to embrace her: *Get out. I told you Claire. I told you
how it stands. Please now. Get out.*)

Gib stretches his arms wide to embrace the tree, gropes for
hand-holds and fights the springing, scratching needles and
cones. He finds two stronger branches and grips. Pulls. Inhales
the pine's festive, bitter incense.

Claire, God damn it, I didn't think you'd really—

Pull, Evan calls, his voice muffled as if he's climbed down
into the hole. As Gib guesses he must have. Yes. To lever the
root system back as far as he can while Gib pulls from the
other side, then to step down, a boot into the pit, both boots,
pressing with his knees and whole stocky frame – his father
who has never done a thing by halves and whose energy once
seemed boundless.

Hang on now. PULL.

The pine shudders in Gib's hands as Evan slashes the tap-
roots. A sudden droning: Gib glances over his shoulder as the
red car tops the hill a stone's throw from the house.

You're easing up! A voice from the ground. *Gib!*

He turns back to the tree and wrenches harder. His father

must be hearing the car too.

Let go, he thinks. *Let go.*

(Claire turning round and rushing back to her car leaving
their front door open – leaving unfinished the climactic scene
she must have meant to play out. But Gib has seen enough.
He's almost a fucking lawyer after all, and the evidence is
pretty clear. Blinding. The headlights – footlights – pull away
and fade. Icy air howls into the house as Evan strides to the
front door and slams it shut.)

PULL. WE'VE GOT HER.

Let go.

The long red car has passed the house and stops by the
fence-line where they've already replanted six trees.
Whoever's in there is looking out at the fields, sharing their
view down the escarpment to the city or else watching two
men, dwarfed by distance, one of them half-buried, struggle to
uproot a pine.

Gib slipped, his treadless boots scrabbling over wet grass,
loose stone. He pawed out at the branches as he
tottered – called out a caution – the tree
rolling back Gib digging heels in deep & clutching
boughs to break its fall. A cry of pain, a gust
of slurred cursing from the other side:
                              through rustling
5   *boughs Gib glimpsed his father buried to his chest*
in the ground, spade crushed against him, handle
rammed into his throat. Gib, frantic,
heaved & ripped the tree back to free him & felt the last
stubborn root give way. He dragged the whole pine
down with him as he fell, its barbed branches
all around him, clawing, whiskering his skin.

His father's strong hands on his arm, tugging him clear.

You all right? Gib? Evan winded, shaken, smeared to the
chest with wet soil. When Gib rises they're face to face. The
red car has disappeared.

Was it Claire? Just now, in the car. Father?

Don't be a damned fool – Evan's face clouding over – she

won't come back here. It's done with.

That wasn't her car?

That was a Mercedes for Christ's sake. She's a secretary.

Well, you could have – helped her out. So she'd keep away.

I told you before I've got no money to throw around these days, you got that? Not on her – pausing, his big hand slicing the air for emphasis – and not on you either.

Another pause. Gib eyes his father's hand. Then the words are churned up from inside him and past his teeth in a hot unstoppable stream, like out on the ice those times, sick after pushing too long, too hard. For his father, watching in silence back of the glass. His father's love. For fuck-all:

You do. You really do make me sick.

You son of a *bitch*, the old man gasps, clumsily winding up to slap him but before he can follow through Gib shoves him hard two-handed on the shoulders and he crumples back into the dirt. Gib frightened again like in the guest room two summers back, or in the nightmares he now has where he finds he's accidentally killed some faceless man then struggles to revive him, mouth to mouth, the blank face icing over, Gib suddenly aware of his hands clamped on the stranger's throat. *Please. Oh please.* Are you all right, he nearly says – cries – feeling his torso and head chafing towards his father while his legs stay planted firm. But Evan, the top of his head flushed, is listing to his feet and Gib holds back, bolstered by anger and a stubborn faith in his father's powers.

Gib turns, lets his legs unwind numbly downhill and stumble up the next hill and over and up two more hills to the house. Through the front door, almost slamming it closed. His mother, pale in the grey light, looks up at him from behind the counter where she stands reading, a book in one hand while the other hand absently stirs a pot.

Oh good, I was getting worried.

Then as her eyes focus: Gib what's wrong? Where's your father?

He's fine. Kicking off his boots and wet socks and bounding upstairs and down the photo-lined hall. A regular rogue's gallery of lost forebears – in the big frame his grandfather and great-uncle smoking, scoffing at the camera in a kind of sepia limelight on the deck of a troop-ship taking them to war. Other long-dead men, mostly bearded. Then his own life flashing before his eyes: MTHL team photos, the cast of the grade-school Easter pageant his mother helped with, Sunday school then high school graduation, the Varsity squad. Into the guest room where he's ringed by other faces – his father beside a stack of lumber in the yard, his father at his desk in the office, his father in uniform, three times over, inspecting him through glass – like those rings of glassed-in faces watching him skate onto the spot-lit rink for some championship game.

Gib! Where's your father!

He's FINE, Gib shouts down the hall, slamming the guest room door. Grabbing his backpack and starting to stuff in the clothes he'd strewn on the floor three nights back, on arriving. Then he stops. Edges over to the window by the gunrack, parts the curtains and peers out at the fields.

Gib!

His mother at the door, knocking.

Gib, what's wrong!

> His father trudging down the hill, stumbling
> sometimes, lurching like a drunk man, mud-covered, somehow
> hauling the tree behind. One fat root bent across
> his shoulder as he clutched the wood
> with tight pale fist & hunched to cross
> the furrows while the pine
> 6   shuddered overground. Even from where he stood
> Gib could tell how red his face had grown
> against the thorn-crown
> of matted hair. The wind-driven hail was salt
> & the window a wound – in Gib – panes blinded, the whole scene
> impossible to see. His own fucking fault

Gib, please, what's wrong! What's this on the door – Gib, honey, are you hurt!

His father sinks out of sight between hills. Gib looks down at his hands, pocked with broken blisters, smeared with drying soil, blood.

His mother's footsteps fade down the hall and the stairway

as Gib studies his palms. His father is still out of view. He swears, turns to the old cabinet under the trophy shelf and kneels down and grips it open – as he almost did at Christmas – to rifle through the files. Blood daubs the sharp edges of folders. Gib's report cards from school and Sunday school and hockey camp, Evan's business records. Letters. Such a thin folder. But they will be here if there are any at all, he would never be afraid of someone digging through his files – who would have dared? Not his wife – my mother. Not me, until now. Blood on the envelopes, blotted addresses. Here, something – this address in a woman's hand.

Gib! Where's your father? The voice sounds so far away. She must be at the kitchen window, scanning the fields.

HE'S COMING, Gib shouts, HE'S JUST BACK OF THE HILL.

But he should be over the top by now.

What? Gib? Where's your father!

Fumbling the letter open:

Evan,

Your 'last letter' came just now and though the 'noble thing' would be to say, Yes, you're doing the right thing, I'll respect your decision, it's hard for me Evan, this is so hurtful. I love you, 'foolish' as it may seem. Our ages, you say, and your wife who would be alone in her old age (as if you can be sure she can't stand on her own, or find someone else, someone who shares more of her interests!) – and your 'bad heart', you bring that up again too. And your son. I've always known that's the main thing for you, Gib is, and how afraid you are of letting him down. And I believe you when you say it is more for him than for anything else that you 'must give me up.' But Evan sometimes you have to think of yourself and what you want most, and not only

My mother's footsteps on the stairs, in the hall. I threw the letter into the filing cabinet and rammed it shut.

Gib? The door flew open. Still kneeling I spun around. 'Gib, I can't see your father.'

Eyes blurred I squinted out the window, just as blurred, and checked the fields. He still hadn't reached the top of the second hill where he should have been minutes ago.

The window rattled as a gust shook the house. A cold draft breathed in from the glass.

I stood and slipped past my mother down the hall and the stairway and barefoot out the front door, leaving it ajar. Cold gusts slowed me, stones, thorns and dead roots tore at my feet as I ran through the freezing fields. *Father!* I shouted – or remember shouting, it's years now and since his death I've been free to revise every scene we ever played out together – *Father*, I think I shouted as I ran down a slope, spattered through a pool of meltwater, rushed on. Uphill. Winded, a stitch stabbing into my side. Slapped again by the wind at the crest. Down another slope and up the last hill he should have topped ten minutes ago.

> *Gib struggled over the bare crest where the wind*
> *& exhaustion drove him to his knees. Evan was there*
> *a stone's toss below him*
> *on the cold slope sitting hunched, turned away,*
> *head down, but alive. & the high winds brought to Gib*
> 7 *for the first time ever the sound*
> *of his own father crying, & the clear*
> *sound came in gusts with the driving rain, & it swept away*
> *his own useless words.* **Father, Father.** *The bald head*
> *slumped forward, the body racked with sobs, the dead*
> *tree lying in the grass beside him.*

The Dead and the Missing

... from the belly of the grave I cried, and Thou
heardest my voice

—JONAH

My grandfather spent a night alone at the end of a mined tunnel, waiting for daybreak and the Germans. At daybreak – Easter Monday 1917 – the mine he was guarding was to be blown under the German lines and my grandfather was to join his company in the attack on Vimy Ridge. It was a cold, interminable wait. Dark, too, after his lantern died. Besides the essentials – a thermos of coffee, bread, two watches, a revolver – he had brought with him a small photograph of the 'high school sweetheart' he intended to marry when the war was done. She was pictured standing on the porch of the cabin he had built in the summer of 1912 just after his parents passed away; Trout Lake was visible in the background, sunlit through the pines.

For me it's on that lake, years later, that the story of his vigil begins.

* * *

My father remembers the stillness of the water, the gentle scoop, suck, and plash of his paddle, the soft clumsy drubbing of its wood against the wood gunwale of the canoe. He sees himself at dawn paddling along the steep shoreline of Trout Lake, west, away from his parents' cabin towards the city. For a moment he rests his paddle across the gunwales to glance behind: he's all alone. His paddle's footprints fade back into the glassy lake; the smooth gleaming whale's-back of the sun, just now breaking surface, exhales a spray of bright beams. My father resumes paddling, his shadow floating ahead of him up the copper path of sunlight leading like a fuse towards the city on the far shore, seeming to ignite its chimneys, spires and steeples to a glowing, molten red. Then he sees the guitar. Afloat on the water, drifting towards him on the slight invisible current that runs from the city past his parents' cabin and on into Turtle Lake. Or is it rather his own motion that makes the guitar seem to glide towards him as if seeking him out? It floats, buoying slightly, a few strokes out from shore: a new steel-string guitar with curved flanks of rich mahogany and a sunburst face, a black burnished pickguard, a cherry fretboard tapering to cut-glass tuning-pegs splashed with sunlight, foam and water.

My father approaches, slowing. Braces his paddle across the gunwales and steadies himself with one arm as he leans out over the lake: reaches, seeing now that the body of the guitar is already half full with water slapping, sloshing inside as the instrument bobs in ripples from the canoe. The faintest chord as the day's first breeze strums over the strings. My father's hand groping for the guitar's neck and the canoe listing, my father pulling back as ripples pumped outward from the rocking hull gently swamp the guitar, its sound-hole like a drowning man's mouth gasping for air but inhaling ripples, waves – water enough for the body to list and settle, begin to sink. My father leans further out and stretches, gasping. His fingers underwater on the neck of the guitar but unable to grip it as it founders, the red face darkening with depth as if choking, the black mouth an O of choked surprise.

Sometimes my father recalls watching till the guitar disappears and then fishing his hand from the water and paddling on, but other times the canoe is tipping and his hands fumble, flail, palms toward the uprushing water as if toward solid ground, body following his outstretched arms into the icy lake then sinking, thrashing in toward shore, so much farther off than it seemed...

My father wondering if the guitar is his own father's, the one he played for the soldiers in the tunnels under Vimy Ridge but never plays anymore.

This childhood memory (or memory of a dream, my father can't be sure now either way) only came back to him a few years ago when his cousin Hal Lawrence, the undertaker, was drowned in a boating accident during a freak spring storm on Trout Lake. This would have been in 1987, fifteen years after my grandfather died and a few years after my grandmother.

Hal, a second cousin and for years the mortician of choice in the small city of North Bay, was twenty years older than my father, and, as far back as my father remembers, a close friend of the family. Sometimes as a boy my father helped out on Hal's less grisly errands; years later, after Hal's drowning, he delivered a eulogy over the lost man's empty coffin.

'Damn sad about the family business,' he said out at the cabin during the reception after the service. 'Hal's cousins are going to have to sell. There's no one to take over now.'

'It was all so sudden,' my father's Aunt Arva supplied.

'A shock,' I added inanely – though as I scanned faces in the cabin I realized everyone did seem less grief-stricken than surprised. Maybe none of us, I thought, really expects an undertaker to die any more than we expect a doctor to fall sick. As if Hal, through his years in the profession, should have acquired some sort of mortal immunity.

My father was staring toward the cabin's open door where guests were constantly coming and going. In theory, of course, it was still possible that the lost man was alive and would enter the cabin at any time – my grandfather had told stories of such things happening with missing soldiers after the First World War.

'To Hal,' my father toasted, not waiting for a response before he drank and finished his rye.

At previous gatherings – parties, weddings, funerals – Hal and my father had liked to tell stories of how it was in North Bay in the years after the Second World War, when the city was really just a big town and Hal's hearse had been forced to moonlight as a kind of back-up ambulance. There were stories of Hal driving my father down to the beach in summer (the hearse looming up behind a line of sunbathers, black fins shining, like some huge, amphibious shark) or picking him up after babysitting as a favour to his parents (slapping on the detachable flashing light and leaning on the siren to clear the streets and get back to my grandfather's as soon as possible for a rye); there were stories of Hal dropping him at school as well, my father surprising his friends by throwing open the black shiny rear doors and bursting into the daylight with claws upraised and a vampire's fiendish cackle. My father saw Hal as a guardian, his natural adult powers enhanced by the eerie, cryptic calling that he alone followed in the town; my grandfather saw him as family and as a friend who, by virtue of his youth, could keep up with the old man's drinking while at the same time being less likely than a peer to nod off when it came time for more Tales of the Great War. Take for example the one about the rich coincidence that bound the old man even closer to the young mortician: Hal's being born in North Bay only hours after the end of my grandfather's night-long vigil at the end of a tunnel charged with explosives, six thousand miles away in France. (My grandfather liked to claim that Hal had been born at the very instant they blew the charge and went over the top at Vimy, but everyone knew that that wasn't quite true.)

What's known of Hal's last outing: early on a May morning soon after the ice had gone off Trout Lake, he and two friends had paddled out from the city towards Turtle Lake to fish. They had spent the unseasonably hot forenoon on Vimy Island, a mile or so out from my grandparents' cabin, fishing off the island's steep granite banks; much later that day the searchers were to find the doused remains of their cookfire and, swarming with ants and flies, the fresh skeletons of a half-dozen trout. Hal and his friends had last been seen a few miles east of the island struggling into a rising wind and spitting rain and steep murky waves curdling into whitecaps. They might have been visible – just – from the porch of the old cabin, but now with my grandparents gone and the season still so early, the cabin stood vacant. And even if any of our family had been there, Hal and his friends and their silver canoe would have been hard to glimpse at that distance through the deepening rain.

The last people to see the canoe told the searchers of a lightning flash followed almost at once by a great crump of thunder, the clouds seeming to split open and let loose a cold stinging downpour, everyone driven back inside. They had all felt badly for the poor men out on the lake but not especially afraid, as the men when last seen were not rushing in to shore but forging confidently eastward, undeterred.

The storm passed quickly and left the grey air purged and

calm. Within twenty minutes the witnesses were all back down at the shore scanning the lake for Hal and his friends, but the calm surface was empty in all directions. Miles to the west, near the city, a yellow cone of sunlight angled through the breaking clouds to sweep like a searchlight-beam over the water.

It was a few days later, as my father and I paddled upshore east of the cabin alongside a motley armada of searchers in canoes, outboards, kayaks, skiffs, rowboats and police launches, that he first remembered the guitar on the lake. For over an hour he had said nothing, his presence behind me signalled only by sporadic grunts, by the powerful, steady impetus heard in his paddle's splash and felt in our forward motion, and by his silence – primed, bated as held breath. For a while now I'd babbled inanely at the air and lake fanning out before me in a vain effort to defuse that silence, to propitiate and avert a storm that never did break; finally I just shut up. When a long black shadow formed suddenly and glided under the bow I said nothing, just gasped, gestured with my paddle. A police diver. My pulse was still racing when my father finally spoke and told me about the guitar.

It was only later in the cabin after the funeral that Aunt Arva and Hal's ex-wife Nancy told us he was recalling a dream, he must be, he'd not have been allowed to take the canoe out alone as a boy, not till his early teens at least, and if he'd been running off to the city like that, well, surely they'd all remember? Besides, Aunt Arva was convinced, he'd have been much too afraid; she fought off a smile as she reminded him how he'd felt back then about giant beavers. (Just after the war, it seemed, several specimens of *Castor horribilis*, extinct since the end of the last Ice Age, were exhumed by gold miners in the hills near North Bay. A noted paleontologist had come up from the University of Toronto to give a talk at the library, and, notwithstanding his cautious descriptions of the creature – *'the largest specimens of which may have approached the size of a small black bear'* – the North Bay *Nugget* soon published 'speculative drawings' in which an immense rodent the size of a woolly mammoth was shown hewing jack-pines in one fell bite and flattening whole Indian villages with its saurian tail. At first, before the findings were verified, Hal and my grandfather had anointed this unlikely relic the Loch Ness or Piltdown Beaver, and over whisky they had speculated on the deeper significance of the country's national mascot having devolved so drastically in a few thousand years. Predictably, my grandfather blamed the Liberals. My father was too young to follow such banter and not old enough to accept assurances that no living fossils still lurked in the lake or above in the pine-forest, so sightings of giant beavers continued for several summers and my father refused to swim in the lake alone.)

'So you see,' Aunt Arva could not help smiling, 'it's none too likely you'd have been out there on your own.'

'A dream,' Nancy insisted again, 'it happens to me too – I'll remember something from when I was a girl, or when Hal and I were first married' – her voice thickened and she paused, sipped her whisky, pressed on – 'and suddenly I can't be sure it happened to me at all.'

'*I'd* imagine it was a dream you had after hearing your father play his guitar, dear. He still did play a bit back then.'

'Or one of his stories from the first war,' Nancy said. '"The War to End All Wars' – do you remember he used to call it that even after the second one?'

'We all kept hoping for the Story to End All Stories.'

Nancy hid a smile in her glass.

'Always on about playing his guitar in the tunnels at Vimy,' Aunt Arva went on, '"Playing for the other men, just like a piper". You recall what I liked to tell him when he'd say that? "Alex," I'd say, "if you'd ever sung your songs over as often as you've repeated those words, I doubt you'd ever have come back alive."'

Nancy smiled again. And then, to be polite, so did my father.

'His own men would hardly have stood it the way we had to,' Aunt Arva declared. 'Not for long, surely. They were better armed.'

My father had to admit to his aunt and to Nancy that their explanations did hold water, but I knew he was still unconvinced. He had told me how clearly he could picture the guitar

– and his words, his certainty, had made me see it too. Adrift on the current with its cargo of mute songs; sinking slowly like a red autumn leaf. Sharp strings that glowed and bit like barbed wire into his fingers. The sound hole like an open mouth, singing.

* * *

In early April 1917 my grandfather was a sergeant with the First Canadian Division at Vimy Ridge, on the Western Front, where he and thousands of other men had been working and living throughout the winter in a maze of tunnels cut into the chalk under the trenches.

Dozens of saps, as they were called, had been dug under the German lines by men like my grandfather who would work up to sixteen hours a day in a darkness eased only by lamps and bare bulbs and a silence cut only by the muted scratch of scrapers and spades. Of course the Germans were busy too, digging counter-saps, trying to detect the Canadian tunnels; to destroy them. So it was dangerous work. Sometimes the sappers hit underground springs and the tunnels flooded and caved in and drowned them like those coal mines under the sea down east, and on occasion two teams of engineers, German and Canadian, would burst through into each other's saps and there would be a brief and savage battle in the darkness, spades and scrapers jabbing, knives, pistols fired point-blank and the shots lighting up the saps like lightning, deafening as thunder. Grenades too, at times. Terrible. Like tunnelling animals meeting underground, no way for either side to back out....

My grandfather was never actually involved in any such battles but he'd heard plenty of stories firsthand from other men and he'd seen the dead and the wounded on stretchers being jostled past into the big cave that served as a field hospital or on into the long tunnel that led all the way to Arras a dozen miles to the south.

Like a giant's bones, those tunnels, my grandfather told me the summer before he died, no doubt knowing this fanciful analogy would appeal to a small boy in love with old books and legends. His clipped white military moustache twitched facetiously, his pale eyes twinkled as he sipped his rye. As usual he had on his navy-blue veteran's beret. *White as bones, and hollowed out. Thousands of us at home there. And every day we made it bigger, that home, and pushed those tunnels farther and farther under the German lines.*

That summer, the summer of '71, I was reading the wonderfully subterranean *Lord of the Rings* so my grandfather's words were especially real to me, vivid. Of course by that time he spoke so little that anything he did bring out, no matter how banal or rehashed, seemed somehow crucial, clairvoyant, profound. So as I wolfed down his rationed words I almost felt myself back in that underworld, hunched over, running my palm along tunnel walls that were always bathed in cold sweat as I sweated too, and swore, and heaved my huge pickaxe down into the chalk....

But for a while I was unable to tunnel deeper into fantasy as I heard nothing more from my grandfather, whose waning renown as a storyteller seemed likely to beat him to the grave. His reputation as a singer, meanwhile, had long since faded out, and his old guitar leaned ornamentally against the wall by the fireplace under the glass case containing his war medals and chevrons and the fang of shrapnel that had wounded him at Vimy. Then one time near the end of summer, an hour after I had been ordered to bed (arming myself with flashlight and the last volume of *Lord of the Rings*), I heard Cousin Hal's deep voice boom through the worn inner walls of the cabin. Perhaps hoping to postpone their gloomy last get-together in the basement of the funeral home, Hal was trying to breathe new life into the old man by urging him affably to 'give us a song'. Nancy and Aunt Arva and my parents and big sister, cheering and clinking glasses, were quick to second the request, and even my grandmother, who must have welcomed the last few golden years of silence, seemed happy to back them up. But no, my grandfather muttered. No, he was years out of trim and on top of that the guitar never had been much good after the war, the damp of the tunnels had got into the wood, the neck. Fifty years now, gone. Would you think of that!

No, my grandfather said, voice stronger, he wouldn't play them a song. But if they didn't mind hearing it again (his voice already bound, determined as the Ancient Mariner's) he'd tell them one more time about his night in the tunnel. That tunnel under Vimy Ridge.

Through the cabin walls a gracious murmuring of encouragement, the clink of ice as more drinks were poured. Like a tot of rum before some dreaded mission. Yet by now a mission they were rarely called on to perform – which made it still harder to refuse.

I didn't want them to refuse it. I'd never really heard the story before. Setting down book and flashlight, I pushed my pillow flush with the wood and leaned my ear into the wall.

It was a long night in the tunnel, my grandfather began; it would have been better if he could have taken his guitar. He guessed they all knew how in the nights leading up to his vigil and the attack he'd done his best to ease the lot of the other men by playing guitar for them, just like a piper, and leading them in song? This was well back of the front-line tunnels, mind you, since sounds carry as clear through chalk as they do through water, or just about. As for the tunnels themselves they were low and narrow and they deadened all sound, but off the tunnels, in the caverns where the men ate and slept, the acoustics weren't bad at all. And there was one particular cavern where the acoustics were so good that when he sang there and played his guitar the chords echoed with an uncanny grandeur, and the rough, dissonant voices of the men were somehow mellowed and richened, remarkably – harmonized. Maybe it was the ceiling – it was concave, almost vaulted like a cathedral, though of course the cavern was pretty small, more like a small church – a chapel. Lit by a lone ring of candles once the generator was cut for the night; an incense of tobacco smoke hanging over the men. Boys, really. 'Amazing Grace', 'The Flowers of the Forest', 'Michael Row the Boat', 'The Water is Wide', they sang them all as the cooks refilled their tin mugs with sweet tea and in the dimmer crannies the other boys sat on blankets playing poker with bullets for chips, and smoking, and humming along, while others who couldn't hum any more laid their heads down on their blankets and drifted off, too tired to even cover themselves up.

I pulled the quilt tight over my shoulder, deliciously chilled by the contrast between my grandfather's dark tunnels and my own warm bed. It made me think of something my father, laughing, had told me one time after I'd leapt out of a closet to surprise him: how once out of curiosity he had climbed into an open, empty coffin in a back room of Hal's funeral parlour and, finding it comfortable, had opted to settle in. After testing the lid to see it was not too heavy he had pulled it shut. It was very dark inside, but snug and warm. My father, a lover of small spaces, was soon happily picturing himself a boy-pharaoh in the inner sanctum of his pyramid (he thought then the pyramids were palaces, not tombs) or a bold stowaway in the hold of a pirate ship, or a Royal Navy destroyer. Then footsteps in the hall. At the door. Suddenly afraid of discovery my father shoved upward with panic-strong legs and the coffin flew open and he sprang out into the room: surprise could not quite lift the solid Aunt Arva off her feet, but she did drop her feather duster and, perhaps for the first time in her life, retreated two steps, while the new mayor – receiving his first tour of the home – groaned, his small glasses slipping down his nose as he slumped back into Aunt Arva's arms.

Some nights, the battle approaching, my grandfather would lead the other men in rougher, raunchier, more festive songs like the new hits 'Tiperrary' or 'Wait Till the Sun Shines Nellie' or even 'The Wild Rover' – a fiddle and harmonica joining in – but always in other caverns, never in 'the chapel' where boisterous choruses like those would rouse up a storm of overlapping echoes which built to a kind of kettle-drum roar and drowned out the lyrics and every other sound. My grandfather admitted that even after the war – when he was still young and his voice still good – he found it hard to play those songs because the otherworldly harmonics of 'the chapel' still seemed to ring in his ears and, whenever he tried to play, kept mocking, drowning out whatever sounds he made. So with time his guitar was set aside and became an ornamental fixture of the cabin, bumped and knocked over during the busy summers and in winter left to the frost and the mice who had nibbled scars in its body and around the sound-hole and sometimes left behind tiny, flattened, fuzz-tailed mummies my grandfather shook from the guitar each spring.

Years later, during the reception after Hal's funeral, I slipped down to the dock with the old guitar and tried it out again. It wasn't easy to play – the five remaining strings were ancient and painfully brittle and pretty much dead, the tuning screws frozen with rust, the neck badly warped, while winter had etched deep fissures into the wood of the back so any notes I did exhume from it sounded hollow – not chords but the weak echo of chords.

A mile out, in the lee of Vimy Island, an outboard was cruising slowly, line trailing behind it. After squinting awhile I made out the police markings. I looked away, down at the guitar, the water.

When I heard footsteps on the dock behind me I was hoping it wasn't Hal's widow.

Is that a police boat? My sister's soft voice.

Damn it – my father, voice a bit slurred – *I asked them to leave off for the afternoon. I called them twice.*

The two of them sat down heavily beside me. For a while they watched the water and sipped their drinks and said nothing as I strummed. Then, when I stopped, my father muttered, 'You remember in Twain? Huck Finn? On the Mississippi the searchboats fired their cannons along the surface. To make the bodies come up.'

I set the guitar on my lap and studied the black water a few strokes beyond our dangling feet where the lake floor sheers off from the flat tepid sand of the shallows and dives to a gulf of green, icy springs, caverns where huge fish stare blindly, craters full of bones and oars and wreckage.

'Let's go out in the canoe,' I urged my father. 'Show us where you saw the guitar, where it sank.'

* * *

The two men who led my grandfather to his post at the end of the tunnel kidded him that he must wish he could have brought along his guitar. But of course he could not have – an absolute rule of silence took effect as you neared the ends of the tunnels, the guides themselves leaving off their banter as the tunnel tightened and forced them to stoop and then kneel and proceed at a crawl. It was almost eleven and the generator had been off for an hour; in the wavering half-light of the guides' mine helmets my grandfather followed the lead man around a sharp bend into the tiny rounded cell that was the 'sap'. Here the first man hunkered against a large pine crate that filled most of the cell. From inside his greatcoat he took a thermos of coffee and a small battery-lantern. When he switched on the lantern the tiny space was flooded with light – dazzling against the chalk walls and the wood of the crate after the darkness of the tunnel.

My grandfather glanced around. There was nothing in the sap but this crate from which a fine black wire, stapled into the chalk, led back into the tunnel. Just before it disappeared it bulged into a small metal box – an emergency transmitter. My grandfather stared dumbly at the crate. It seemed strange to him that such modern munitions should be housed in a receptacle so crude, so humble and homely; why, even the copper wire through which the charge would be blown resembled an old-fashioned ignitable fuse.

Make yourself at home, the first guide whispered with an audible smirk, hands cupped at my grandfather's ear. *You know when to leave.*

Five twenty-five, my grandfather recited. Then took from his greatcoat pocket a chained watch and held his wristwatch up beside it. The two guides held out their own pocket-watches to compare.

Not a sound, the man whispered, hands cupped again. *Or smoking. Sound of the matches, eh. Be sure and crank the lamp on the hour. Quietly. You've pissed?*

My grandfather nodded. He knew his job. He was to spend the night guarding the explosives and the tunnel and listening for any sounds through the chalk. The enemy sappers were always at work, trying to detect and destroy the Canadian tunnels and saps, and a breakthrough into any of them would give away the plan before the charges were blown and the attack launched. So my grandfather was to monitor the Huns' approach. And, if they seemed likely to break through, signal for help using the small transmitter. And if they did break through try to slow them down – with one revolver, a knife, and a grenade.

The two men saluted farewell and squeezed back into the tunnel. By bright lamplight my grandfather watched the second man's hefty ass wriggle away. He shook his head, smiled. When you're born you emerge to a circle of old faces, when you die you sink away from a younger circle round your bed; a hopeful last image. But if he died tonight, humanity would have left him no more than this unflattering last impression. And perhaps that was apt? Even the dullest, least thoughtful among them had reflected more than once on the bestial stupidity of their lives underground....

The men were gone. My grandfather sat himself tightly on the floor, on his greatcoat tails, in the narrow space between the chalk wall and the crate. His back rested against the rough pine. He set the lamp on top of the crate, directly behind his head. After a few minutes he took from his greatcoat pocket an instrument that resembled the stethoscope his company medic used, and then a small book – a volume of Kipling his father had given him in 1910. His first winter in the trenches had tempered his reverence for the poet, but the book did serve to protect the photograph he had brought with him from Canada and still looked at whenever he was alone. Susannah, on the porch of his cabin; Trout Lake in the background through the pines. He propped the photograph against the wall atop his jammed-up knees. The lamplight – slightly fading now, more yellow than white – was like the glow of votive candles in the cave he sometimes paused by, where the Roman Catholic chaplain celebrated mass and sat behind a curtain to hear confessions and performed – more and more often these days – the last rites.

After a minute my grandfather put the photograph and the book away. He inserted the earplugs of the geophone and wedged the coin-sized receiver between his knees against the wall: at once a faint current of scraping, gnawing, a steady burrowing as of mice in a wall or large rodents underground. Some of the tunnels seethed with rats, he had the teeth-scars to prove it, and he could almost believe he was hearing them now – but he was hearing men. Sappers. Far off, and reassuring – for it was nearby digging he had to fear, or, if the nearby digging stopped, the primed silence of a mine set to explode.

With his fingertip my grandfather drew dim fading lines on the damp wall, for the first time understanding the need of solitary prisoners or sailors wrecked alone on islands to leave behind some trace of their lives. His finger sank into a small scalloped depression and when he looked closely there was a fossil in the chalk.

As quietly as he could, he trickled coffee into the tin cap of his thermos and took a sip. From his greatcoat pocket he drew a slab of army bread and dipped hunks of it into the coffee. In the cold dim confinement of his cell it tasted as good as anything he had ever had – but soon the sound of his own chewing, amplified by the geophone and drowning out all other sound, made him uneasy – afraid – and he slipped the bread back into his pocket.

He held his breath and listened. The same steady scratching. Somewhere off in the tunnels the clock-like ticking of water.

He reached behind his head and fumbled for a moment, then pulled the lantern down between his legs and cranked till it grew brighter and set it back behind him.

(The bedroom where I lay eavesdropping seemed suddenly darker, colder than before. I wanted to turn on the bedside lamp but I knew the gathered adults would see a crack of light under the door and I did not want to disturb them, for my grandfather's voice had not sounded so clear and strong in as long as I could remember, and I may have sensed it would not sound this way again.)

In the sap, as the hours passed, my grandfather tried to fight off sleep and the cold by holing up in a tight, heartening circle of memories. The previous night's singing, for one. It had been a special night of course, the eve of battle – every man given a double ration of rum, the various chaplains busy – and the sing-along had been a kind of vulgar, supplementary communion. He had played for two companies in separate caverns, starting in a low-ceilinged, smoky space (like the dingy Paris bistro that he and his friends had practically lived in on their last leave) where they had brawled out songs that made their young Rosedale lieutenant blush and sputter and storm off to his own quarters after he had asked them to desist, and they would not. Then in 'the chapel' he had played a very different repertoire yet with equal gusto, feeling a kind of chastened, bashful enchantment, like the cocky young soldier who weeks before in Paris had sauntered whistling into Notre Dame and was ambushed by awe, a sense of wonder revived from his boyhood, that made him slouch and bow his head and try to vanish, blend in, ashamed to be so moved.

Two a.m. It was now Easter Monday, three and a half hours till the attack. The same distant scraping through the wall. The thermos of coffee was more than half finished but seemed to be having little effect: several times already he had caught his eyes closing, chin slipping onto his chest. He had noticed before how tired he always felt a few hours after performing, the exhilaration finally dying down; he pinched and shook himself but it was difficult to find space or leverage. For a while, demoted to boyhood by necessity, he amused himself shadowing hand-creatures on the wall – a dog, a cat, a fish, a beaver – reasoning he could hardly fall asleep as long as his hands were engaged, arms up.

But soon he felt his arms sinking, eyes closing again.

He was wide awake, heart pounding. Three a.m. Something had happened to the lamp behind him, like a torch in a windy cave it was guttering, projecting wild diabolical shadows on the wall. For a moment he thought the crate had caught fire – then realized the lamp batteries were dying. He groped with his hands behind his head and gripped and realized too late that his hand was asleep, the lamp slipping from his grasp, toppling onto his shoulder, sliding off into the wall with a brittle smack.

My grandfather had caught himself before he could swear out loud but the lamp's breaking, amplified by the geophone, had been loud enough – a gunshot, an exploding grenade. In reality it may have made no more than a soft tinkling, but he could not be sure. He slumped back against the crate in total darkness and tried to catch his breath – tried to hold it so he could listen for any reaction through the wall.

Then he recalled what had jolted him awake: a sound, like singing. He'd been having a dream. He was swimming in Trout Lake a long way out from shore, shivering in the icy water of early spring or late fall when he first saw the ships looming toward him – a great grey fleet of battleships and destroyers steaming along in close formation, quite silent and very fast. Coming west, out of the narrows and Turtle Lake towards the city. Towards him. He slashed at the water trying to swim and barely seemed to move, yet somehow he avoided the razor prows of the giant passing ships and the suction of their churning props. Then he heard a voice from the deck of the last ship, high above him. Singing, very faintly, in a language he could not place.

German. Suddenly he had known the soft distant voice was singing in German, it had seeped into his dream and it was a real human voice and coming at him through the wall. He had felt himself deep under water, choking, thrashing to reach the sunlit surface and wake up.

He sat stiffly now, alert and afraid. Shivering with cold, moving the receiver of the geophone over the wall as if searching for a patient's heart. For a while there were only the same far-off scratchings and the ground bass of his own pulse. Still racing. Then – perhaps it was only the slowing of his heart, and breath – he heard it again. Someone was humming, very softly – now singing a line or two of words in German – now humming again. The voice so faint he could not make out a tune yet he did catch occasional ripples of notes and he knew it was no song he had ever heard.

The voice died out for a while, then recommenced. So faint. My grandfather sat in the darkness perfectly still. Whenever the voice started up again he would cease breathing for as long as he could – sometimes until the humming, the singing, stopped.

No doubt the man was singing under his breath and believed no one could hear him. He must be close – a dozen yards away, no more.

My grandfather thought his singing was the most beautiful sound he had ever heard.

He knew he was meant to use the small transmitter on the far side of the cell if he heard Hun sappers approaching, or if all sounds of enemy digging died out, but this, he thought, was different. It was clear to him that the man singing a dozen yards away must be doing just as he was: keeping a vigil in a cold cramped dugout, possibly in darkness, and listening for the enemy. And this new conviction forced upon my grandfather certain unavoidable questions: was the man guarding a similar cache of explosives – a kind of counter-mine – and, if so, at what time would it explode? If at five a.m. then my grandfather was sure to be blown to pieces, buried like a fossil in the chalk; if at six a.m. or later the German himself would be killed.

And why was the man singing? Softly – even through the chalk my grandfather could sense the soft tone – yet singing nonetheless.

Why, to keep awake, of course. To keep off the cold and the fear – fear of the dark, fear of daybreak, fear that he really was the last living thing on earth, as my grandfather had almost felt himself to be before the other man had broken the silence.

Even if the German thought that no one else could hear, he must be aware of the danger. Perhaps, if he was overheard by his superiors, he would be courtmartialled and shot. And somehow this raw defiance of orders and all common sense made the faint singing seem still more beautiful to my grandfather. The voice was bolder now, it no longer stopped and started but pressed on – though softly – through one song after another and once or twice my grandfather heard tunes he thought he knew, either because he had heard the Germans sing or whistle them in their own trenches a few yards from the Canadian lines (so sometimes, as at Christmas, the enemy troops would actually sing together, verse after verse of the same song in different tongues) or because they were German versions of common songs. Then the voice began a song my grandfather knew well, knew by heart – 'Michael Row the Boat Ashore'. 'Michael,' he kept hearing among the German words, and then a word that sounded like 'boat'. *Hallelujah.* My grandfather found himself hunching forward, back stiff with cold, until he had pressed his ear and the side of his face up against the wall and the geophone receiver. At first, of course, he thought the moisture he felt over his cheeks was from the sweating chalk as he trembled with the cold and the beauty of the voice and the strain of not joining in with a harmony he knew well and had sung just a few hours before. He felt his fingers, bunched up inside his greatcoat sleeves, moving stiffly, unconsciously, and knew he had been forming the chords with one hand while the other hand plucked at invisible strings. Pressed up against the wall he could hear the enemy soldier even more clearly: he had a fine tenor voice and sang steadily, firmly, no doubt convinced by now that nobody could hear. Now again his voice grew louder, in bald violation of orders and duty and, if it came to that, of the whole war; my grandfather felt a sudden, irrational, indefensible conviction that the man was doing this for him, risking his life to keep him company through the night and the long vigil. Amplified by the geophone the voice now seemed at large in the sap all around him. My grandfather's fingers moved less stiffly now, more surely, firmly chording the air above his palm then pressing right into it with his fingers, nails, as if to urge music from the flesh. *The river is deep and cold and wide, but milk and honey on the other side....*

Strange how the words should be in English, my grandfather thought – then realized the singing he had just heard was not only the German's. He froze, his fingers rigid claws, like that sentry they had found dead of cold one morning up in the trenches at Christmas.

He listened, but the voice had stopped. So my grandfather was sure. He had let a line slip out, in his fear and fatigue, the way men were said to do on night-watch or in solitary confinement or anywhere else they found themselves awake late at night, and alone.

The tears on his cheeks had chilled to cold sweat. He realized he was not breathing. The German must be doing the same. Or was he busy in silence signalling others about what had just happened – transmitting coordinates, sending the code for help? My grandfather's cold face flushed hot with shame. The fine soft voice had been the voice of a siren, a lorelei luring him into the rocks and along with him twenty thousand men. What difference did it make that he had not meant to join in? The outcome was all that mattered. He had fallen asleep on duty then let himself be tricked and he would die alone in this cold tomb and the attack, thanks to him, would fail.

The unlikelihood of the Huns' trying to suborn Allied sentries into singing along with German folksongs only occurred to my grandfather days later in his hospital bed, but at that moment of blinding panic and fatigue he felt certain he had been tricked into betraying himself, and the enemy sentry's performance now seemed sly, diabolical, a kind of enchanting, melodic propaganda....

Shivering, suddenly more afraid of the time than of any noise he might make, my grandfather half turned from the wall and lit a match: 4 a.m. He blew it out as reluctantly as a child, on a parent's orders, turns out a bedside lamp. He listened carefully for any sound. Besides the far-off steady scraping there was none. Perhaps he was mistaken and the German, like him, was merely afraid? Or had he gone to bring back sappers who would quickly gouge through the chalk wall into the cell?

The hard wooden crate at his spine felt more and more like his own casket. It was not till days later in hospital that he realized the German, by singing, had pulled him from the depths of a heavy sleep and saved his life.

And lost his own. For my grandfather sat utterly silent for the next hour and a half – sweat oozing from chilled pores, his pulse drumming in his earplugs and amplified around him like a huge heart in the chalk – determined to wait out his enemy. Wondering if the German sap were about to explode. Afraid even of crawling around the crate to the transmitter because he was sure the German was listening for the faintest sound and because he knew he would have to lie about falling asleep, about the noises he had made, about putting off the call to begin with. So he waited, smelling his own sour sweat, desperate to piss, guts griping with fear – imagining the German a few feet off doing the same.

He risked another match at 4:24, then began counting, slowly, by thousands. When he hit 3000 he lit another match: 5:10. He counted to 800 and risked one more: 5:23. Squeezing his body round, away from the wall, he crawled toward the tunnel. *Christ* how he had to piss! Like playing hide-and-seek as a child and burrowing into a closet and waiting and hearing the seekers nearby and closing in, coming up the stairs, closer, and the whole time your empty bladder seems ready to explode.... For a moment my grandfather's backside felt terribly exposed, helpless as he squeezed headfirst into the tunnel. He began to crawl. Poorly, stiffly at first, then with frantic, feral speed, cutting palms and knees and smacking his head where the tunnel curved and tasting blood but squeezing on. A few seconds later, where the tunnel widened, he was dazzled by a blaze of light and for a moment he thought the charge had gone off then realized it was only the electric bulbs, the generator grinding on. He squinted, saw he could stoop now and began to lope hunched over as if running under fire. He glanced at his watch as he passed another light: 5:27.

A few minutes later, my grandfather safely back at the command post, that buried world of chalk tunnels quaked and rumbled as the saps were set off and overhead a morning storm broke, the cruellest barrage of the War to End All Wars plummeting on the German lines. In their own trenches, in the darkness and driving sleet under the massive whale-back of the ridge, the Canadians troops fixed bayonets, and rose. More than one of them would later liken the barrage to 'a terrible rainstorm crossing a lake....'

I turn from the wall and burrow under the covers, relieved, as if the story could have ended any other way. How exciting it must have been, I think, to watch that storm explode and go 'over the top' and take part in the great battle! I am ten years old, and I wish I had been there. Nothing the old man or anyone else might say can change or dissuade or discourage me.

I've wondered, though, whether the whole thing happened at all. I've wondered sometimes. If I wasn't asleep the whole time.

My grandfather's concluding words – or my father's words, years later? Already I'm half-asleep and sinking through the bed and the pine floorboards into undergrowth and soil, stone, green springs deep underground. Into dreams of being older.

* * *

I push out from the dock, settle in at the bow. My father is in the stern, as he always will be, though I'm stronger than he is now and in the years to come the gap between us will grow.

On the dock my sister, feet dangling just above the water, strums absently at my grandfather's guitar. As we round the point I glance back: she hoists the guitar above her head in farewell.

'I don't think any of us would have heard the full story,' my father booms from the stern, perhaps thinking it's hard for me to hear – 'the full story of his watch, if he hadn't distinguished himself the way he did – later on, in the battle. Those decorations. Sometimes, you know, I think he wouldn't have done what he did to win them if he hadn't felt so ashamed of what happened before. In the sap.'

I nod. I've thought the same things. I know that seven hours after the battle started he and other men of his company were suddenly called 'up top' into the wind-driven hail and cold and thrown in near Hill 145, where the attack had run into 'stiff resistance'. And there he had led a foolhardy but successful charge, seizing an important trench and killing a German officer with his bayonet. Moments later, trying madly to rally a fresh attack, he was pierced by a chip of shrapnel and plunged face-down into a trench streaming with meltwater and muck and blood; they found him and pulled him to safety just in time.

As a boy I'd heard him recite that brief story to Hal and my father when he was drunk, and even my mother when he was especially drunk, and it always spilled out like a kind of confession, not a boast. Yet he was always poised for sentimental reactions and when he saw them – in my mother, in my sister, in Nancy – he was quick to pounce and remind us all that those were different times, it was war then, it was *kill or be killed*. The same old stuff. I'm not sure he really believed it. I'm not sure he cared much either for his beret or his neat little military moustache, but he had been ferried home a hero and, jaded, worn and shell-shocked as he was, he never seemed to muster up the energy to break free of that narrow post. Which in some ways must have seemed a secure place to stay – like the cabin.

It's wildly far-fetched, of course, but the possibility always remains that the officer my grandfather looked in the eyes and stabbed was the German singer, escaped from his tomb, thrown up top like him into a crucial part of the fray. A one in ten thousand chance, at best – but adding urgency to the old man's proud, pained confessions.

We paddle west along the shore, towards the city, as my father recalls paddling in his dream. We haven't agreed out loud to do this but we find ourselves doing it all the same. And of course it does make sense to go that way, it's better, quieter, everything a mile west of the cabin is Crown land and the shore is still untouched, as wild as it would have been forty years ago when my father first spied the guitar, or dreamed it.

'Here,' he says, laying his paddle across the gunwales, resting as he does so rarely – so at last I can do the same.

'Some place around here, I think ... I do remember that outcrop in the background ... Vimy Island to the left, about there ...'

'So it must have happened,' I call back to him, eyeing the police launch near the island, trolling. 'It must have. I mean, how could you have placed everything so perfectly in a dream?'

But he must know as well as I do – he could have done it. Then or after. Now. We surge forward as he digs his paddle back into the lake and nearing the shore I can see the rocks and rotten logs of the bottom sloping up to meet us. I lean over the side: a dim underworld looms up through the red reflection of our canoe. Really I would have liked to ask my sister for the old guitar and brought it out here with us, then set it adrift – somehow that would have seemed apt, inevitable, like the predictable, perfect last chord of an old song. But a gesture so densely, dramatically symbolic would have embarrassed my father, and me as well; I could only do it alone. But I won't. The guitar is as much a fixture of the cabin as the parade of chevrons, pins and decorations in the glass case above the fireplace, and besides that the guitar's parts are all rusted, the old wood is cracked, it wouldn't flash and bob gracefully but just settle and sink – a bathetic burial at sea for all the mice and spiders and moths and insects trapped inside over the years.

There was another time I overheard my grandfather through the wall long after I should have been asleep. He was telling Hal and Nancy and Aunt Arva and my parents about an old chum from his company who had died of the Spanish flu on their way home from France – how they had had to 'bury him at sea'. Shivering in my dark bedroom I pictured Cousin Hal – who could not have been there, of course, who had only just been born – nailing shut the poor soldier's pine casket, then the crew lowering it like a lifeboat onto a grey sea studded with giant headstones of drifting ice. For a few years I kept thinking such 'burials' were carried out that way and picturing my grandfather and Hal and the sailors all leaning over the railings, saluting sadly as the ship steamed west and the coffin bobbed and drifted off into a maze of chalk-white floes.

About the Author

Steven Heighton was born in Toronto and raised there and in Red Lake, Northern Ontario, and has lived and worked in Alberta, British Columbia, and Japan. His work has appeared in many magazines and anthologies in Canada and abroad, including *The Second Gates of Paradise, Best English Short Stories, The Journey Prize Anthology, Agni, The Malahat Review, Best Canadian Stories*, and *Revue Europe*, and he has won a number of awards for his writing, including the Air Canada Award, the Gerald Lampert prize for best first book of poetry, and the gold medal for fiction in the National Magazine Awards. He is the author of three books of poetry, most recently *The Ecstasy of Skeptics*; his first book of stories, *Flight Paths of the Emperor*, was a finalist for the Trillium Award and appeared in 1994 in French translation. Currently he lives in Kingston, Ontario, where from 1988 to 1994 he edited *Quarry Magazine*.

Acknowledgements

Earlier versions of some of these stories have appeared elsewhere. The author is grateful to the editors of the magazines and anthologies cited below.

'To Everything a Season' was published in the *Malahat Review* and reprinted in *The Second Gates of Paradise* (Macfarlane Walter & Ross, 1994, ed. Alberto Manguel).

'On earth as it is' was published in Canada in *Exile* and in the USA in the *Northwest Review*. The opening section, 'Father', was reprinted in *Books in Canada*.

'The Patrons' was first published in 1991, in a very different form, in *The Antigonish Review*, appeared in its present form in *Nimrod* (USA) in 1994, and was reprinted in *Best Canadian Stories* (1995).

'Townsmen of a Stiller Town' was published in *The Fiddlehead*.

Parts of the novella from 'Translations of April', appeared in *subTERRAIN* and the special Arctic issue of *Nimrod* (USA).

'End of the Festival' was published in *Yak* and reprinted in *Parallel Voices/Voix Parallèles* (Quarry Press/XYZ, 1992, eds. André Carpentier and Matt Cohen).

'Everything White is Closed' first appeared in 1988, in a very different form, in *Matrix*, and was published in its present, longer form in *Geist* in 1994.

'Downing's Fast' was published in Canada in *The New Quarterly*, in the USA in *Confrontation*, and also in *Kunapipi* (Denmark).

'Root-Fires' was published in Canada in *The Canadian Forum* and in France in *Paris Transcontinental*.

'The Dead and the Missing' was published in *The New Quarterly*.